The
Last Man
Standing

The
Last Man
Standing

PHILLIP A. MOSES

ALLEN & UNWIN

First published in 1999 by
Allen & Unwin
9 Atchison Street
St Leonards NSW 1590
Australia
Phone: (61 2) 8425 0100
Fax: (61 2) 9906 2218
E-mail: frontdesk@allen-unwin.com.au
Web: http://www.allen-unwin.com.au

National Library of Australia
Cataloguing-in-Publication entry:

Moses, Phillip A., 1967– .
  The last man standing.

  ISBN 1 86448 951 0.

  I. Title.

A823.3

Set in 12/15 pt Garamond by DOCUPRO, Sydney
Printed by Australian Print Group, Maryborough, Victoria

10 9 8 7 6 5 4 3 2 1

We all went up
to Gettysburg,
the summer of '63,
and some of us
came back from
there, and that's
all except for
the details.

—A Confederate officer's
account of Gettysburg

Year One

A LONELY ARRIVAL

As the plane taxied towards the terminal of Canberra airport, I peered out of the window at the expanse of washed tan grasslands that were the Australian Capital Territory in summer. My eyes were drawn to the short, steep hill only two kilometres from the tarmac. As the aircraft came to rest, the flight attendant politely requested passengers to stay seated until the 'fasten seat belt' light was turned off. The majority ignored her. They always did. It was just a ritual. The attendant dutifully played her role by ignoring all the passengers standing in the aisle and reaching into the overhead lockers. Everyone had to be the first off the plane to show how busy they were. Busy had status. Then all the passengers would queue for half an hour waiting for luggage.

I clip-clopped across the tarmac with my eyes looking to Duntroon and Mount Pleasant, about two kilometres away. The dry slopes had four or five reddish brick buildings which I knew from a previous visit was the Royal Military College. It was not an unpleasant sight but it was not attractive either. There was a brutality about the sharp functional lines of the construction. Above the buildings I could see an incongruous red earthen scrape which was untidy and out of place.

I moved into the terminal building. There was nowhere else to go. I was wary and looking for options, but there weren't any, so I contented myself by floating with the crowd. In the terminal, some other new cadets and I were met by a sergeant who directed us to collect our bags and then ushered us onto a khaki coloured bus. I can't remember how the sergeant knew which of us were cadets, or whether I approached him. My confidence was not high and I can't recall having enough courage to have presented myself to this towering, tattooed stranger. I just remember that we all gathered around him like some oversized family. Perhaps all of our attention had been captured by the sergeant's boots, and that was what drew us together. The boots danced in the light, though the owner's feet stayed firmly planted. I could tell the boots were black but they were like chrome, reflecting every shard of light. I was certain I'd be found wanting when asked to emulate such feats with polish and brush. I don't think those boots were meant to intimidate, but they certainly had that effect.

The bus struggled to RMC as if the uncertainty of its passengers had somehow been transmitted to its engine. When it finally came to rest Sergeant Boots stood in the door, directing us to pick up our personal belongings from the rear of the bus before waiting for our names to be called by a cadet sergeant.

There were several cadet sergeants, who proceeded to call names until my fellow passengers, myself, and our mountains of baggage were assembled in front of each one. The sergeant I stood in front of was a tall broad-shouldered man with ginger coloured hair and a full moustache. He informed the small knot of people to his front, in a low growl, that his name was Sergeant Starch but we were to address him as 'Sergeant'. He was a member of the senior class and we were now all members of Beersheba Company, which was currently the Sovereign's Company. 'You'll find out what that means later, but simply it means we are the best. Do not include yourself in that for the time being,' he said, glowering at us.

All of the cadet training companies were named after famous battles in which Australian soldiers had fought. I recognised Beersheba from reading military history as the scene of a mounted charge by the Australian Light Horse during World War I. It

4

was the last great cavalry charge and I was glad to belong to a company honouring such a battle. Beersheba, where the Australian soldiers had shown courage, dash, tenacity and a little recklessness to win against odds. Beersheba, I thought with satisfaction, I like that name.

'You are Fourth Class, I am First Class. We are both cadets, but we are a world apart. I'll explain it to you like this,' rumbled the sergeant. 'Imagine you are on an Indian train. First Class are valued customers of Indian rail. They are looked after. Second Class have the potential to be valued customers of the future, so respect is given to them. Third Class have paid their fares and have been allocated seats. Fourth Class are seated on the roof of the carriages. You have not paid a fare, so you are of no particular value to Indian rail. You are there only on sufferance. Fourth Class passengers have to hold on tight as the train comes to corners, lest they fall off. Hold on real tight, Fourthies, because no-one cares if you're on that roof when the train reaches its destination.'

Sergeant Starch turned and we picked up our bags and followed him through twisting walkways, up stairs, between buildings, to a powdery white path which ran steeply up a hill. We struggled in pursuit. The sergeant appeared not to notice we were all carrying quite heavy loads. He never slowed the pace and the crude arrogance of his behaviour was unfamiliar to me. It was not until we topped the rise and stood before a double-storey white brick building that I had a chance to catch my breath. A fire-engine red sign proclaimed Sovereign's Company and the buildings were obviously new. Sergeant Starch gave us all somewhat confusing directions to our rooms. As I moved down a short flight of stairs in what I hoped was the right direction, an uncertain face peered at me from above,

'Are you a Fourthie?'

'I suppose so,' I replied slowly, 'I'm new.' The sound of my voice gave me courage.

I received a relieved smile and the rest of a body appeared.

I shook hands with a nondescript individual who introduced himself as Andy Bird. 'Thomas. Thomas Sneyk,' I managed. Andy scurried away, making some senseless comment about not being seen by the senior class. I watched the retreating Andy. Most peculiar, I thought.

ISOLATED IN A SEA OF CONFUSION

A fog descended on me. It was the fog of battle. A fog that distorted, and through fear made my perception very different from the soldiers who stood beside me. I can recall clearly the overwhelming desire for sleep and craving for food, but everything else remains a haze of jumbled facts that have no order. I was not starving. It was just that my body required inordinate amounts of energy to go on. Sleeplessness, however, was the major problem. With sleep deprivation came a painful cloud that descended not only on my mind but my whole being. I strove to concentrate when my body just needed to shut down. This fog dominated my every waking hour. Sometimes it was so thick it required every ounce of energy to force my eyelids open. It clouded my ability to think, it swirled before my eyes and confused me. All the Fourthies were the same.

Each day began with Reveille at 0600 hours. The process consisted of standing at the door of your room and shouting, 'Reveille, Reveille, Reveille' at the top of your voice. Echoes of other Fourthies' voices would resonate around the building. There was cold comfort in hearing those voices. Other cadets conducting what appeared to be a faintly ridiculous procedure made it somehow normal. You then waited at your door standing to attention, until your section commander's head poked around the corner of his door and told you to continue with your duties. The idea was to yell loudly, otherwise your section commander would not wake up and you would be left at attention for some time. The alternative option was to conduct your yelling directly outside the section commander's door and dash back to your room, so you were back in front of your own door when his head appeared. By doing this, I was often able to solicit a compliment from my section commander, a First Class cadet, on the loudness of my voice.

The purpose of Reveille was twofold. The first was to ensure all the Fourthies were awake, the second to ensure all the new cadets slept in bed. This was done by making the junior cadet stand outside his door with a sheet over his shoulder, indicating his bed was unmade and therefore slept in.

My section commander never worried about the sheet. In fact I don't think he ever worried about anything, due to laziness, so to save time in the morning I slept on the floor beside my heater, with a woollen dressing gown as a small blanket to keep me warm. It was an uncomfortable arrangement, but it allowed me to save precious minutes in the morning. These stolen minutes were used to scrub showers and ablutions to a meticulously clean standard. Less than spotless bathroom areas normally ensured your first dressing-down by the senior class for the day.

The problem with Fourth Class cadets not sleeping in bed had surfaced a year or two previously in bastardisation allegations levelled at the College by the *Age* in Melbourne. Amongst the allegations made by former cadets who had resigned was that they had not slept in beds for weeks after arrival. This was because the senior class made such demands of the Fourthies' time that they couldn't waste any moments in the morning making and remaking the bed till it reached the required standard of the senior class. Through the procedure of Reveille and the sheet checking ceremony, the military hierarchy believed that they could assure the inquisitive media that all Fourth Class cadets were now sleeping in their beds.

There was feverish activity after Reveille, with Fourthies cleaning mirrors, vacuuming floors, scrubbing tiles and latrines before finally appearing outside in uniform, ready for an inspection prior to

7

breakfast. The system of 'fives' now came into operation. If as Fourthies you were told to parade at 0620 hours, the fives system required you to be ready to go at 0615 hours. At 0615 hours we would begin to appear in the car park, which was Beersheba Company's designated form-up point, the 26 Fourthies in Beer-sheba Company scurrying, individually or in groups of two or three, doing up belts, adjusting ties, tucking in our shirts or combing fingers hurriedly through our hair.

Of course, someone was always late, and the senior class would then launch into a fearful tirade, the favourite topic being our lack of group cohesion and spirit. Not only were the individuals who turned up late at fault, but the selfish individuals who turned up on time obviously had not offered any assistance to their struggling mates. Further to being selfish, those who were on time obviously wished to show the people who turned up late in a bad light, which made them even more loathsome. It was a confusing situation and it was difficult to see how you could win, but I think that was the idea. Some of my classmates grumbled in quieter moments about our inability to do right as a group, and were obviously taking the situation to heart. I never took it to heart. To me the behaviour was part of being new. It happened to new children in schools all over the country, and the only part I found surprising was that my classmates appeared to be shocked by it. Surely they realised that when they had tormented a new child at school this was the turmoil it caused. They must understand that. Why else did the ritual continue?

After the torrent of abuse subsided, a dress inspection followed. Failings in your dress would be pointed out.

'Dust in the welts of your shoes. Show parade to your section commander at 1800 hours.'

'Your belt is not correctly aligned. Look down . . . Fix it now.'

'The ends of your tie are not the same length. I strongly suggest you get someone to show you how it is done properly.'

'Creases are not sharp enough in your sleeve. Show parade to your Platoon Sergeant at 2000 hours.'

These proceedings finally drew to an end and we would march to breakfast, down the steep white 'Kokoda Trail' to the Corps of Staff Cadets' Mess. Before being fallen out we were given a time at which we had to be formed up ready to go to our next activity. Normally about fifteen minutes was allocated to each meal, but because of the fives rule you really only had ten minutes.

I recall forming-up for lunch at 1145 hours on one occasion. However, some classmates were late and we weren't ready for inspection until 1150 hours. We then had a dress inspection that took ten minutes, followed by a tongue-lashing on the subject of punctuality that took a further ten minutes. We finally embarked on our ten-minute trudge to the mess, arriving at 1220 hours.

'The Sovereign's Company Fourth Class . . . Halt.'

'The Sovereign's Company Fourth Class will advance. Left . . . turn.'

The First Class cadet who marched us to the mess peered at his watch and a look of consternation crept slowly over his features. Then he looked up slowly, consternation changing to disbelief, and then rage.

'Being a magnanimous person with your welfare foremost in my mind, I formed you up at 1145 hours so we could reach the mess at 1200 hours. I would have then been able to give you all a leisurely twenty minutes for lunch. However, it is now 1220 hours, the time I wished to have you reform. The untidy thing in my mind is that, if you were supposed to be reformed here at 1220 hours, by the rule of fives we should all have been out the front of this mess at 1215 hours on this exact spot, ready to go. This clearly has not happened. Gentlemen, you are screwing me around. What, however, upsets me the most about this whole affair is not your lack of punctuality, but the fact that you as a group seem to think you can take advantage of my pleasant countenance.

'Left . . . turn.

'Quick . . . march.'

We marched back whence we had come. Willie, a Fourthie who was marching beside me, muttered 'Bastard' under his breath. It didn't overly worry me, and although I was hungry I could see a funny side to the whole charade.

A NEW WORLD TO SURVIVE IN

The Corps of Staff Cadets' Mess holds a special place in my memories, not least for the appalling quality of the food. The much loved staff were known as 'seals'. I was told the name derived from their black-and-white uniforms, though all the seals I'd ever seen were murky brown. In any case, the important point was that the seals went to special lengths to ensure the bread was always stale, and on special occasions mouldy. The jelly was either so mercurial it defied efforts to stay on your spoon, or so hard it bounced like a squash ball. In the first five weeks, the priority was to get food to mouth.

As we were dismissed to march into the mess, each Fourthie pulled a cloth and a toothbrush from his pocket to wipe the white dust of the Kokoda Trail from his shoes. Visible dust on your shoes would immediately secure your ejection from the mess and a punishment parade of some description. Invisible dust occasionally got the same result. After you were satisfied with the state of your shoes, you took a deep breath and climbed the brass-railed stairs, past rows of officers caps that were a part of our uniform, into what the military staff called our 'home'. If a Fourthie was supposed to feel at ease in this home, no-one had bothered to tell the senior members of the corps. Rather, they ensured we always felt like a pile of shit that had somehow landed on their doorstep.

Once inside the mess, which was a large H-shaped eating area with long dark wooden tables, the greater proportion of your time was spent queuing in a line which normally extended from partway down the stairs, through the entrance door to the food point. First Class cadets pushed in at the front of the line. We Fourthies said nothing and looked to the front.

The food point was a noisy clatter of pots and pans bashing together, with an accompanying odour that made you wince. After collecting your meal, which was a simple matter of selecting the meats and vegetables from huge bains marie, you made your way to a table.

Each of the six companies had an area set aside for members. Beersheba Company's area was ten tables of constant pandemonium. There was an unwritten rule that no more than four members of Fourth Class could sit at any one table. This ensured that a ratio of about three to one was maintained in favour of the senior class. Students of the military will be aware this is the minimum ratio we require in planning for an attack. It is also an ideal ratio for harassment.

A source of endless amusement for the senior class was a game which, surprisingly enough, had no name, or none that I can recall. Mindful as my classmates and I were of avoiding the wrath of our seniors, good manners were the order of the day in the mess. The manners required were nothing special, and would be familiar in Australian households. We were required never to talk with our mouth full, and to place knife and fork down prior to speaking or when spoken too. The RMC culture distorted these most innocent of conventions.

A hunk of meat would be poised on the end of your fork, ready for consumption, when a Second Class on your left, in an unusual display of civility, would ask, 'Where are you from, Staff Cadet Sneyk?'

Down would go the fork with the morsel untouched. The question answered, the fork would just about have returned to your mouth when the next person, from Third Class, would ask, 'What does your father do?'

Down would go the knife and fork as you answered. Up would

go the fork when the next cadet from Third Class asked, 'Do you have any brothers and sisters?'

Down would go the fork again. I was now decidedly suspicious, so there was a flash of silver as my eating utensils raced for my mouth. Victory! I have food in my mouth.

'Staff Cadet Sneyk, how old is your sister?'

I swallow quickly, so I can answer the question promptly, and a large piece of meat sticks in my throat. A slight gag and the meat bounces into my empty stomach, causing tremors before finally coming to rest. Learning fast, I now select a small piece of potato which I am certain will be kinder to my digestive system if by some accident it should reach my mouth. A blur of potato and metal whirls towards my mouth, but the Second Class cadet whose turn it was to ask the next question is up to the challenge.

'So what does your sister do?'

SWEET LIFE

The mess was the theatre in which the single most frightening event occurred in my time at RMC. A Fourthie who was being harassed very loudly rounded on his assailants and told the Second and First Class cadets involved that they had no right to treat him in this manner. Stunned silence ensued for a moment, for the harassment was taking place centrally, and many people were listening to this particularly loud sideshow. The quietness, incongruous against such a normally noisy background, was broken by an indignant roar from the senior class. The young lion who had raised his voice for all of us disappeared under blows from twenty odd of the Second Class. He appeared briefly for a second as he sailed through the air and crashed into the solid wood of the mess doors with a frightful crack. He was then dragged down the stairs yelling and screaming in agony.

I averted my eyes quickly and tried to shrink inside myself as

I realised my vulnerability. I kept my eyes firmly fixed on my plate, not daring to look to left or right until it seemed opportune to excuse myself from the table. Fear, frustration at my own impotence and shame at my lack of action all descended on me as I walked into the sunshine outside the mess. The overwhelming emotion, however, was relief that my own life was still preserved.

Weeks later I discovered we Fourthies had been victim of a cruel hoax. The lion in our midst, who I had not seen again—significantly reinforcing the sense of the senior cadets' power over our lives—was actually a Second Class who had dressed up for the occasion. But the point by this stage had been well made. Our lives were completely in the hands of the senior class.

NEW IDEAS ON INTEGRITY

As for bastardisation, it didn't happen in my time at the college. As one Second Class cadet explained it to a group of Fourthies, 'If you want to complain about bastardisation, let me assure you it doesn't happen. If you prove to be an idiot or a grot we might bish you out of the Corps. But bastardise . . . never.'

After the *Age* newspaper printed allegations of bastardisation, many earlier activities were banned. 'Leaps', for example, was forbidden. Leaps was a process where Fourth Class cadets were paraded, given three minutes to run to their room, change into a different type of uniform which had been stipulated by the senior class, and return in inspection order. Punishments were awarded for any faults in your dress and senior cadets harassed you to, from and in your room for an hour or more. I never saw leaps the whole time I was at RMC. However, I do remember Andy, who I'd met on the stairs during the first day, running through a glass door while conducting 'splits', which was effectively the same activity. A military staff member asked the senior class if Andy had injured himself while conducting leaps. 'No,' they said truthfully. Get the terminology right. This was integrity, Duntroon style.

SURFING 300 KILOMETRES FROM THE BEACH

One evening the word was passed by the senior class that all the Fourthies were to be in the central common room—the Rec—at 2000 hours. We were to be dressed in board shorts and sunglasses, and were to carry our ironing board and iron.

Members of the senior class stood around the front of the room with knowing smiles on their faces. All the chairs had been moved to one side.

'You Fourthies have been working long hours so we have organised something to release a little tension,' began their leader. 'If any staff ask you, this is not a "beach party", this is "ironing practice", 'cause we all know you can't bog for shit. All you have to do is stand on your ironing board, which has magically turned into a surfboard, and surf away to the music.'

The senior class had set up a ghetto blaster for the occasion, and it began to pump out Beach Boys favourites. Somewhat self-consciously, we began to imitate surfers on the coast.

'Come on,' yelled the senior class, 'put a bit of life into it. A new set of waves is coming. Get down on your boards and paddle out to meet them. Oh no! You've just been tipped off, back on quickly. Quick . . . turn around, another set's coming. Paddle hard now. You've caught it. Stand up. Not too quickly or you'll lose your balance. You're riding that wave. Feel the exhilaration.'

I looked around warily, but the activity appeared harmless enough and no danger was evident.

'Let's go, Fourthies,' encouraged the seniors. 'The music's coming to an end, you have to ride that wave all the way to the beach. *Oh no*,' yelled the senior class in unison. 'Wipe-out!'

At that instant more of the senior class came running into the room with fire hoses and buckets, showering water to left and right. They shoulder-charged us, knocking us flying into walls and chairs.

The commotion finally died away and we Fourthies began to pick ourselves up off the floor. One of us was nursing a bleeding nose and several others were holding their shoulders.

'That was fun wasn't it, Fourthies,' said a senior class at the head of the room. 'Nothing like a day at the beach and a bit of surfing to release tension.'

There was no answer.

'Disappear, Fourthies, and remember this was just ironing practice.'

I walked away feeling silly and humiliated. Not from the idiotic activity of surfing on an ironing board, but for being so stupid as to be caught off balance by the senior class again.

A LONELY SOUL

A cadet by the name of McKay was caught crying on the telephone to his parents. Use of the telephone by Fourthies in the first five weeks was banned. The senior class explained that contact with loved ones during this important period wasted valuable time and caused homesickness.

A senior class cadet stood in front of us prior to marching us to lunch.

'That wimp Staff Cadet McKay was found on the telephone yesterday, having a sook and a whinge about being bastardised. The sneaky little shit has broken the rules. I strongly suggest that none of the rest of you are found in the telephone box. As for his whingeing about bastardisation, staff will back the seniors. For a start, you girls wouldn't know what bastardisation is, so grow up and learn to stand on your own two feet. You're supposed to be soldiers, not mummy's boys. If you think you're being bastardised, I suggest you do the honourable thing and resign.'

With that the senior class marched us down to lunch.

What a strange fellow McKay was, I thought. I wonder who picked him to come here. McKay was physically fragile, and he had the most annoying whiny voice. Duntroon was a super critical environment, and a whiny voice was the last thing needed to focus more attention. I looked across at McKay, who was trying to shrink into himself. He seemed on the verge of tears. Yes, he was a wimp, but I vaguely felt sorry for him. It seemed unnecessary to humiliate him like that.

Staff Cadet McKay tried to commit suicide that night by slashing his wrists. This only confirmed in my mind that there was something wrong with him. He just wasn't all there.

A senior class stood before us again.

'That wimp McKay attempted to gain attention last night and you will not see him again. You will notice that I don't use the words "attempted suicide" because it wasn't. All McKay wanted was attention. If you want to commit suicide, do the job properly. We don't tolerate failures here at Duntroon.'

I couldn't help thinking that if McKay had actually killed himself, he might have been allowed to stay at RMC because he wasn't a failure.

Staff Cadet McKay was our class's first casualty.

A CHANGE PROCESS

The majority of our time during these early days was spent on medicals, inoculations, issuing of books and uniforms and getting haircuts. Spare moments were spent studying for the 'screed' test. Points such as the charter of the Royal Military College, the name and rank of every key person in the army, from governor-general to the cadet sergeant in charge of every platoon at the college, had to be on the tip of your tongue in case it was the whim of a senior cadet to ask you. We learnt the height of the flagpole, allowing extra millimetres for expansion in hot weather and excrement from stray birds. The meticulous senior class emphasised this last point as the top of the flagpole was one of the few areas of RMC not to be cleaned by Fourthies.

We also learnt the 'seven wonders' of RMC. I would tell you what they were if I could remember any of them. And we learnt the college history. The Royal Military College Duntroon had been opened on Tuesday, 27 June 1911. Its first commandant and founding father was Major General William Throsby Bridges. Bridges had attended the Royal Military College in Kingston, Canada, and had established Duntroon along similar lines. Kingston's course itself had been based on the military academy at West Point in the USA. We learnt that along with Sandhurst and West Point, Duntroon was the finest military college in the world. No evidence was brought forward to support this theory, but none of us doubted it. I also learnt that the Sovereign's Banner had been presented by the Queen to be carried on parade by the champion company. This company was known as the Sovereign's Company.

Learning to iron a perfect uniform, tidying your room, placing socks in the correct shelf for socks, jocks in the correct draw for jocks, was all important information imparted to us. Other tasks included learning how to answer the telephone politely, how to leave a message in the correct format, and completing show parades awarded for any deficiencies in dress that had appeared that day.

The cadet language became more familiar. There was a host of new words and I thought them peculiar. 'Bogging' was a curious term used to describe cleaning, spit-polishing and ironing. If you thought about it, 'bogging' ran off the tongue far more easily than 'cleaning brass'. A show parade consisted of turning up to a specified area, usually the room of the senior cadet who had awarded the extra training, and having the item that had been found deficient reinspected. On one of these occasions I turned up to a corporal's room for inspection of a shirt at 1755 hours as the corporal had stipulated 1800. I waited till the second hand of my watch reached six before rapping smartly on the corporal's door and announcing myself.

'Excuse me please, Corporal. Staff Cadet Sneyk reporting with a shirt for show parade as directed.'

'Staff Cadet Sneyk, there is no requirement for you to turn up to a show parade five minutes early,' said the corporal in an obvious effort to be pleasant. 'Just punctual will be fine.'

Gosh this place is confusing, I thought. The rule of fives is applied at all times, except now. But you let me stand around for five minutes anyway, arsehole.

I gathered myself and replied politely, 'My apologies, Corporal, I didn't know there were variations as to when the fives rule applied.'

'Don't apologise!' yelled the corporal in a furious change of tone. 'A cadet is never sorry. Are you going to be sorry when you kill half your soldiers because of a mistake? A fat lot of good it will do them. Just get it right.'

'Yes, Corporal,' I replied. 'I'm sorry. I was just trying to be polite.'

'There you go again,' raged the corporal. 'Don't say you're sorry, and there is no requirement to be polite in the army.'

'Sorry, Corporal, I didn't know that either. Thank you for telling me about that.'

'Stop apologising,' the now livid corporal yelled at me. 'Just get out of my sight.'

'Yes, Corporal. I'm sorry, Corporal. Excuse me please, Corporal,' and I beat a hasty retreat down the corridor.

MATESHIP, AN ANZAC TRADITION

After the initial days of administration at the college, the time came to do our basic military training at Majura Field Firing Range, or

'Club Med Majura' as our senior class called it. Majura Range was only eight kilometres down the road and was looked forward to with anticipation, as no senior class would be with us, just military staff.

Club Med was a stepped hillside, the lowest step being a rectangle 300 by 150 metres made up of fine grey dirt that clung to everything. The dust was whipped up by the smallest breath of air. This step was the parade ground. The next two steps housed rows of khaki tents. Staff accommodation and administration areas took up the top two steps.

Showers were of the bucket variety. It was a Spartan existence, but far from uncomfortable. Concessions had been made to the twentieth century by the military and a corrugated-iron hut had been erected, with electric power and ironing boards. Every military necessity was catered for.

As I was the only cadet in my class enlisted in Tasmania, I had somehow been omitted from the class roll. On arrival, a parade was held on the grey square. Names were read out in groups of eight and Fourthies were allocated to a corporal who led them off into the tented area. This process continued until only I was left.

'What's your name?' asked Sergeant Boots.

'Staff Cadet Sneyk, Sergeant,' I snapped promptly.

Sergeant Boots had a discussion with several corporals for a period. I had an awful feeling that I was going to be told that a mistake had been made and I really shouldn't be at RMC at all. After much discussion I was relieved when a Corporal Flecks decided he'd own me and I was allocated to his section. Flecks was a quiet ex-sergeant of the British Paratroop Regiment. He was a no-fuss, no-frills operator with whom I instantly identified.

Corporal Flecks settled me down in a tent with seven other people, all from Beersheba Company. Most I knew by name already. Four of them had organised themselves in a clique which went by the name the Musketeers. Their stated goal was to work as a team to graduate. This surprised me, as I had not struck up a solid

19

friendship with anyone at the college as yet. The only person with whom I had a regular conversation was Jude, who lived in my section back at the college. Jude was a hyperactive livewire who had already completed a year at RMC, but was repeating Fourth Class because he had failed academics. He popped into my room now and then to give me advice, but that was about as far as our relationship had developed. As it happened, I felt no particular need for companionship. In my childhood I had been comfortable with running by myself for hours, or reading quietly.

I watched the Musketeers closely. Each contributed a little to the whole and I admired the ease with which they had fitted their roles. I spent many hours with them and was flattered when I was asked to join the brotherhood, but I hesitated before accepting. By joining the Musketeers I was pledging my complete help to four strangers for four years.

Could I trust them?

Could I assist them or would I hinder them?

Did they understand the pledge?

Were they my kind of people?

I knew in a moment that I must accept. There was no room at Duntroon for a loner. No place for reservations about my comrades. I'd joined the army, and the army was based around the idea of mateship. It was time to grow. I was part of the Anzac tradition and that tradition was about strangers pulling together to survive in battle. Well we had our battle—that was to graduate—and I knew we could do it.

It was a solemn 'yes'. There was nothing theatrical. No swapping of blood. But it was a vow nonetheless. We all understood that and I was determined that I would never put the Musketeers asunder. Matthew 'Willie' Wilson, Mark 'Archie' Andrews, Luke 'Squizzy' Taylor and John 'Bluey' Harding were, like me, honoured to be part of Duntroon's tradition, and that was enough. We all knew that on average only 60 per cent of the college's entrants could expect to graduate, and we were all determined that four long years from now we would stand together on the same parade ground. We did not understand the fog of war yet, and did not know that those of us who survived the years ahead would each have a different story to tell.

It didn't occur to me that the Musketeers were just like me—lost, disoriented and isolated.

EXERCISE OF THE BODY AND MIND

The day at Majura started at 0555 hours. We quickly pulled on our physical training attire of white T-shirt, blue shorts with a red stripe, white socks and running shoes and made a mad dash to the parade ground one step below. There we stood in neat ranks waiting for roll call, shivering, not because it was cold but because it seemed the right thing to do at that time of the morning. After roll call we headed off in groups, under command of staff, for physical training. This generally consisted of a run down the dusty gravel trails of the Majura Range. I enjoyed these runs, as for me they were never physically strenuous and I felt a link to my life before joining the army when daily runs were an integral part of my routine.

My mind would wander off across the soft pre-dawn hues of the grasslands to the distant twinkling of Canberra's lights. As I watched the last glimmer of the stars, before they faded into the orange tinge of another sunrise, I imagined what activities other people were undertaking. Walking off to a bus stop? Kissing the wife goodbye? Drinking a cup of coffee? Sleeping? The activities of other people, not us.

My mind's meanderings were encroached upon, on one of these morning runs, when our group was halted every 500 metres and instructed to do push-ups. On each downward movement we were instructed to kiss our rifle butts which were laid across our hands. On the upward movement we were told to chant, 'I love my rifle'.

I manoeuvred into a position so the sergeant couldn't see me and chose not to get involved in the recital. I never said anything to anyone, but I just hated the sergeant after that. Love was a word I felt should not be abused in this manner. Love was sacred and personal. No-one had the right to make me love, or to use the word like that. I dreaded seeing that sergeant, as this so-called training was his specialty.

After the morning run there was time for a quick shave and shower, which was followed by breakfast. Instruction was then given for the rest of the day as we learned drill, navigation, first aid, field craft and how to use military weapons.

A MATE TO HELP THROUGH

Toad was definitely the weak link in our tent. He was a know-it-all who constantly reminded us that his father was a colonel in the army. That was an interesting fact, but it told me nothing about Toad, other than perhaps he thought this might have been a free meal ticket.

I sat down with Willie, who was helping Toad with his shoes. I had some of Toad's brass and was polishing that for him. 'Like this in small circles,' Willie said. 'See? Make sure your cloth is stretched tight across your finger. Only a little bit of polish at a time. No, don't spit! Use water.'

'Here, I'll show you a picture of my car,' Toad said. 'My parents gave it to me for passing my Higher School Certificate. Look, it's a beauty isn't it?'

I knew Willie would be grinding his teeth, so I stopped for a moment to look.

'Yes, nice car, Toad. Let's try to concentrate on the job, though. Otherwise we won't be ready for inspection tomorrow.'

'You're right, Tommy,' said Toad, using a form of my name I usually reserved for friends. He looked over my shoulder at the brass. 'My that's a nice job you're doing. It shines like my girlfriend's eyes when she sees my dick.'

I looked at Willie and he looked at me. I kept polishing as a sign not to give up. There was death in Willie's eyes.

I stood rigidly to attention at the left-hand end of my cot. My rifle was stripped for inspection and laid out like every other rifle in the tent, on a folded blanket directly beside where I stood. My metal security trunk was opened and my shoes gleamed back at me, though not as much as I would have liked. My trousers and shirts were heavily starched and folded into the trunk. They'd now require re-ironing before I wore them but the thought of the wasted time didn't worry me.

What did worry me was who would conduct the inspection today. I hoped it was Corporal Flecks. Otherwise it would be Corporals Bill and Ben. I didn't know their real names. Everyone just called them Bill and Ben because they were always together. Bill and Ben, the crackpot men. I heard a movement at the end of the tent and surreptitiously glanced out of the corner of my eye to see who it was. My heart sank.

They stood in front of Toad. Bill started firing questions while Ben picked up Toad's rifle.

'Yes, Corp . . .' was all Toad could manage before he was cut off by—

'Bullshit. I don't even have to look at it to tell you're lying. It is filthy.' Bill glowered at Toad for a minute before turning to Ben.

'Don't bother looking at those rifles. These people just aren't learning.'

Bill then took Toad's rifle and dropped it on the ground before kicking dirt all over it. He and Ben repeated the process with all of us.

'You people are not pulling together as a team,' announced Bill. 'You will not survive here unless you help your mates out. You will learn because I will teach you. I am now going to pay special attention to this section.'

They left and we all bent down to pick up our rifles. I didn't look at anyone else, I couldn't look anyone in the eye. Again, I had done nothing.

'Pricks,' Willie almost sobbed.

'Don't worry about it,' said Bluey. 'It's nothing.'

THE BUILDING OF OUR TEAM

The morning inspection started more positively the next day.

'My that's good,' said Bill. 'Your brass is 100 per cent on last time and your shoes are looking good.'

'Yes, a much improved effort,' confirmed Ben. 'Unfortunately spoiled by the potatoes growing in the barrel of your rifle.' He held the rifle out for Bill to inspect.

Bill glared at the weapon for a moment before dropping it. Then he picked up Toad's cot and overturned it. After that he kicked over Archie's cot, mine and then Willie's. He threw Bluey's cot out the tent flaps.

'Teamwork. That is all we are after. You people are going to be officers. You're supposed to be smart and you can't even get a simple concept like teamwork,' sneered Bill. 'God help us.'

TOGETHER AT LAST

A portion of the class was required for swimming and athletics training two mornings a week at 0500 hours. Those of us involved would get up early, travel by bus into town, do our training and return to Majura. This activity was an extra burden on those involved as it took away sleep. On one of these mornings when we returned to Majura we were told that our presence was required on the parade ground for splits.

'On the command "Go", you will disappear from here, re-appearing four minutes later in PT Dress Code two,' barked Corporal Ben. 'Go!'

One hundred and forty bodies hared off, scurrying up the embankments that led to the accommodation tents. People tripped over guide ropes leading from the tents, which only added to the frenzy. Inside the tents we threw clothes everywhere in an attempt to find the correct dress, changed hurriedly and then raced down to the parade ground.

'You three slugs are late. Everyone can get down and give me twenty push ups. Go.'

'On your feet, up,' bellowed the corporal. 'Not quick enough. On the ground . . . down. On your feet . . . up. On the ground . . . down. On your feet . . . up.

'Obviously I do not have your attention yet. Start switching on, people, or we'll be here all day.

'On the ground . . . down. Push-ups, begin.

'On your feet . . . up. On the command "Go", you will dis-appear from here, reappearing four minutes later in Polyester Ceremonial. Go!'

After half an hour of this I became aware through the muttered bitching of Bluey and Willie that Toad was the cause of this surprise activity. He had made no effort to iron his uniform or clean his rifle for the morning inspection.

Group punishment was the form most commonly used at RMC. One effect this had was to make us all work together as a team. The staff knew this, and group punishment was a tool they adopted to achieve team identity. The other effect of group punishment was bastardisation, for as soon as the group decided an individual was beyond help, they were left with little option but to weed out that person. Peer group pressure is a powerful and dangerous weapon, and by administering group punishment the staff were in fact giving seventeen- and eighteen-year-old boys the authority to discipline their peers.

Toad had caused much heartache and his platoon was constantly being rebuffed for his inadequacies. I had earlier been involved in a heated discussion with the rest of the platoon, who were vastly in favour of bishing Toad in the time-honoured RMC fashion. With the Musketeers in support, I had suggested that bishing was contrary to class spirit. We should help Toad. Eventually the clamour was quieted. This was not due to any remarkable skill I or the other Musketeers had in the art of persuasion. Rather, it was due to the fact that no-one other than Jude knew how to go about bishing.

The class's current predicament, I felt, was very much my responsibility. It was as if Toad's lack of improvement was meant as a slap in the face to me personally. I felt angry. It was only proper that I should seek retribution on behalf of the group. Being new at this game, I was not really sure how I should go about bishing Toad, but advice was not hard to come by. It seemed that everyone had a fantasy on how best to solve our dilemma and to pay Toad back for the trouble he so regularly caused.

Dinner time saw the germ of an idea implant itself in my head. With Willie's assistance, I filled several empty milk cartons with a rice pudding which, in the best tradition of Duntroon catering, was already slightly off. The sickly odour which had triggered the idea developed nicely over the next three days of 40 degree heat.

On the allotted evening, Jude, as the senior cadet of our class, contributed by organising a parade to the front of our tents. Not surprisingly, the only person missing once we were assembled was Toad. This helped fray my last shred of sympathy for him and the mob was in a veritable frenzy when Toad eventually strolled into view. Willie and I moved simultaneously. Willie emptied a carton of stench on Toad's head while I pushed past and poured the contents of another through his sleeping bag and other belongings. Mixed emotion made me hesitate for a moment, but I had committed myself to this course of action, since all other forms of assistance to Toad had failed.

As I stepped out of the tent to the quiet applause of my classmates, Toad directed a punch at me which I sidestepped easily. My classmates encouraged me to deck him but I held back. Years of fighting at school had taught me repugnance for physical violence. My reflexes were quick but I always refrained from physical retaliation unless someone was good enough to get through my defence and land a blow to my head. Schoolyard assailants could usually be humiliated into stopping a fight after their first eight or nine punches had been evaded. Toad threw two more punches which I also sidestepped. Bellowing like a wounded bull, Toad then rounded on Willie. It was an unwise move. Willie didn't appear to have such complicated hang-ups about throwing punches and with one swift blow sat Toad on his backside. We all turned our backs and walked away.

However, the episode was not quite over, for Toad had sworn vengeance. The next evening he hoisted a sandbag into a tree to form a makeshift punching bag, which was entertainment in itself for the large group of us watching. He fell over several times under the weight but, encouraged by hoots of derision, he persevered and was eventually successful. Toad then started to dance around, throwing bare-knuckle punches at his sandbag in what he thought was a professional and businesslike manner. A private school boy from Sydney's affluent Knox College, Toad saw the noble art of fisticuffs as the gentleman's way of evening scores. Unfortunately I am not a Knox boy, and most definitely not a gentleman, so no fight eventuated. What did eventuate, however, were infected hands for Toad, who had cut them open on the dusty sandbag and had to wear bandages for the next week.

THE THINGS THAT BIND US

Senior cadets and staff often talked about homesickness and the fact that it would make everyone want to resign at some time during the first five weeks. Like all generalisations, however, this was not entirely true. Never once did the thought cross my mind, although the person in the stretcher next to me wanted out. I thought he was wet behind the ears, a mummy's boy, and hardly said a word to him. In fact I treated him as if he had a dangerous contagious disease and my fellow Musketeers did likewise.

Generally, I enjoyed the companionship of the cadets, although I missed the freedom of being by myself. My world began to shrink and the Musketeers became more tightly bonded. There was no-one else. We had no adult figures to turn to. We all agreed that Corporal Flecks was a good bloke, but no-one trusted the military staff, as they were the people who could throw us out. There was a general lack of approval of everything we did, and this was wearing on our spirits. We were eager to please, but no-one cared enough to be pleased. It was as though the rest of the world had failed to exist and the planes we saw overhead, approaching or taking off from Canberra airport, were a cruel trick, sent to suggest there may be normality elsewhere. I came to accept that no-one really cared about Fourthies and the fact that we breathed at all was a freak of nature which inconvenienced both staff and senior cadets. I was on my own. We all were.

The Musketeers entertained ourselves by writing letters and pining over photos of our girlfriends. Ridiculous conversations developed around which one of us was going out with the world's most beautiful vision. Consensus was never reached and we'd eventually all go back to our individual cots, lie on our backs and look up in the half-light at the woman we loved. While lying there one night, Bluey broke the silence that had engulfed us.

'You know, this is crazy,' he said.

'Oh, we've got a genius in our midst,' snapped Willie irritably.

'No, it is,' continued Bluey, undeterred. 'You know we lie here every night looking at these photos and I haven't had a hard-on once. Can you get a hard-on, Squizzy?'

'I can't rightly say I can,' he replied. We could all tell it was bothering him.

'I had a soft-on the other night,' I said hopefully, 'but it took fifteen minutes of deep concentration and gave me a headache.'

'It's because they're putting bromide in the food,' Archie contributed. He had done chemistry at school.

'Rubbish,' said Bluey. 'No chemical can keep my little fellow down. He usually pops up any time.'

'I'd like to agree with Bluey,' I said. 'But my pecker's about as hard as a cheese stick.'

'Everyone quiet,' said Archie. 'Let's have twenty minutes of dirty thoughts and silence. It simply takes willpower, gentlemen.'

The results were a nil balance of hard-ons, but five headaches. Still, hard-on training became our regular piece of stupidity each night. The women of Canberra were looking safe, and whether it was bromide or plain exhaustion I'll never know.

NOT EVERYONE IN THE FIRE BRIGADE HOLDS A HOSE

The dry grasses of Majura Range were a constant bushfire hazard. One day a thick cloud of brown smoke could be seen on the far side of the range. Lessons ceased and the whole of Fourth Class assembled on the parade ground. A buzz of rumours floated through the assembly. It was a plane crash. A farmer was back-burning. These were finally laid to rest when Corporal Flecks informed our section that Second Class had started the fire while firing anti-armoured weapons.

Corporal Flecks and the other section commanders began delegating tasks, and cadets were sent to pick up beaters and water packs. While on one of these errands I passed close to Sergeant Boots, who had gathered the section commanders around him in a huddle.

'You're going to have to get a hold of these lads. Control them tightly.

They're not trained soldiers and they've only been in the army for three weeks, so use caution at all times. If you lose one you'd better die trying to rescue him because there'll be hell to pay.'

I was surprised to hear corporals spoken to in this abrupt fashion, but more surprised to hear that someone cared if we lived or died. I liked Sergeant Boots.

Trucks arrived. There was urgency in the way they rapidly did U-turns to face the way they had come. We piled in the back, some hanging off seats, others crouching on the floor and some standing. The trucks then jerked into motion, gathering momentum as we wound our way down dirt trails at breakneck speed. I felt we were driving excessively fast and I studied Corporal Flecks closely. He was the leader and I trusted him. His face wore an alarmed expression and grew paler as we skidded around each corner. My judgment was right. We were awfully close to rolling the vehicle. I watched in amazement as classmates whooped at the unexpected fun.

We lurched to a halt and rapidly dismounted, looking wide-eyed in each direction for the fire. Corporal Flecks disappeared towards the front of the vehicle, presumably to have a word with the driver. Blackened ground and smoking stumps showed that a fire had recently swept through the area, but any fire worth fighting had passed on. The starters of the fire, Second Class, were seated nonchalantly a short way up the hill. Reclined in a comfortable position on the only visible patch of unburnt grass, they seemed not at all perturbed by events and looked almost proud of their handiwork. A few derisive comments floated down the hill on a gust of wind.

'You're late, Fourthies.'

'There's never a Fourthie around when you need one.'

'Don't stand around, Fourthies, get to work.'

Ripples of laughter followed each comment. I didn't feel angry although I vaguely felt I should. I continued to look at this unusual scene and was the last person to climb aboard my truck. Strange. Fourth Class drove off to fight the fires while Second Class remained to relax.

SWEET RETRIBUTION

The last part of our training at Majura included the digging of a company defensive position on the side of a shallow hill not far from the parade ground. On our last night at Club Med the staff had organised for the film *Zulu* to be shown at an outdoor cinema they had set up on the parade ground.

I appreciated the effort the staff had gone to, but didn't follow as the class glided off into the half-light. Jude and I sat in our fox-holes waiting for them to disappear. As the class senior, Jude was constantly being harassed by the staff about Toad's laziness, and they made it clear that his attitude must change. Assistance had again been tried by class members, but Toad didn't want any help. He knew it all. Our only choice was to bish Toad again, hoping he would either change or leave.

All was quiet as we strolled down to Toad's foxhole. We emptied the contents of his pack into the bottom of the hole and refilled it with dirt. Then we dragged Toad's sleeping bag from one pile of dirt to another until it was full. When the pair of us were staggering under the load and the seams of the sleeping bag began to break, we flattened the world's biggest sandbag over the top of Toad's foxhole and camouflaged it with tufts of grass and dirt.

On return Toad stumbled around the position for an hour and a half before he eventually found his sleeping bag. I knew he'd found it because there was a squeal, like that of a wounded pig, followed by the sound of frenzied digging.

INDOCTRINATION COMPLETE

The following morning we were given our first report at the college. These reports were commonly referred to as 'pinks', after the paper on which they were written. Terminal test reports came on green paper and practice ones on blue. Military efficiency. Couldn't you get to love it? My first report was a C+—C being average. Sergeant Boots gave me my report.

'A satisfactory report, Staff Cadet Sneyk. I really can't say much more, other than that you have a good sense of humour and you're always smiling. Some people won't like that but don't lose it. Too many people don't have a sense of humour around here.'

'Yes, Sergeant.' I beamed gratefully and sincerely. I vaguely wondered why people didn't like smiling but dismissed it without more than momentary thought.

After we'd received our reports we marched the eight kilometres back to Duntroon. As we neared the front gates I pulled myself up to my full height for the benefit of anyone watching, but no-one watched. It didn't matter. I was still here.

Those who wanted to leave were allowed to resign. The class suffered casualties two through eleven.

A TENNIS PARTY WITH NO TENNIS

Life was more relaxed on return to the college. The senior class only berated you when you did something wrong. There was still a great deal to do wrong, but the situation was an improvement on being yelled at when you had done nothing wrong. Our thoughts now turned to the start of the academic year.

At about this time Jude had to arrange the last Tennis Party to be held at Duntroon. The Tennis Party was an old tradition, arranged in the hope that new cadets would get off on the right foot with the 'right kind' of Canberra women, and invitations were extended to the young ladies of Canberra's private schools. Jude thought it would be sound planning for me to travel on the bus from one of these schools, acquaint myself with the best looking of the students and thus give him and the Musketeers a head start over the rest of the frenzied mob. The plan was good, but the outcome was less than brilliant. Even after five weeks in an all-male environment, the majority of schoolgirls on my bus seemed less than attractive. However, one particular brunette was gorgeous and I struck up a conversation with her. It turned out she was only hitching a ride and intended to disappear as soon as we arrived to see her boyfriend, who was in a senior class. Heartless bitch, I thought. I haven't seen a woman for five weeks and you want to go off with an arsehole from the senior class. But my roving eye saw no-one else I wished to talk too. On arrival at Duntroon I waved goodbye to this beauty, much to the dismay of the rest of the Musketeers.

'I wouldn't look for a pearl amongst that lot,' I said to Bluey. 'I suggest we try somewhere else.'

The Tennis Party was a curious institution. Gracious old Campbell House, Canberra's original building, was the venue but no-one played tennis. The coat and tie, which were the minimum dress standard for cadets attending, were not my usual tennis attire. At least the food was sumptuous, as was always the case when the college was on display to the public. My imagination didn't stretch so far that I could think of where those good cooks came from. The party moved sometime in the evening to the Cadets' Mess. Many a bawdy joke was made by the senior class about our chances with the innocent little schoolgirls, but to be honest the mood was less than perfect for romance. One hundred and forty overly eager shave-headed cadets who have not seen a lady in five weeks and 200 giggling schoolgirls did not make for a roaring party.

I made one long-term friendship from the night's activities. Alison and I talked for a long time and eventually I took her for a tour of our accommodation area as she was curious about the new academy buildings in which we lived. Absolutely nothing happened and I never intended that it should, but I will always be able to boast that at the Royal Military College's last Tennis Party I entertained a young lady in my room. As a gentleman I would never tell any more than that. I had picked up a sound value of the corps. That is: Never ruin a good story with the truth.

AN INTRODUCTION TO ACADEMICS

On the day following the Tennis Party, a morning tea was organised on the lawns, again at Campbell House. The gentlemanly proceedings gave us an opportunity to meet our academic lecturers in an informal environment. We were supposed to discuss preparation for our university study. The idea generally had merit, but to a class of ravenous cadets, talking to professors and doctors assumed a very low priority compared to eating. By this stage, many of my classmates and I skipped breakfast to devote more time to cleaning the section area. I didn't go to dinner, so I could avoid harassment by the senior class, and only ate lunch because it was compulsory.

I remember descending on the tables at a dignified canter before stuffing as many cream puffs into my face as possible. My classmates did the same as we swarmed from table to table. I took brief respite to burp and have a gleeful chat with Squizzy and Bluey before re-entering the throng. It really was exhilarating watching the class work as one while the academics stood in a defensive huddle off to one side. Andy, who I'd met on the first day, was the only cadet within coo-ee of them. After the food on the table was finished we set ourselves in ambush along the path the waiters were following with more food.

When that supply of food had also been exhausted we trickled away to whence we had come, with barely a word spoken to academics by the whole class. At the time I was self-consciously aware of our bad manners and expected a rebuff from the military staff, who were surely aware of the class's barbaric display. It never came.

I spoke to Jude about this.

'Look, Tommy, you'll soon work this little love triangle out,' he said. 'The military staff hate the academic staff as much as the cadets hate the military. There's three groups here. Cadets, military staff and academics. At best we all compete with each other, at worst we all hate each other. Forget the seven wonders of RMC, the only wonder is that the place doesn't blow itself apart.'

MORE INDUCTION, LESS VALUES

Before receiving our first night's leave in Canberra, the RMC screed test had to be passed. The screed consisted of 40 useless questions about Duntroon's history. I studied the set material diligently but was never really confident with the rote learning which was required. It was uninteresting and my attention span was limited as a consequence.

As a repeat, Jude had already passed the test and had many friends in the senior class. He waltzed in one evening with a copy of the exam in his hand. 'Here you go,' he said. 'Keep this under your hat. It should be of some assistance.' He was obviously pleased with himself.

'Thanks, cobber,' I cautiously replied.

'Not a problem. What are mates for?' And he was gone.

I felt uncomfortable about this gift. What about integrity? I toyed with using it for a moment before hiding it by taping it to the bottom of my drawer. I was even careful not to look at the paper as I hid it, as if it might somehow taint me. I thought about destroying it, but something stopped me.

When the results of the screed test were announced, only half a dozen people in the class had passed and I was not one of them. We were allowed to get three questions out of 40 wrong and I had failed four of them. 'What's wrong, Tommy?' asked Jude. 'How come you didn't pass?'

'I didn't use the exam you gave me, mate.'

'Why not?' he exclaimed indignantly. 'Don't you want leave? Stop being a dick. It's an idiotic test any way you look at it. Let me tell you something. This place is a game and it depends on how you play it whether you win or lose. You must play the numbers, go with the odds. This place has rules for everything. If you're going to stay sane you're going to have to break some rules over the next four years.'

I could sense Jude had a real need for me to understand his point of view and he continued his lecture.

'You only break them when you have assessed your odds, and made sure the chances of not getting caught fall in your favour. Of course if you do get caught you cop it sweet. No whingeing.

'All the staff are ex-RMC. They know the game because they've all played. You can lie your arse off, as long as you don't get caught. The only time you don't lie is when someone says "integrity question". That is an indicator that the staff want to know the truth. The rest of the time you can presume that they don't.

'It's the way things have been, the way things are, and the way things always will be. Just like this shitty screed test. The staff don't care about it. No-one's going to mind if you use your initiative a little bit. You're an officer in training, that's what you are supposed to do. Don't steal and don't go jack on your mates. After that, anything goes.'

I thought about it and Jude was right on all counts. I was being a dick. It was a stupid test. What the hell! Jude gave me a copy of the retest and needless to say I did quite well.

THE BROADENING OF THE MIND

The greater part of the year at RMC involved university studies. The military aspect of our education took a back seat: it consisted of the morning parade and an afternoon devoted to military instruction. In Fourth Class's case, this was Wednesday. Saturday morning was totally dedicated to military instruction.

The atmosphere in Beersheba Company became noticeably lighter as everyone went about their business with a minimum of fuss. I had not set the world on fire with my academic ability at school and I was worried about my ability to cope with tertiary-level study. However, Duntroon required me to complete a degree to become an officer, and so academics I would do, and do well. The two highest awards at Duntroon were the Sword of Honour, awarded for leadership, and the Queen's Medal, awarded for academic excellence. I wanted both.

I strictly adhered to the study hours each night from 1900 to 2200 hours in my room, as required by RMC rules. It was the first time in my life I had studied, and my first History paper for the year showed immediate progress. I received a distinction. This was quickly followed by a high distinction for my first Philosophy essay. I started to feel new confidence. There were often knocks on my door as classmates sought me out for advice on some piece of work or other. I developed a reputation as a 'conshi acca'—RMC speak for conscientious academic—and found myself besieged the night before the second Philosophy essay was due. The text that was causing such confusion was a particularly intricate novel called *The Tempest*. I spent an hour explaining the themes of the book to Jude, Andy and another classmate, Simon. Blank looks were my only response.

I'd been up late the night before putting the finishing touches to my essay and felt no inclination to spend another late evening, so I wrote an essay for Simon and then dictated essays for Andy and Jude. This was a relatively simple process and I produced three totally different essays within two hours, each one laying emphasis on different themes. It never crossed my mind that this may be considered academic misconduct. It was a combination of helping out your mates, as we'd been taught to do, and the quickest way to get to bed.

When the results eventually came back, my four essays had received a high distinction, a distinction, a credit and a credit minus. I was slightly put out as the essay with my name on it only received a distinction while Andy, who'd had his typed, received a high distinction. I knew my essay had more substance to it, but I wasn't in a position to debate the issue with my lecturer. I just accepted that the lower mark was the penalty I paid for having spidery writing.

A HABIT FROM PREVIOUS TIMES

I waited a couple of weeks after the academic term started to see when I could fit in my daily run. No time seemed satisfactory, for as long as there were people awake there were people making demands on my time. From 0600 hours till 2200 hours I couldn't find the time to go for a run. The joy of running comes from either having a wandering mind or a mind that is totally focused. Neither can be achieved when you are worrying about an unfinished task, or a show parade for some minor misdemeanour, or an interview of some description. The only real option was to wait until after 2200 hours, when the college started to fall asleep.

Eventually it became my regular habit to go for my run at 2300 hours. My route took me through the academy construction site, up the side of Mount Pleasant, down to Russell Offices and from there across to the bicycle path that surrounds Lake Burley Griffin. Once on to the lake, I crossed two bridges before returning to Duntroon. The course was eight kilometres long and took in some magnificent views. This was especially true on quiet, windless nights when the lake's surface was a mirror. For company I had the wallabies, rabbits and occasional fox that reclaim Canberra's streets at night. We looked at each other with curious eyes, each wondering what strange twist of fate made us companions. I swore by the therapeutic effects of these runs and asked Archie, Willy and Jude to join me on several occasions. They did so once or twice, but quickly trailed away, convinced of my insanity.

I was determined, however, to persevere. My run gave me a sense of normality. It was an activity which I did independent of the army. The run took determination to complete, especially in mid-winter when the temperature was below zero and every gasp for air burnt my lungs, or I was so tired my body was pleading for me to go to bed. Most importantly, the runs gave me a chance to put a perspective on what I saw each day. Running was an opportunity to think, free from others' views that crowded me and came from all directions.

I would come back from my runs and sit. Normally, my ideas and thoughts were settled by that stage. I would gather them and send them off to the people I loved in letters. I especially enjoyed writing home. Dad would understand, he'd been around the military all his life. He knew what kind of soldier I wanted to be and I began to recognise how my parents had guided me in life. Every belief and hope I held for the military had been carefully sewn when I was a child. For others it may have been different, but I realised that I had come to this vocation out of respect for my father and his friends.

NEW FRIENDS

The Musketeers were not as tightly bound as we had been at Majura. The strong necessity to survive was not as apparent and we all felt a loosening of the bond between us. Still, those pledges made in the hard times of the first five weeks stood as links that we were determined should not easily be broken. Squizzy, Bluey and Willie became best friends and I spent most of my time with Archie.

Archie was a sensitive kind of person who was unpretentious and lacked guile. He was a poet and an idealist, a dreamer and a lover. We spent much of our time plotting our weekend trips to Sydney, where he had a girlfriend whom he adored. Archie and I talked about all issues to the last detail.

With our Sydney trips we had to choose between applying for leave and going there legally, or not applying for leave. The tricky part was that if you applied for leave and it was refused, when you went to Sydney you could be charged not only for AWOL, but also for disobedience of a lawful command. If you didn't apply for leave and were caught, you could only be charged for AWOL, so no leave application was ever put in for our trips. Besides, I hated paperwork.

Bluey, on the other hand, never cared what people thought of him. I always felt certain that Bluey would do what Bluey thought right and that he would never bow to peer pressure. Bluey was strong willed, often arrogant, and insensitive to other people. I hate all of these characteristics, so I found it strange that I could like him, but he was his own man and that was his redemption. Bluey was one of the few of my 156 classmates who never moralised to me. He did what he liked and I could do what the hell I liked. Bluey was obsessive in nature. He was love. He was hate. And he was both with an intense fury that seared people who didn't understand emotion. A lot of people feared Bluey.

Squizzy was often judged by classmates who knew him less well to be an adjunct to Bluey's personality. Having known him well I could understand that opinion, except that Squizzy cared what people thought which sort of spoiled the final result.

Willie was a complex character. Introverted, he came to the college to please his father, who was a graduate. Willie resented the behaviour of the senior class towards us as juniors. He was always loyal to our class, and capable of being very good fun.

I had strong reservations about us, but the Musketeers filled a need and I knew it.

EIGHTEEN YEARS OLD AND I STILL BELIEVE IN THE EASTER BUNNY

Easter was the first major leave period of the year, when cadets could expect four or five days at home. Everyone except Fourth Class, that is. We were required to go on a camp. The senior class said that if we were allowed home on leave we would all turn into mummy's boys and wouldn't come back. It was probably true. The Easter Recreational Camp we were obliged to attend was abbreviated to Easter Rack Camp, 'rack' being the cadet word for sleep. Half of the class went to Batemans Bay to get their Bronze Medal in Surf Lifesaving and the other half spent five days in Jervis Bay camping on HMAS *Creswell* golf course.

I went to *Creswell* and we spent our days lounging on the beach, catching the last warmth of the summer sun, windsurfing, running or playing tennis. It was a relaxing time and the staff did their best to stay out of our way. Two things weighed on all of our minds, however. The first was the fact that we would rather be at home; the second was that the Easter Bunny might visit.

The Easter Bunny was another Duntroon tradition. For some reason the bunny only visited Fourthies. For the uninitiated it might sound nice, but what things appeared to be and what they were were always two different things at Duntroon. The Easter Bunny that visited Duntroon while we were at the Rack Camp was a little uncoordinated in his hopping and could cause a frightful mess if he visited your room.

When we returned to college I approached my room with a feeling of trepidation. I opened the door and realised all was intact. The bunny, however, had definitely visited some people. Toad's room looked as if the bouncy visitor had had an epileptic fit there. The bunny's movements had not exactly been random and in my opinion he had only visited people who deserved it. The Easter Bunny, I decided, was a good tradition.

The most interesting effect of the Easter Rack Camp was the fact that I was so well rested I stayed awake for three academic lectures in a row. For a Fourthie, this was a major miracle. After attending these lectures with a totally alert mind I realised that I could now sleep through the rest of them with my mind well at ease. I'd felt guilty up until then about the amount of information I was missing when I nodded off. But the best way to absorb information was of course by my previous method of having it seep into my subconscious.

EARTH IS THE CENTRE OF THE UNIVERSE

After Easter we had a different Philosophy lecturer. His name was William Crick and he was new to our class, but his lecturing style was the subject of much comment around the college. William spoke only to the back left of the lecture room. This was patently ridiculous, as the lecture room was designed for 100 students, yet he never established eye contact with anyone bar the back row, and only then if you were in the left-hand side of the last line of seating. Although Philosophy had well over 100 students enrolled, there was never any danger of not getting a seat. An average class would have the usual eight or nine regulars turn up, with perhaps six or seven stray students who were feeling guilty.

William's lecture style meant that the class was split into two groups. The first gravitated around the left back of the class: the other to the right-hand front. Those who sat at the left back, I later discovered, were destined for distinctions or credits. The other group, of which I was a prominent member, indeed sometimes the only member, was heading down another path.

My group used to delight in trying to get Mr Crick's attention to the right-hand front. Initially this was easy, but he became adept at ignoring sudden loud noises. After much experimentation, I discovered the best way to get William's attention was to throw balls of paper at him. This invariably caused a head movement in my direction, even if it was only to look daggers at me. I wanted to excel in academic studies but my sense of fun overrode all else.

A BIRD AMONGST THE SNAKES

A new section commander, Corporal Finch, arrived in my section. During his first day as our commander he called us all into his room. We perched on his bed expectantly.

'I am here as your commander and I intend to command,' the corporal told us. 'We are here to get a job done—that is, to graduate as good officers—and we will. This section will work hard and work together. I expect that, and I also expect that we won't take life so seriously that we lose our sense of fun.'

Corporal Thaddaeus Finch was one of the college's fittest cadets.

He didn't have a nickname, which was surprising when you considered what a mouthful Thaddaeus was. He was just referred to by his class as Finch. He was an outstanding academic who threw all his energies into achieving excellence in everything he did. Thaddaeus Finch was a man of integrity and honesty. No-one in his class trusted him.

A MATE

I looked on with interest. The arrow went hurtling through the air and Archie deftly knocked it to one side. We were in Sydney and I was watching him go through his karate routine in a park with a group of other enthusiasts. People often seemed to place their bodies in the way of unnecessary danger. There had to be an attraction, but I couldn't see what it might be. Archie wanted me to get involved with karate but I had politely refused. Trouble always found me without much effort and I didn't see any particular need to stand in the way of an arrow on my weekends. Self-destruction. Why were people fascinated by the idea? I shook my head and watched closely.

I'd known people who had learnt karate at school. Usually they had just enough knowledge to get their heads kicked in. There's nothing like anger correctly directed to tear someone apart. Still, Archie was interested in the 'spiritual side', he told me. This was generally a throwaway line, but in Archie's case I think it was true.

Archie was an interesting fellow, no mistake. I'd never met anyone with such a soft centre. Sensitive was not a correct description, for he had an ability to be cruel if you watched carefully. Yet he had shown me some of his poetry one night. It displayed an intricate and complex character. He'd given it to me like a fourteen-year-old girl asked to give her teacher a love letter she had been reading under the desk. It was all shuffling and embarrassed looks. I took it as a sign of acceptance and trust. That was a nice feeling.

The squat little frame with glasses that was Archie was a real surprise package. He'd also represented New South Wales in schoolboy rugby union. Archie was a gifted person but in terms of Duntroon, he was just your average cadet.

ANOTHER DEPARTURE

One day while walking back to the company lines, I passed a classmate, 'Blowie' Wilson, packing up his utility with suitcases and other personal belongings.

'Where are you off to, mate?' I asked as I stopped.

'I've resigned, Tommy. I'm off home.'

All I could blurt out was a 'Why?'

'I've had enough. I don't need this any more. They can play their silly little games with someone else. I've got better things to do with my life than sit around here with some power-hungry fools telling me what I should and shouldn't think.'

I stayed and talked for a while before shaking hands, then went straight to Archie's room to chat about the shock news. Blowie had it all. One of the most motivated people in the class, he was fit and intelligent and he was doing it easy. After talking with Archie for a while I reached the conclusion that to resign like that was probably the hardest decision a man could make. It took courage to walk away from RMC and accept the social stigma of being regarded as a failure when it was all there for the taking. More courage than I possessed.

He was the twelfth member of our class to leave.

LOYAL TO THE CORE

Writing a letter in my room one morning, I was disturbed by a knock at the door. I looked up to see the commanding officer of the Corps of Staff Cadets, Lieutenant Colonel Pat Goode, walk in. I immediately stood to attention, trying to look as smart as possible, my mind racing as I wondered what had brought on this visit.

'Sit down, Tommy,' he said pleasantly. 'What are you doing?'

'Writing an essay, sir,' I lied easily.

'What's the topic?'

'Oh, ah, Geography, sir.'

'Where is everyone, Tom? The company appears to be awfully quiet. Probably sleeping I dare say.' Sleeping during the day was forbidden, only because everyone did it.

'No sir. I'm sure everyone would be at lectures. This is a rather hectic time, what with exams coming up. Tuesday mornings tend to see everyone at one lecture or another.'

'Quite right. Keep working on that essay,' and he was gone.

I was amazed. The commanding officer knew my name, an insignificant Fourthie. The senior class often talked about being in 'Pat's family', and right at that moment I was happy to be a young son of Daddy Pat.

THE SPIRIT OF ANZAC

I kicked in Jude's door. He lay semi-conscious on his bed. 'Get up little buddy, drill in half an hour.' Saturday morning military training was always hard on hangovers and Jude was a mess.

'Cover, Tommshie,' was the only response from the floppy doll.

'Let's go, mate. It ain't that easy,' I said, shaking Jude. He pulled the sheets up over his head.

I left. He wouldn't be much good anyway. As the class senior, Jude was responsible for the handover to the training staff of each lesson. He could hardly do that in his present state, so I called the class to attention and marched across to the sergeant.

'Good morning, Sergeant. Posted strength 136, one in hospital, four medically rest, 131 on parade and all accounted for,' I said quietly and clearly before handing over the parade state sheet to Sergeant Boots. He scrutinised it carefully.

'Jude's in hospital?' The sergeant raised an eyebrow.

'Yes, Sergeant. He was ill last night.'

Sergeant Boots looked me up and down. 'I'll bet he was. Have a little too much to drink, did he?'

'No, Sergeant. Food poisoning, I believe. Jude's a teetotaller.' This was going a little too far, but an unusual and unlikely fact like that often distracted the staff from the real issue. It wasn't often that a cadet abstained from the demon alcohol.

'I'll be checking on his health then,' the sergeant said. 'Right after lessons are finished.'

The lesson over, I tore back to the lines, washed Jude's mouth out with Listerine and took him down to the hospital. The matron didn't look convinced by my story of food poisoning, but Jude was propped up in a hospital bed by the time Sergeant Boots appeared two minutes later.

TOAD FINALLY IMPROVES

Toad came down to parade one Friday and everyone in the Sovereign's Company noticed that his boots were shining for the first time since our arrival back in January. Much banter was directed at him.

'Who'd you pay to do those, Toad?'

'Toad didn't pay anyone, he just stole them.'

My curiosity was aroused and I gave Archie a nudge. 'Watch this,' I said as we formed up into our ranks and I ensured I was in the rank to Toad's front. The parade was in the usual RMC format of a march around the parade ground in slow and then in quick time. To change direction on the parade ground, the cadet body did forms at various points, which required you to stamp your feet on the ground and move in the direction commanded.

On one of these forms I dropped back slightly and drove my foot down and back into Toad's toecaps. There was a satisfying yelp as I found my mark.

Once we were dismissed from parade, I went up to the limping Toad and apologised profusely. 'Sorry, mate. You all right?' I said as I looked with satisfaction at my handiwork. I'd driven my heel through his toecap, leaving a large gash in the leather. I walked off and Squizzy came up to me.

'You're an arsehole, Tommy,' he said with a smile and a shake of the head.

'Why thank you,' I replied genially. Other people walked past and patted me on the back in congratulation, but not Sergeant Starch.

'Did you do that on purpose?' he asked.

'No, Sergeant,' I replied indignantly. 'I couldn't do that to a classmate.'

'Well done. That's the attitude.'

He smiled at me and walked on.

A LITTLE BIT OF FUN

My head was pounding. I sat at my desk struggling with a book on Freud. It would not normally have been my first choice for reading material, but I was still missing something in *The Tempest*. I might have achieved a distinction for my essay but I was not happy and I still didn't really understand the book. I was fairly sure my inadequacies were based around my lack of understanding of Jung and Freud. The author was trying to tell us something about these two figures, but I couldn't quite grasp what it was.

The door opened and a bag full of double happys and Tom Thumb crackers came flying in. The bag bounced around, twitching as each cracker went off. When I jumped up to extinguish my smouldering carpet I knocked my brew mug against the wall and broke it.

'I'm going to kill you, Jude,' I yelled at the top of my voice.

I wasn't so much angry about the firecrackers and burnt carpet; it was the brew mug. RMC superstition stated that if you broke your brew mug you would never graduate. I was fuming.

'You little bastard, you're dead meat,' I yelled for good measure.

THE WORLD IS FLAT

I approached my first exams knowing that I had so far achieved good academic results. I had already accrued many marks and was usually a good performer in exams, so I felt confident.

Unfortunately they were a minor disaster. The good work I had previously achieved was eroded and I was extremely lucky to pass. Philosophy in particular, where I was hoping for a credit or perhaps a distinction, was a dismal performance. My mark when posted was a 'Q', or a 'query' as it was known. This was a marginal performance of either 49, 50 or 51 per cent. I was so dismayed by this turn of events that Corporal Finch suggested we go down to the Philosophy Department and clear up where I had gone wrong. However, I was far from keen on this suggested course of action. As a cricketer, I had always accepted the umpire's decision as final. I had always been taught by my dad, 'Don't question it, fix it.' It's a good rule, too, and is often the right thing to do. At other times it is simply obeyed because it is easy to obey rules.

At any rate, we went down to the Philosophy Department, Corporal Finch holding my hand. This is scarcely an exaggeration for at this stage of my life I did not know how to confront people with an issue. I'd learnt to keep my own counsel and to work around problems, but I'd never had anyone else take an interest in them before and was uncomfortable with the feelings that Finch's interest had aroused.

Corporal Finch did the questioning and I merely watched as we sat in the cluttered office of the first-year Philosophy coordinator. The coordinator said that my poor exam performance had been a surprise to him too. My exam essays, he went on to explain, were very original, so original in fact that the marker, William Crick, couldn't decide if I was a genius or completely befuddled. Faced with this difficult decision, and having never met a genius before, Mr Crick decided that I was fuddled. The coordinator was careful to keep my three exam essays out of my sight. When the interview drew to a close it was suggested to me, with a meaningful look, that I wouldn't have a problem with passing Philosophy at the end-of-year exams. I stood up to go, and as I left the office I noticed my distinctive scrawl on my exam papers. 'Exam average 26 per cent' was circled in red ink on the top right-hand corner of the top essay. It was a large coincidence that this mark just happened to take me from a high distinction down to 49 per cent. I said nothing and kept walking. Mr Crick had his revenge.

As I returned to my room, I felt betrayed. I'd always believed that the abuse of power was perpetrated by ignorant, petty people. And I had also always assumed that the military spent money providing us with an education to ensure that, with the broadening of our minds, we would better understand the responsibilities that went with authority. I'd been naive enough to think that people who abused power were monsters like Hitler and Stalin. It came as a shock to learn that everyone abused power, even academics who were leading us in the search for a better understanding of the human race.

SIMPLE SOLDIERING

The military program had taken a back seat in the weeks leading up to the exams. This was to allow the cadet to focus on study. After the exams the military staff needed to remind us that we were still in the army and their means of doing this was called Exercise Ben Hur, ruefully known as Ben Hurt to the unfortunate participants. We rummaged around attempting to find our temporarily abandoned military equipment. Greens were ironed, boots brushed and patrol packs dusted off as the corps readied itself. At 0530 hours on a Friday morning we were assembled on the parade ground, in the light of a cold pre-dawn, and steeled ourselves for the challenges ahead as we waited to march off in our section groups.

A brisk eight kilometre walk followed out to Majura Range, and then the 30-odd ten-man sections split, each one to go to a separate area and commence the 'start' activity. The activities were designed to test group cohesion, military knowledge, and quick decision-making ability. Our section's first task consisted of crossing two four-metre high walls with two logs and a piece of string. The activities were conducted at a ferocious pace as both company and personal pride were at stake. Casualties mounted. Jude, who was in my section, almost lost his manhood after jumping off a precariously suspended log in an attempt to cross an obstacle. Archie went down with a sprained ankle. And still the activity continued. Lunch was eaten running between areas and we lost another member of the section in the afternoon. Each activity was short but required maximum output of energy. The sun was a red orb on the horizon as we dragged our tired bodies up to the last activity. Our last exercise of the day required us to attack an enemy, through obstacles of barbed wire and trenches, rescue a casualty and evacuate him. This had to be repeated ten times for each member of the original section. Unfortunately our section now numbered only six, but the course still had to be completed ten times.

The popular commander of Beersheba Company, Major Grey, stood to one side to watch our efforts. In truth, no-one really knew him because he never took much interest in any of us. He was popular mainly because we seldom saw him and this meant we could do as we pleased.

When Corporal Finch, our section commander, looked at us he wouldn't have seen a very promising sight. Five of us stood before him, leaning on our rifles or bent over double from muscles that were too exhausted to support our backs. Our uniforms were ripped and dirty. 'Let's give Grey a hard-on,' was all he could manage by way of inspiration. We were off, hitting obstacles with speed and precision as we drew on the extra adrenalin one gains to compensate for fatigue. The barbed wire tore at our greens, which hung in tatters. The barbs slashed our skin. Major Grey caught the mood and started jumping up and down like a schoolkid as we crawled and limped on our last ounces of energy, dropping as we hit the finish line. For that last exercise, we completed the fastest time of any section through the day. We were proud and elated.

It meant nothing to anyone except us, and I knew that. There was no point in writing home to anyone about it. What was there to understand? My values were moving further away from society's. I knew it and knew it was uncontrollable. You either believed or you left.

Events concluded, the sections all gathered at the Rifle Static Mechanical Range about 400 metres from Club Med. Section results were read out and my section finished fourth. We trudged the kilometre and a half to the front gates of the range, muscles aching, minds numb. Thankfully, buses were waiting and when they dropped us off at the college at 1830 hours we creaked slowly towards our rooms. Ben Hurt had lived up to its reputation and had left me physically and mentally exhausted. I had a shower and went into town to do some late-night shopping.

Curious looks followed my movements as I shuffled around like a 100-year-old robot. Unusually for a late shopping night, I did not see one cadet. After much pain I finally found the right birthday present for a friend in Sydney. My mind was racing, even if my body was not. If all the cadets had gone to bed, it followed that the two nightclubs they frequented, the City Club and the Private Bin, would be devoid of competition. Off I shuffled to the City Club, where I found a seat at the bar and ordered one or two anaesthetics.

The following night my simple gift caused an eye to light up for a brief moment, and that was reward enough. The truth was she could never appreciate the effort that went into buying such a trivial gift, and I knew it. I drew further into myself and the corps, not wanting to explain, but aware of the fact that if I did wish to, I couldn't.

A PARTING

Toad was thrown out a week after mid-year exams as he had failed everything. I was happy to see him go and there was not one sad face in the company, but I was also melancholy. I was disappointed in my own behaviour. I understood it and would do the same again, but I was disappointed for myself. When the Fourthies of Beersheba Company went to the Ainslie Hotel to celebrate, I stayed behind. Classmates were startled by my refusal to attend. 'But you did more to get rid of Toad than anyone,' they said.

I shrugged. 'I've nothing to celebrate.'

The class lost its thirteenth member.

PART OF A GRAND TRADITION

Queen's Birthday Parade was to occur in the weeks just after June exams. Besides Graduation, this was Duntroon's biggest parade and an occasion much talked about. For the Fourthies this would mark our final acceptance into the fold of the Corps of Staff Cadets. After this parade, life was expected to become markedly more relaxed and the last of the off-handed behaviour of the senior class was expected to disappear.

Around about the time of QB, as it was called—our thirst for acronyms was insatiable—the corps became obsessed with the fact that RMC as we knew it was going to disappear. The opening of the tri-service college, the Australian Defence Force Academy, was due at the end of the year and Officer Cadet School Portsea was to close. Duntroon's name would change to the Royal Military College of Australia, much to the dismay of the corps, and have two graduations a year as it took over Portsea's role. With the proposed Mid-Year Graduation, this QB was expected to be the last. It was billed as such and in a sense it was.

I invited my family, who travelled from Tasmania. Jock, a friend of mine and my father's who had graduated from RMC in the '60s, came with his wife, Sue. A friend from Melbourne, Steph, also came. A week of drill preceded the parade and the corps' already sharp drill was honed further.

The parade started on a foggy, chilling Canberra morning. The Fourthies were first up, as we went down in layers of tracksuits to scrape the ice off the guests' seating. This appeared to be a futile task and I am assured by Mum that it was. The ice had returned by the time the guests were seated, but Fourthies had been doing this since time began, so we scraped ice one more time.

The drill on parade was sharp and impressive from start to finish. Afterwards morning tea was held in the Cadets' Mess and Jock found a captive audience, as he explained some of the 'goings on' in his days at the college. I knew nothing had changed, and I wondered if I would one day return to tell stories in a similar fashion. Just enough detail to make them funny, not enough detail to make them tragic. The rest of the day was spent with my family, before enjoying dinner and the QB Ball. Archie and I spent the evening dancing and drinking before heading back to the college where we sat in my room with our ladies, watching the sun come up and talking of nothing. Dreaming and believing in dreams.

The following day the festivities continued as each company had a party in various venues around Canberra. The Sovereign's

Company party wound up early and we moved back to the college lines. The company was a madhouse. Being a romantic at Duntroon is often a trying business. My door was banged on by an hysterical classmate. 'Go away,' I yelled. 'Tommy, I've cut my finger off,' floated through the still-locked door. I didn't care, but realising I'd look callous in front of Steph if I didn't, I reluctantly decided to swap passion for compassion. When I grudgingly opened the door I was confronted by Bluey, who had a finger dangling from a thread of skin. 'You're bleeding on my floor,' I growled harshly as his finger dangled independent of any bodily control.

Off we went to hospital. How Bluey managed to chop off a finger remains a mystery to this day. My duty to him over, I hurried back to my room, hoping the mood hadn't changed too dramatically. However, someone had started a bishing war while I was away. People were running around throwing buckets of water in windows, firecrackers were going off, doors were slamming. Sometimes you have to give up. Who needed love when you had the corps?

The grounds of RMC looked splendid at QB and I enjoyed showing my family around. I enjoyed Jock's tales of days gone by, all of them funny, and I felt as if I belonged to something greater than the sum of its individuals. I also received the first unqualified compliment by a senior class in six months. The simple words, 'Good turn-out, Tommy' on the pre-parade inspection had made me swell with pride. I had arrived. I was accepted as an individual and I belonged to the corps.

MATESHIP

My academic work never quite picked up again after mid-year exams. I don't know if this was the result of a conscious decision, or just a loss of interest. Indeed it may well have been subconscious.

But the fact is I changed. I started to miss lectures, which I had never done before. And I took the path that many a cadet had trodden, sleeping during the day rather than listening to lecturers I was beginning to despise. I went to Sydney virtually every weekend, often returning in the early hours of Monday morning, and I discovered TOC.

Tea or Coffee was a grand tradition that I had hitherto avoided. Corporal Finch, however, was a great believer in the mid-morning institution and encouraged me to go. TOC consisted of several tables set with jugs of hot water, tea and coffee, of course, along with some loaves of bread, jam and Vegemite. It was all rather crude, but it definitely fed the starving hordes. Each class ate TOC separately, with Fourth Class outside in the chill of the Canberra weather.

On the morning of my first TOC I turned up punctually at 1000 hours, salivating slightly at the prospect. All that greeted me were a few remaining classmates having a chat and the remnants of food strewn everywhere. Everything at Duntroon has rules and I was becoming a little bit more perceptive. Aha, I thought. Obviously the first rule of TOC is he who is punctual is late. I found a used cup and some coffee but not much else, so I made an evil-smelling brew and was in the throes of taking my first mouthful when a shower of sugar landed over me, thrown from an upstairs window where Second Class had their TOC. I looked up and Corporal Finch's grinning face greeted me.

'You're late, Tommy,' he called out. 'Remember one thing. TOC is war.'

I could relate to that rule and, as in warfare, all was fair. One of the contentious issues about TOC was that engineers, who had a full academic program, could rarely get away from lectures early enough to get a feed. Artists, by contrast, often had free periods and could get to TOC early. The whinges of the engineers and the anguish on their faces when they arrived to find you stuffing the last piece of bread in your mouth provided pure satisfaction. I started getting to TOC earlier and earlier, until eventually a group of stalwarts would lie in wait for the seals to appear with the food, rip it out of their hands and pig out. I encouraged the Musketeers to come to TOC and we often ate until indigestion set in. Then we'd throw everything that was uneaten in the bin that was always beside the table, pouring milk and throwing Vegemite over the top to ensure the engineers would understand that TOC is war.

BUREAUCRACY

After mid-year exams many classmates dropped one of their academic subjects to ease the burden of their workloads. I intended to follow suit but was told flatly by Major Grey that he believed I could pass all subjects at the end of the year. Therefore he would not allow me to do what the majority of my classmates had done.

NEW LINKS

Bluey and I became closer friends during the second half of the year. We both did Geography practicals, which took up our Friday afternoons. These had become a real drain on my willpower, for by the end of the week I had had my fill of academics. This was not an uncommon feeling amongst cadets and the Geography staff, who were well aware of the problem, stipulated that we must attend 80 per cent of practicals to pass the subject that year.

One Friday I turned up to Geography, picked up the practical and shuffled over to a bench where I flopped down next to Bluey. I put my name on the top of the exercise and started to read a language that faintly reminded me of Upper Amazonian Swahili. I looked at Bluey, who by his expression had encountered the same language barrier.

'I'd rather be in Sydney,' I deadpanned.

Bluey nodded. 'Let's go,' he said.

I stood and Blue followed. Twenty pairs of eyes watched us boldly walk up to the front desk, toss our evidence of attendance in front of the lecturer and turn to leave. I paused on the way out to let Jude know where we were going and to cover us in the military lessons in the morning.

OURS IS NOT TO REASON WHY

Besides cleaning your section each morning, there were also area duties. These included polishing the brass handrails in the mess and picking up rubbish outside the buildings or in the car park. One of the area duties we most disliked was looking after the Rec Room. The room was used by the whole company as a common area for watching television, TOC and relaxation.

One morning when Squizzy and I turned up to clean the Rec Room it was an unholy mess. Meat pies had been wiped around the wall, leaving gravy stains on the cream painted brickwork. Eggs had been exploded in the microwave oven or thrown around the room, and broken chairs littered the area.

'Well, I'm not cleaning this up,' I said.

'We've got to, Tommy,' Squizzy replied. 'It's not like there's any choice. Who are you going to complain to? The senior class? They're the ones who made this mess, dopey.'

'I'm not cleaning anything,' I replied heatedly. 'They can bash it.'

'Tommy, don't cause trouble. You know we can't win.'

'Leave that to me,' I snapped fiercely. I turned around and went straight to Corporal Finch's room.

'Excuse me, Corporal. I refuse to clean the Recreation Room this morning,' I managed to say. Emotion was straining my voice. I'd never questioned a task before, as I believed very much in accepting responsibility for your duties.

Corporal Finch looked at me. 'What's the drama, Tommy?' he asked calmly. Any surprise he may have felt was well hidden.

'I'm not cleaning up after pigs who think they can do anything and have Fourthies clean up after them. I'll take the charge.'

'Let's have a look,' said Corporal Finch. He stepped through his door and down the corridor, indicating I should follow. Corporal Finch looked into the room, 'Don't worry about it, Tommy. You are not to clean here this morning.'

At parade that lunchtime, some Second Class who had made the mess gathered all the Fourthies together to say their piece.

'There's been a group of you Fourthies whingeing about the mess in the common room this morning,' said their spokesman. 'Let me tell you a few facts. When I was a Fourthie I did my turn at section duties and my senior class used to leave the place like a brothel. Now I'm a senior class, I'm leaving the place like a brothel for you, and fairly shortly you will be able to do exactly the same thing to your junior class. You can now see that the system is fair, and it all evens out in the long run. So I suggest you stop your whingeing and bitching and being stroppy and get on with your job.'

ALONE

Archie perched like a fat Buddhist monk on the window ledge looking out over the new Defence Force Academy buildings. It was ridiculous to think of Archie as a monk. He was neither old nor wizened, and he was definitely too well fed, but there was something religious about his squat stance and the way he held his tea mug. It was tea, of course; monks didn't drink coffee. I watched Archie. Archie stared into his brew mug.

The orange orb of a winter sun was low on the horizon. The hills were turning nondescript shades of grey and the shadows of the nearby buildings closed in around us. I shivered involuntarily. The sun's warmth disappeared in palpable waves and I wrapped my hands up under my armpits. The white bricks of the academy buildings glowed a yellow orange as if they had an inner life. This was an illusion, of course. They were dead. The whole place was dead, waiting for humans to make it function.

I watched Archie as his hand absent-mindedly picked up the exercise book full of poetry that was beside him before putting it back down. Archie had given it to me to read and I had done so with interest. Not because I liked poetry, in fact I found it pompous and ridiculous. It was, rather, a rarity that someone of my age would openly display much enthusiasm for such a melancholy activity, so my mind became alert.

What was I missing? I reached across and picked up the exercise book once again. What made Archie want to spend his spare time so? Did he have something to say? If he did, I really couldn't understand it. He did seem awfully confused. What was he saying? Did he know himself? I read a piece entitled 'Oppression':

Let me out
Listen to my voice
Life I need to enjoy
Disdain I don't need it
Despise, detest myself
Death, freedom.

'You're a morbid little bastard. Have I ever told you that?'
A long silence ensued.
'Tommy, Angie's pregnant,' Archie said eventually.
'And . . . ?'
Archie finally looked around. 'And we are going to have a baby.'
'Good . . . Congratulations,' I replied, trying to convince myself, as if I was the father.
'Yeah,' said Archie without enthusiasm.
'You're staying, of course.' It was a statement needing an answer. We both knew that cadets couldn't get married.
'Of course.'
'What does Angie think about that?' I didn't know Angie very well, in fact hardly at all, and it was not really my business. But

it was a question that had to be asked and there was no-one else to ask it. Archie was going to be an eighteen-year-old father with a seventeen-year-old girlfriend, and he was completely alone. He had the Musketeers, of course, but I was realistic about our limitations. We didn't know anything about life, families, love. We didn't know a lot of things.

'Oh, she knows being here is for the best, in the long run.'

'That's sensible. Have you talked to your parents about this?' I didn't want to know the answer.

'Don't know how. I don't really think I could say it on the phone or in a letter. Thought I'd wait till I saw them next.'

I couldn't have discussed it on the phone either and I sympathised with the problem. He was alone.

'I thought about seeing the padres, you know . . . in confidence,' he stammered.

I was doubtful. I didn't trust staff, not even the padres who were supposed to be a confidential outlet for the cadets' worries. However, I didn't share my doubts with Archie. He was religious. We'd had theological discussions before, but the time was not right to start them again.

'Sounds good,' I said, but it didn't.

FORAGING

As the year drew to a close, the empty buildings of the new academy began to fill with equipment. The doors were locked, but that did not deter the cadets and the soon-to-be-opened academy looked like the promised land. There was an abundance of every item, which was certainly not true of Duntroon.

One building was found piled high with microwave ovens. A few disappeared. Some cadets decided they would make good Christmas presents for their mothers.

Another building was full of computers, and yet another with chairs. Still more buildings were found full of blankets and heaters. More items disappeared, to the amusement and benefit of Beersheba Company.

Jude assured me that my use of the word 'stealing' in relation to the disappearances was overly harsh. Besides, armies had been foraging for centuries; it was a respectable activity for a soldier. The appropriation of equipment was all the staff's fault anyway, Jude went on to explain. How could they expect normal people to resist a temptation to take such lucrative goods? Jude almost made it sound as if the cadets of Beersheba Company were doing the staff a service. If they hadn't stolen the equipment the staff would never realise their error and might make the same mistake at a later date. Although I didn't fully subscribe to this logic, I said nothing. I knew that was wrong too, but there was nothing to say. I just watched and learnt.

A LONER

'Look at that knuckle,' proclaimed Bluey. 'Can you believe him?'

I followed Bluey's gaze to the First Class in question. He had an unathletic frame and a docile expression that could only be described as crushed domestic. He wasn't married, of course, but I could imagine his future wife taking his hard-earned pay off him and generously leaving him ten dollars for drinks with the boys. Unfortunately there would be no boys and he'd save the money to buy his wife a tatty bouquet once a month. He was downtrodden, and his face was unanimated as he played a beat-up old piano in the corner of the mess. The music he played was a beautiful piece called 'Jukebox Dancer' that I usually loved. I didn't love it now. The First Class spoiled the music. His fingers were sure but listless and the music sounded disconsolate.

'No, Blue,' I said. 'I can't believe him.'

'If I ever resign three months before graduation, do me a favour and help me commit suicide, because you'll know that I have no grasp on life. What gets me is that it has taken that moron three years and eight months of hell to work out the army is not for him. He must be awfully slow or hasn't thought for the last four years.'

DIVINE INTERVENTION

Archie was sulking. I'd come up for a brew and a chat and found him lying on his bed, staring at the ceiling. He barely moved as I walked across to the brew urn on the corner of his desk and started to help myself.

'Want a brew?' I asked.

I didn't get an answer, nor did I expect one. As I waited for the water to boil I read the little sayings that Archie had written out in his ornate handwriting for the hundredth time. Experience is always experience of oneself. It cannot therefore make others wise. John Spalding. Amazing, I thought. Every dullard who ever walked on the planet feels the need to leave some asinine statement behind. John Spalding ought to read a little Bismarck, who had managed to come up with a quote that completely contradicts Mr Spalding. *Fools learn by experience. I learn from the experience of others.* Who is this Spalding anyway? I wonder why he thinks he has the right to leave that legacy.

The water started to steam and I made myself a bitter black coffee. Truly horrible, I thought, and took a loud slurp to remind Archie I was here. I waited.

'The company commander knows about Angie,' he said at last.

'Who else knew?' I asked.

'The padres, who bloody else?'

I didn't say a word but sat in silence, watching. There was not much else I could say.

After a long time, Archie broke the silence. 'Angie's getting rid of the kid,' he stated as a matter of fact. 'It's too much hassle, especially now the military's breathing down my neck.'

'Sorry,' I said. It was final. I didn't want to know any more.

You bastard padres, I thought. You'll sit there and justify everything you've done. The military staff are here to help, you'll say. They can't help if they don't know. Cadets shouldn't keep secrets from the army, which has a right to know. It pays good money to educate you here.

May you rot in hell.

'I'm truly sorry, mate.'

The silence sat between us till I could bear no more.

'Let's go for a run.'

THE RECLUSE

I screwed up the piece of paper because it was only that. I had tried to turn it into a letter but it hadn't worked. It was full of 'I went to Sydney on the weekend', 'I'm tired', 'Exams are coming up in a month'. It was full of nothing. It didn't tell Dad that he was wrong, that the last 30 years of his life had been dedicated to a fabrication, that soldiering was not what he thought it was. I didn't tell him that so few people shared his beliefs, and that they didn't count. That I had failed and that I couldn't live up to his ideals. Or that they had me beaten and I didn't know how to win. I didn't know if I had the will to win.

I turned off the light and went to bed. I lay awake. Where do I go from here?

The courage to resign, I thought. I had said that once.

I remembered a day when I was eight years old and Dad brought home my first compass. We'd go up to the mountains each night after he'd finished work and he'd taught me how to navigate.

'The creek lines are easy to find but remember the ground is always the steepest there. The bushes are also thickest. It's probably best to stay on the ridges and high ground, that's how Blaxland, Wentworth and Lawson first crossed the Blue Mountains.'

Or the day Dad brought me home books on the Maori Wars to read when we lived in New Zealand. On the following weekends we'd visit the battle sites.

'Look at this ambush site. It's superbly chosen. There is no easy escape route and the British would have had to charge across open ground to get close to the Maoris.' Or, 'Look at these defensive works. They have carefully considered where to place the fortifications. Notice how you can't approach without being observed and then every route is covered by some defensive works. That must have been where they had those walls that channelled the British attacks in here . . .'

I'd enjoyed it all. My mind was hungry and I wanted to take in as much information as I could. Yet despite this education, Dad had not taught me how to iron or spit-polish. All the other cadets whose fathers were in the army knew how to spit-polish and iron. Maybe Dad was trying to tell me something.

Dad had also told me Duntroon was one of the finest military colleges in the world, if not the best, but I hadn't learnt any tactics yet. No-one had even mentioned them. I'd been yelled at a lot, though, for not having shiny shoes. Maybe I thought too much. No, you can never think enough, must use the brain . . . I fell asleep.

BATTLE SCARS

I tried to interest Willie in joining me for my late-night runs. It was good to have the company and seemed to improve his increasingly frequent dark moods. Willie was having problems with academics, which made him more introverted as he tried in vain to keep abreast of his workload. He withdrew further into himself with each passing week. The problem was not helped by his senior class, who were a group of bullies who usually had either a skinful of whisky or were doped to the eyeballs. Willie became very sullen, and resented the behaviour of the senior class. He confided in me that one night, while in a drunken stupor, his senior class had whipped him across the stomach with a bicycle pump until he bled.

The whole experience was obviously scarring Willie mentally, yet the code of the corps meant that we Fourthies never considered saying anything to the authorities. The truth was that we all realised to say anything would bring no results. The corps would close ranks and the complainant would be ostracised. To be honest, I never thought much about the beatings Willie had been subjected too. There was not much point in dwelling on events about which you could do nothing. We had all been disempowered a long time ago. Physical violence happened in all societies and I had witnessed it at all the schools I had attended. A lot of things happened at Duntroon, and Willie's problems were just one of them.

We all have different buttons. Willie's had been pushed by the demeaning behaviour of the senior class and the beatings he had received. Mine was pushed by the issue of marijuana smoking. Different horses, different courses. Part of my section duties each morning, besides polishing the mirror, vacuuming the floor and cleaning out the showers, was to pick up my Third Class, Bart, from the corridor, drag his lifeless body into his room and put him to bed. Bartholomew was a big boy who played First XV rugby and it was no easy task wrestling with the dead weight of this awesome teddy bear each morning. Despite the extra drain on my time, I never resented this extra duty. Bart simply was a nice guy. He was a victim whose button had also been pushed. Each morning after I tucked him into his doona and was about to leave, Bart's face would light up with a silly smile and his red eyes would blink at me before he mumbled, 'Thanks, Tommy.'

I could only feel sorry for Bart, who was always a true gentle-man, was never arrogant or rude and actually had a brilliant mind when it wasn't hazed over by alcohol or marijuana. Bart was an interesting person, and typical of the many who simply lost direction in the quagmire of the college.

As time went on, I had started to notice the distinct aroma of marijuana floating down the corridors, and I started to tally up the number of cadets I knew who had a smoke, either regularly or occasionally. My final tally included nearly half of Beersheba Company. The other companies reportedly were not as bad.

Beersheba was probably the worst hit company because the main supplier was a member of our fold. Another member grew plants at his girlfriend's house. The corps was rotten with dope and it played on my mind. This was the Royal Military College. These people were potential officers. What of integrity? Yes, I knew the word was a joke in the corps, but surely there were some restraints on cadet unruliness. The army had a no-drugs policy, yet the people who would enforce it, the future officers, were compromising themselves. At the very least they would end up hypocrites. I spoke with Archie about all this at some length. Archie smoked. He was still my friend. I didn't know what my course of action might be, but I warned him to leave the smoking alone for a period.

I thought about the issue in depth on one of my Sydney trips. The staff must have known that dope smoking was prevalent in the corps. I couldn't believe that so many cadets could be involved without the staff knowing. So what was the point of telling them something they already knew? If they didn't know and I told them, could anything be achieved? I was only a Fourthie and would easily be discredited. The corps would close ranks. What was integrity? Should I leak the story to the press and ruin the corps' reputation for no discernible gain? After all bastardisation was still prevalent. The staff appeared not to care. Should I? Did I believe in RMC any more?

The decision on what to do was not easily made, and I talked the issue over with some family friends. There was no-one else. I still couldn't decide on anything concrete. I put a pack on my back

66

and went for a long run around Sydney's bays. The rhythmic beating of my feet on paths, sand and rocks was good therapy. My troubles began to take some sort of shape. Occasionally I stopped to look at the view and felt envy for the seagulls flying overhead. They did not have to confront the issues I faced. I felt it was unfair that I had to make these decisions, I was not old enough. On I ran. The army was supposed to be fair and just, but it wasn't. The army was supposed to have rules and it didn't. On I ran. I thought back to the selection procedure, a long time ago. Maybe I should have seen signs then that I would not belong.

Recruitment, Melbourne

Defence Force Recruiting in Melbourne was located in Little Bourke Street, a narrow one-way lane in the CBD. The building was tatty and untidy, with years of accumulated smog darkening its original cream colour. The paint was peeling and rivers of grey were smudged around the gutters and windowsills. Water from the last rains had streaked the grime into tears, and the building was sombre and forbidding. As I stood in the busy lane no-one showed any inclination to walk up the short flight of depressing stairs that ushered the visitor into the unknown. As I trudged up the stairs I was deep in thought. It was scarcely believable that I was old enough to attain my dream of applying for the Royal Military College. Anticipation of long-held dreams reaching fruition added a tinge of excitement, but my steps were weighed down by the thought that I was competing where I had no right to compete. I wanted with all my heart to be accepted into RMC, yet was conscious that I had not done one piece of work to help achieve this aim. I was floating through school and knew I shouldn't be. I had a slight queasy feeling in my knotted stomach and a light head fighting to concentrate.

I don't remember when the idea of becoming an army officer first entered my mind. However, to go to Duntroon was a long-held ambition. To lead men was the goal. The idea of being a professional who defended my country struck me as being the noblest of occupations. An honour above all others.

I recall a television advertisement recruiting for the Royal Military College and the words, as best I can remember, were:

The greatest thing in life is to do your very best,
To look the world right in the eye, the mark of a man,
There is hard work that must be done by men of high degree,
It is not an easy road to go, but you're in good company.

They were idealistic words, rather naively put, but they were sung to a catchy tune and to me they summed up everything good and challenging about RMC.

The assessment procedure began with a medical board. I was seated in a reception area with a dozen other applicants for an RMC scholarship. The room had no natural light, just a cluster of fluorescent tubes. Wood veneer panels were used to divide what once must have been an open-floor plan. Sitting in an olive green vinyl chair with very little to do, I read old Woman's Day magazines that had retired on a coffee table in the centre of the room.

The medical consisted of taking your clothes off and putting them back on several times and being poked and prodded by doctors.

The first incident of interest to me in these completely forgettable proceedings was a little playlet acted out in front of me, and it remains firmly fixed in my mind. I was seated in my olive chair, studiously reading an article on the Princess of Wales' latest fashions, when a door opened and a grossly obese sergeant waddled into view. The sergeant cast his docile eyes, which had long since surrendered any pretence of life, around the expectant throng. There was a momentary glimmer of recognition as he fixed his target and changed direction, wallowing like a supertanker in rough seas. The tanker finally came to rest to the front of a pleasant-looking fellow who had just completed another round of medical checks. The sergeant was most apologetic as he informed the applicant that he was five kilograms overweight. I had trouble containing my mirth and buried my thoughts deeper into the Princess of Wales' eye-catching red hat.

Later, I told Dad this story. He was aghast, and immediately wanted to notify someone in recruiting about the situation. I was horrified that Dad was prepared to make such a scene. It was the last thing I needed if I was to be successful in my application and I tried to placate him. Eventually he admitted the whole affair was 'all quite funny really', although there was no smile on his face. Parents—they can be such problems.

There were aptitude tests to be completed and the last event of the day was an interview with the army psychologist. At this time of my life I would honestly say that I was addicted to running. I ran between 20 and 30 kilometres each day, a fact which it appeared had not gone unnoticed.

My childhood had been shaped by a succession of moves from state to state, and country to country. After attending eleven different schools with different sports, and different social groups, I felt a keen need to belong. But being a new boy so often, I found that almost impossible. Over time, I began to worry less about what other people were doing. I also discovered that when I had no-one to play with, the easiest way to entertain myself was to walk out the front door and go for a run. It was the perfect activity as it required no friends, allowed me to explore my new environment, and gave me an opportunity to think.

I read a great deal on athletics, and was familiar with a paper written by three psychologists on the subject of running. It had only been recently released. The basic premise of the article was that athletes often used the daily run as a means of avoiding life's problems. Constant pounding of the pavements meant they avoided confrontation with people back home. You could have bowled me over with a feather when the psychologist asked me a series of questions that suggested he had read the same article.

How are things at home?

You don't get on with Dad?

You're always fighting with your brother?

I hope the psychologist threw the article in the bin the minute I left the room. Of course I didn't get on well with Dad, and of course I was always fighting with my brother, but if you can find a sixteen-year-old who doesn't you've found one seriously sick individual.

My tales of domestic bliss really must have done the trick, because not long afterwards I received a letter stating I had successfully completed phase one of the selection process. I was invited to sit a Selection Board.

Around this time the Melbourne Age caused a nationwide furore by revealing allegations, made by former cadets, of bastardisation at the Royal Military College. I read the articles avidly, keen to glean as much information as possible, and discussed the issue with Dad. He was anxious to know my opinion.

'It doesn't seem too bad,' I told him. 'I don't see any problems in lasting through it, that is if it happens. The army hasn't admitted to any wrongdoing.'

Dad did not look convinced. 'You do realise there might be some substance to these allegations.'

Despite knowing of his 30-odd years in the army, it never occurred to me that he might know more on the subject than me. I was getting testy at this probing.

'For a start, I don't know if it happens,' I repeated. 'But if it does happen I don't agree with it and I won't be involved with it.'

The following weekend I went camping with my father's friend, Jock, a graduate of Duntroon and a Vietnam veteran. We were with a group, but as the day wore on we became lost in conversation and separated to the rear. I tried to tap his memory on RMC, soldiering and war.

The trail we walked on was a brown scuff mark, and the remainder of the landscape was black from bushfires. As the sun slipped to the horizon the shadows lengthened and the world became darker. We slipped further behind the trampers in front. As a distance runner, I knew that the chains that had linked us to the pack of people in front were broken.

A snake rustled across the trail to our front, weaving between rocks. It seemed oblivious to us and I didn't falter from my stride, instinctively knowing there was no threat. I thought of the snake and wondered what else could have survived the firestorm. The birds, of course, but they had never faced the full fury of the flames. They had just returned to sing their songs, preen their feathers and mock the snake. In return the snake was oblivious to the birds. The snake lived in the dirt. It was not gifted by nature. It could not flee from trouble with the flick of wings.

Society had taught me that Vietnam veterans were different, that the whole subject was somehow dirty, yet I knew that war was the key element of soldiering but was rarely discussed. It demanded my attention.

I took a deep breath and dared not look. 'Vietnam—what was it really like? No-one ever talks about it. How can I know what war is all about?' I faintly expected something bad to happen as a response to these questions. Nothing did. We just continued walking with the steady beat of boot on trail.

'This reminds me of some of the country,' said Jock finally. 'B-52s had been doing high-altitude bombing in the north of the province. It was a shambles. Everything was burnt. Trees were thrown everywhere but there were no leaves, just black stumps.'

I looked at the country with new eyes. The soldier continued.

'We'd been sent in to count the bodies. We laughed. There wouldn't be any bodies, just some torsos and limbs that were once human, before they were blown apart. My platoon was on the left of the company as the scouts began up a slight slope. Not more than that one there.' The soldier pointed and I turned and stared. First at the slope, then at Jock. We walked again.

'The crack of bullets began,' he said. 'I'd heard them before, but not like that. It was like a swarm of bees suffocating you with the buzz of death. I had two dead and four wounded. I could hear old Bull Blakemore's platoon copping it on my right. I felt the rockets exploding over there, and realised with a start they were exploding amongst my platoon too. I didn't know it then, but Bull had twelve killed or wounded in those opening seconds.'

We walked on. I was transfixed by that slight slope to the left of the track.

'I was trained to act, but couldn't go forward or back because of the intense fire. I knew fear. The platoon signaller screamed that gunships were coming to assist. They couldn't have been more than four minutes. Seemed like four years. I still resent those pilots for those years in hell. That's wrong, but they weren't sharing the screams, the fear, the confusion.'

Jock paused and walked in quiet for a moment. 'When those gunships left we reached the top of that little slope and there were bodies to count. The problem was some of them were ours.'

The story was remarkable to me in that it contained only facts. Uncertainty was a fact. Fear was a fact. Momentary panic was a fact. Casualties were a fact. Death was a fact. The story was not meant to inspire me to heroic deeds. It conveyed neither bitterness nor regret, and there was no analysis of the consequences of the soldier's actions or the actions of others.

The story conveyed information and I began to realise that I would never *understand the emotion of war until I'd shared the same experience. I did understand, however, that in extraordinary circumstances the maintenance of self was a remarkable achievement. The ability to survive as a human being was an end in itself.*

We walked on in silence. It was neither uncomfortable nor awkward. The silence was filled with thought for me, and I guessed memories for Jock. I peered at the black and tried to imagine struggling for life in this kind of environment. Thoughts jammed my mind. My next question was on the same subject—soldiering.

'I don't really want to go to university. People say, if you want to become an officer and make it a career, you should do a degree course at the Royal Military College, Duntroon.'

'I might sum it up best like this,' said Jock. 'When you finish Officer Cadet School, Portsea, you march out as an officer. You have a party after doing a year's hard work. When you finish the Royal Military College, or RMC, you graduate as an officer and have a party after doing four years' hard work. Both are officers and both have parties.'

The decision was easily made, I liked good parties.

After three or four hours of running I knew that I would have to make a decision. The only consideration relevant to that decision was the fact that something within me loved the college. I did not know why, but I knew that I had to be true to that love. Whatever decision I made would have to be in the college's best interests.

On returning to RMC I went to see Corporal Finch and told him of my intention to resign. He was taken aback and asked me why.

'Dope smoking is rampant and no-one cares,' I told him. 'There is no integrity. Neither the cadets, the military staff nor the academic staff have any. It's very disappointing and I don't want to belong any more.'

Corporal Finch was decisive. That was his way. 'I'll look into the problem, Tommy, and if you're right I'll take the matter to the military staff myself. I'm sure they can't know about it, or they would have taken action. After all, this is news to me, I'm sure they wouldn't know about it.' Corporal Finch was resolute. 'As for the problem with integrity, you will have to deal with that in your own way. It's a problem everywhere, not just here. I want you to stay, and I want you to consider that.'

Corporal Finch had been at the college for three years and not known about the marijuana problem. Maybe he was right. Maybe the staff didn't know about the abuse of marijuana.

'Look, if you want to know more about this, don't just talk to anyone. A lot of cadets won't give you a straight answer. I'll have a few people pop around and tell you about it.'

Archie was one of them. Although he was a dope smoker and in a sense was cutting his own throat, he did it out of friendship.

In the end, Corporal Finch spoke to Major Grey and I didn't resign. That was the last I heard of the matter until some months later, when a padre came down to visit me in my room. After fencing around for a while he finally came to the point. 'The staff are aware of the problem of marijuana smoking,' he told me, 'but their hands are tied. The college just can't afford a scandal right now, so they can't do anything about it.'

When he had had his say I stood up and walked out of my room. I was hurting. I had absolutely no reason to believe in the padre, but still expected more. It was ridiculous of course that I should have to leave my own room, but as a cadet I was not in the position to throw the padre out.

I walked upstairs, had a brew with Archie and sat on his window ledge, looking over the almost finished academy, the 'new order'. We talked about the hypocrisy of everyone, even padres. 'Men of God,' I laughed. 'I've got more integrity and I'm a two-faced arsehole.' I now trusted no staff member. The Corps of Cadets was hypocritical and had warped values, but at least we had enough honesty to admit it.

I walked back from church, humming to myself. The day was beautiful, although a little cool and there was next to no noise. It was a nice day to be living and as I walked through the quiet streets of Campbell I made a mental note to thank God more often that I am alive. I could smell the native plants in the air, I could feel a light breeze caressing my cheek, and the world was pleasantly peaceful.

I enjoyed these walks to and from church. The experience of being happy to be gifted enough to walk was in some ways the most religious experience. Church itself didn't do much for me. Dad said that the important thing about going to church was to worship as a community. He was sure about his religion, a regular at church, and sure there was a God. I wasn't a regular, or even sure there was a God, but I still went to church when I was happy about life. A real joy I could share. A cynical side told me religion was a crutch and I'd noticed Dad became more religious when my brother died. Perhaps my judgment was unfair but I felt he needed reassurance more than anything else. It might have been a cruel and an unworthy thought, but that was my judgment. And I knew I didn't want a crutch. I wanted to live a Christian life and do what was right. The problem was that right and wrong were a little more complex than I had first thought.

When I returned to my section area I ran into Corporal Finch. I smiled. 'Good morning.'

'G'day, Tommy. Where've you been?'

I was tempted to lie. Corporal Finch was a leader in the college's Christian Fellowship and I didn't want a philosophical talk on my personal brand of religion.

'Down at church,' I said. Finch was a committed Christian, but not a Bible basher.

'Really. I didn't know you went. I've never seen you down the bottom,' he said, referring to Duntroon's church.

'No, I don't go to RMC church. I object to it.'

'Really?' he said, genuinely surprised.

'I don't believe a priest can serve two masters, God and the army. It's either one or the other. Just a personal opinion.' I didn't want to go any further.

'Interesting. Come down some time. I don't think it's like that. Of course the church comes first.'

'I'll respect your judgment,' I told him, and I did. Corporal Finch's opinion held great sway with me and I intended to think more about the matter.

A TEST FOR AN EXAMINER

Spider was a revolting creature. He was the kind of person I always imagined with a line of milk on his upper lip and a dribble of sauce on his chin, but milk was far too wholesome for the image of Spider. I was fairly certain that the only liquids that ever passed his lips were beer and Bundaberg rum.

Whichever he had been drinking, Spider was legless again. The only surprising thing about this was that, instead of being carried out of the Private Bin, he was being carried into our final Philosophy exam. He was the last in and two classmates propped him up at a vacant desk.

Spider immediately turned his exam paper over and picked up a pen. This caused a flurry of activity and an invigilator went racing up to him, told him to put his pen down and turned his paper face down.

Spider burst into defiant laughter. 'Surly old bitch,' he rasped.

'Keep quiet or I will remove you for creating a disturbance,' she wailed.

'I'll remove you for creating a disturbance,' he mimicked. Spider's head waved violently from side to side and he laughed uproariously at his own cleverness. Eventually he became so excited that he spilled off his chair. The invigilator retreated and everyone else in the room had a sparkle in his eye.

When the exam started, Spider wrote furiously. I watched him as I stopped to gather my thoughts. After 40 minutes, Spider put his pen down, dropped his head onto the desk and began to snore.

THE HEAD'S FOR THINKING WITH

I can't remember putting in any particular effort for the end-of-year exams, in fact I was busy taking every short cut I could.

In Mathematics, a compulsory half-subject, the questions were given to us beforehand. The lecturer told us point-blank: 'You are all hopeless students. You show no interest in this subject and I consequently have no interest in you. None of you will pass without some help, so I will give you the questions now. I don't hold out any hope, but I wait for the day you cadets understand the opportunities you have missed.' It was really the old story of the chicken and the egg and I wasn't sure which had come first—our class's lack of interest in the lectures or his uninteresting lectures.

There was no point in calling the charade an exam at all. As well as knowing the questions, we were allowed to have calculators with us. This immediately put an idea into my mind. A programmable calculator was still a calculator, wasn't it? Rather than doing any study, I borrowed four programmable calculators from classmates and crammed them full of answers so I had nothing to learn.

During the five minutes allowed for reading the exam paper, the exam-room supervisors started looking at the calculators. I looked for a hiding place for my neat pile of electronic equipment but there was none. The situation looked grim and I was scratching my head in frustration when inspiration hit. I casually took my hat off and placed it over the incriminating evidence. The examiner looked at me inquiringly when she saw I had no calculator and I smiled sagely. 'I keep all the help I need under my hat,' I said, tapping the side of my head.

Harsh people would call this academic misconduct. Harsher judges still might call this cheating. We as cadets didn't care about such people. We were the journeymen on the edges of morality.

BACK TO SOLDIERING

After exams concluded, three weeks of Annual Field Training commenced. Putting aside the worries of possible academic failure, we became soldiers again. The exercise started with Fourth Class digging into a company defensive position on Majura Range. After the first fifteen inches of soil is removed the range is solid rock. We chopped away with picks for a week, blistering hands, breaking tools and numbing our backs for no discernible gain. Jude's birthday happened while we were out in the bush. I took some rum and salami which I had bought for the occasion across to his pit and we sat down in the dark to yarn and joke. This was RMC. Politics behind us, we enjoyed the camaraderie of simple soldiering.

Phase two of AFT was a link-up with the senior classes, followed by a helicopter flight to the Brindabella Ranges south of Canberra. There was continuous rain for the next week and a half. We patrolled all day and ambushed all night, quickly turning into sodden zombies. Towards the end of the exercise, Stripper from the senior class and I were the first on gun picket after lying in ambush until 0300 hours. I distinctly remember the directing staff giving us a debrief about the excellent ambush we had just conducted. He now wanted no-one to fall asleep on gun picket before moving out of our position before dawn.

I woke up as the sun's rays were peeping over the horizon.

'Stripper, wake up. Someone's screwed up. We were supposed to move out before dawn.'

'Don't worry. It's someone else's problem,' Stripper mumbled.

I opened my eyes a little more and stared in horror at the gun, directly to my front.

'Stripper, wake up!'

'Rack off!' Stripper was now really annoyed.

'It's us, Stripper . . . *We* screwed up.'

Stripper sat bolt upright, suddenly alive. I couldn't stop laughing, and nor could he. We woke everyone up in the position and moved out as if nothing untoward had happened. We never mentioned the event to anyone, we just laughed. The directing staff never said a word and we presumed they enjoyed the sleep-in too.

As Annual Field Training drew to a close, exam results crept back into our thoughts. Back at RMC we all crowded the boards where results were posted, our futures hanging in the balance. My results danced before me: Physics—Pass Conceded; Mathematics—Pass Conceded; Philosophy 1—Pass, Geography 1—Pass, History 1—Fail.

I'd failed an exam, but I had enough passes to continue through to the next year. Bluey, Archie and Squizzy all passed too, but Willie had failed.

Spider whooped. He had a high distinction plus posted as his mark in Philosophy. He waved an opened letter. 'They're offering me honours!' He held out the letter to me and Jude.

All he said was true. A letter written on University of New South Wales letterhead stared back at us. And it was indeed from the Philosophy Department.

I patted an ecstatic Spider on the back and left with Jude.

'Can you believe that?' muttered Jude. 'Unbelievable.'

'This place is a joke, make no mistake.' I shook my head. 'And they wonder why we don't take acas seriously.'

THE SWORD IS MIGHTIER THAN THE PEN

Five cadets from Second Class had failed subjects and could not continue into First Class and their Military Year. Their future hung in the balance for a week. Speculating about what was to become of them was the favourite topic, corps wide.

Finally, they were allowed to resit their exams and were passed. The whole corps perked up. I had no warm feelings for any of the five. In fact most of them were rude pigs, but like every other member in the corps I knew that the passes were a demonstration of the military's power over the academics. The rules of the Royal Military College's university charter did not allow for posts.

A TIME FOR FUN

Drill week, before the graduation of the senior class, was a hectic time as we all tried to finalise any administration matters left outstanding by the three weeks of AFT. There were commitments on our time for drill rehearsals, work parties and organisation for the move to the academy. To top it off, Steph, who had visited at QB, decided to come up from Melbourne. This extra burden on my time made me less than happy. Not that I wasn't happy to see her, it was more a case of being unsure of myself, a little tired and disoriented. Steph arrived at the airport at 1400 hours, in the middle of a parade rehearsal. I asked Jude and the Musketeers to cover for me as I wouldn't be at practice.

Squizzy's girlfriend Lynda was down from Newcastle, and by coincidence had the room next door to Steph's at the Ainslie Hotel. This was convenient as we would both set our alarms for 0530 hours, then bang on the hotel wall to ensure the other was awake and head back to RMC, each in his own car. This all came unstuck one morning when I heard Squizzy bang on the wall but I needed five minutes more sleep. I closed my eyes and woke five minutes later to see the digital display on the clocks screaming at me. 0704 hours. I hurtled across the room, pulling on my trousers as I raced downstairs and smiled to the girl behind the front counter. I tried to look dignified in a pair of trousers and an unbuttoned shirt, with my shoes in one hand while the other played with my fly.

I floored the V8, wheels squealing for purchase on the corner near the War Memorial. I passed a truck on the blind hill leading towards RMC, praying briefly as I did so. The car squealed to a halt in the car park and I raced into the barracks, undoing my trousers as I went. My uniform was picked up off the floor, where I had carefully stored it the night before, and I raced down to the form-up point for parade, where I eased myself into the back rank at exactly 0719 hours. A whole minute to spare. What's the rush?

Horror of horrors, Sergeant Boots was doing an inspection of the rear rank. There was nowhere to hide. I pulled myself up to full height and puffed my chest out in an effort to look my best. Boots stopped in front of me as I looked to my front, avoiding his eyes.

'Staff Cadet Sneyk, did you polish your boots this morning?'

'Ah . . . no, Sergeant.'

'Staff Cadet Sneyk, did you iron your uniform this morning?'

'Ah . . . no, Sergeant.'

'Staff Cadet Sneyk, did you clean and polish your brass this morning by any chance?'

'No, Sergeant.'

'Staff Cadet Sneyk, I suppose a shave would have been out of the question this morning?'

'Yes, Sergeant.'

'Staff Cadet Sneyk . . . these things we all must do daily, even cadets who almost run me over as they drive into RMC at 0715 hours after entertaining the little lady all night.'

'Yes, Sergeant.'

'Staff Cadet Sneyk, I would consider being squashed by a half-naked hoodlum behind the wheel of his V8 to be an undignified death.'

'Yes, Sergeant.'

Drill Sergeant Boots walked on. He had made his point beautifully. I never made the same mistake again and I never heard any more of the incident.

A FAREWELL TOAST

The end-of-year dinner of the Corps of Staff Cadets was a dining-in night like no other. This was the last night of the corps as we had known it. Romani and Kokoda Companies were being disbanded as the new 'RMC of Australia' would only have four companies. The drinking started early and by the time the main course was served one classmate had already had too much. He was crawling under the tables, his head occasionally popping up in people's laps.

'I have to find the adjutant,' he would slur before crawling on.

This unfortunate creature had been thrown out for academic failure and he obviously felt the need to discuss the matter with someone in authority. Eventually someone pointed him in the direction of the door and, still crawling, he disappeared.

Romani and Kokoda were trying to out-do each other in song, and there was much thumping of cutlery and of tables. It was a fine night. The only dampener came when a sodden padre tried to engage me in conversation later in the evening. 'We can't do anything about it,' he managed, barely able to stand. I glared at him, thought about saying something and walked off. I didn't like that padre, and I certainly didn't respect army chaplains.

Class numbers were reduced by another 34 members.

ALL FRIENDS IN THE END

Graduation week was a carnival. An occasion to remember.

One night I received a phone call from the bar at 2130 hours. In the background was the usual roar of festivities and it was obvious that First Class were enjoying themselves.

'Tommy, this is Corporal Bailey . . . this bar is a brothel, get all the Fourthies you can find and get down here immediately to clean it up.'

I was not happy. Didn't they ever leave us alone? The last thing I wanted to do was clean up First Class's mess. I did a doorknock and eventually collected four or five mates to head down to the bar with me. We walked down the dusty Kokoda Trail, hands thrust in pockets, a doleful group full of bad language and bad manners.

We stepped into the bar warily. A group of First Class were still partying but the noise quietened down as the disgruntled Fourthies eyed the drunken First Class.

'It's the Fourthies' work party,' cried Corporal Bailey.

'Get in here now,' a steely voice demanded.

We moved inside cautiously, apprehensive about what could happen next. Pop went a champagne cork and more bottles appeared by magic. The party started anew. This was the party I'd heard about so long ago on a forest trail. Fourthies and First Class joined arms singing songs, playing games and swapping yarns. Corporal Bailey decided that a naked sit in the parade ground was the order of the day. He was of the opinion that the cadets who had gone before and who had made the ultimate sacrifice wouldn't have minded the statement he was trying to make about parade grounds, and about drill in general.

A SAD PARTING

For the first night of our Christmas holidays, Bluey organised a party at a holiday house in Terrigal hired especially for the Musketeers. I was heading home to Tassie but Terrigal was on the way. This was the last time we all gathered together. Willie was out, our first casualty. I hardly said anything to him that night. There wasn't much to say. Duntroon had left its mark on Willie. He didn't talk to his father any more and he didn't talk to us. He was in pain, but I had no aspirins. He'd made the break, crossed over to the other side.

I spent most of the evening as an observer, participating only enough to add to the momentum of the occasion so I might learn more. Bluey's girlfriend Helen gazed back at me from across the pool. Her eyes did not dart away in embarrassment but returned my vacant stare with curiosity. I stared for long moments before my eyes moved on. I was not interested in what she was thinking, but I was curious about the fact that she was thinking. She was assessing us all, as I was.

Tired of watching and being watched, I stood up and moved to the back of the yard, where I stared out into nothing. I knew Helen would join me. I didn't want her to but I knew she would just the same. Some people always disappoint me and never surprise me. I looked at her resignedly as she joined me.

'You're very quiet. Aren't you enjoying yourself?'

I thought for a long time before answering.

'Just thinking.' I felt no desire to explain further.

'About?' she persisted.

'About us,' I said, indicating the Musketeers with a nod of my head. 'How we fit together.'

There was a long silence. Helen was gathering herself.

'You're different somehow from the others. You're always off to one side, watching and thinking. It's difficult to explain but you're not really one of them.'

She did not articulate herself any better as she continued. 'You know, Bluey and I have had our ups and downs. It's been a hard year on all of us. Last time I left him he took a gun to my head. He threatened to blow it off if I ever humiliated him again. He's a strange guy, Bluey. You're not like him. Bluey could do anything when he's angry. He frightens me a lot of the time.'

I did not doubt the story was true. Nor was I surprised. We were all of us capable of anything. I was too drunk to care.

'Helen, we are here, which tells you something about me and you. Either we are like him, or our personalities find something attractive about him. I don't know which is scarier, but that's the truth.'

I was being a bastard. She wanted help but I wasn't going to offer it to her. I'd offered help to Willie. He was gone.

Helen left to rejoin the others.

The next morning I woke up with a nasty hangover. Willie was on a fold-up bed, naked. Helen lay beside him, also naked. I didn't want to know about it. Maybe Bluey would shoot them both in a fit of rage.

I dressed quietly and left. We'd come a long way in twelve short months.

Year Two

BACK TO THE BEGINNING

I spent the Christmas holidays quietly. There were no cadets from Tasmania in my class but some senior cadets had suggested I give them a call. I did not do so. This was not because I failed to appreciate the gesture. I simply did not wish to talk shop. Inevitably, RMC would be the only topic we would have in common.

I had only been to school in Tasmania for six months, and that was four years ago now. There were no old school friends with whom I'd stayed in touch. I was very much alone, without feeling alone. I did not feel any desire to seek company of any sort and I enjoyed the opportunity to be by myself. I spent much of the day walking, running and swimming. I was not happy with my fitness level, which had fallen away considerably over the last year, and I was determined to resurrect it.

This was a slow process but I pushed myself a little further each day. After two weeks I was again capable of running two hours non-stop. I knew I was far from racing fitness, but the enjoyment was returning to my strides as I powered up and down Launceston's hills in the soft light of a Tasmanian summer's early morning. The views were pretty without being spectacular and I began to make contact with my soul again.

As the weariness that plagued Fourthies receded into a dull memory, my ability to rationalise returned. I thought through the issues that I had confronted or sidestepped during the year. They would not go away. How would I deal with them in the new year? On I ran, further and further.

What of my integrity? I had sold my values short on many occasions. And I had excused that by blaming the inadequacies of my lecturers, my military peers and superiors. Was this just a cop-out, an easy way for me to sit smugly in judgment over others, while being guilty myself of the biggest crimes—hypocrisy and duplicity?

Control that breathing, keep it deep and regular. Longer. Longer.

How do I really feel about drugs? All my civilian friends smoked marijuana, so why couldn't I accept it in the army? What was wrong with it at Duntroon? Society accepted it, why couldn't I? The military staff didn't mind.

Push it harder, just a little longer, you can relax at the top of the hill, harder, harder.

Would the academy be different? Was this what I wanted to dedicate my whole life to? I still wanted to be a soldier, but did I want to deal with the politics? Could I remove myself from the politics and still be a soldier? Now that I wasn't a Fourthie, surely things would be different. Staff would take more notice of my opinions, wouldn't they?

Relax, easy now, you're on the wind-down, nice and steady. Enjoy the power of your body, let it carry you along.

THE NEW ORDER

The Australian Defence Force Academy's buildings are nestled into the side of a north-facing gully of Mount Pleasant. The buildings are of a white brick with a design that is functional, but not rugged enough for the destructive power of cadets. The central administration area and parade ground are quite attractive if you're looking for beauty, but they are not impressive enough to make the casual observer stop and look. The buildings lack presence and can best be described as pleasantly common.

The academy was opened with the intention of combining the education content of the courses previously run at RMC by the army, Point Cook by the air force, and HMAS *Creswell* by the navy. It was hoped that this common training background would help increase the cooperation and understanding between the services in years to come. The academy was probably also seen to give an economy of scale that the smaller single-service colleges couldn't. RMC, Point Cook and *Creswell* were retained to provide the specific-to-service training in the final year.

One hundred and one of the original RMC class of 156 reported to the Defence Academy. Outside my new room were two cadets in naval uniform who introduced themselves as Salty and Sharky. I shook hands with them as warmly as possible. However, Duntroon had taught me to be suspicious of people who were loitering, especially outside your room. I cast a critical eye over my new friends, noting that Salty was built like Porky Pig while Sharky reminded me of the Scarecrow from *The Wizard of Oz*. This impression was reinforced by the scarecrow agreeing animatedly with everything Porky said. I smiled absent-mindedly at something Salty was saying and thought perhaps Sharky 'Could be another Lincoln if he only had a brain'. I could barely wait for our first lesson in physical training.

Salty told me that the room I had been allocated and had moved into prior to leave was now his, and he made it quite clear that he wanted my possessions moved out by yesterday. I was not happy, and told him to hold his horses while I went down and found out where my new room was supposed to be.

I drove down to the Headquarters building and joined a queue of about twenty other cadets waiting for room allocation, with Archie up towards the front. I joined him, ignoring all the others. I didn't know any of them, I'd been driving all day, and was not in the mood to wait at the back. As I reached the front of the line the captain who was allocating rooms informed me that my dress was unacceptable in the academy. I looked down at my comfortable driving clothes while he told me the minimum dress standard was dress shoes, long socks, shorts and collared shirt.

For a moment I was tempted to explain that I didn't normally drive in my dinner suit, thought better of it and said, 'My apologies, sir, I'll be right back.' I walked quickly to my car and started rummaging around. There was a pair of purple football socks on the back seat and some pink flowered board shorts in the boot. A Paisley shirt completed the picture and I strode back into the Headquarters building, purple socks pulled up past my knees. I stopped in front of the captain, raised my favourite set of pink sunglasses, smiled in my cheeriest heart-winning fashion and reported, 'Sir, if I am now dressed to your satisfaction, could I please get my room allocated?' The captain smiled wanly and handed me my key.

Archie and I chatted outside about our first impressions of the academy. 'That captain was a dick,' Archie announced emphatically. 'He was still shaking his head when you had gone.'

'Stuff him. I'm really pissed about having to move rooms. What's the caper? As if it matters if I sleep in the room next door, which is all they have moved me to.'

'They'll jerk us around just to show who's boss. You wait and see,' commented Archie.

I excused myself. 'I'd better go and see how Laurel and Hardy are going. See you at the bar tonight.'

BUILDING A BUREAUCRACY

The academy was an interesting part of the world to be in during these fledgling months. No idea was too ridiculous. It had only had to be thought of to be tried. Nothing, it seemed, could be borrowed from RMC, or HMAS *Creswell* or Point Cook. If, for example, the staff were questioning the cadets about how to smoothe the passage of information within the corps, a correct answer could not refer to RMC's simple and effective way of dealing with this. Looks of horror would accompany such a remark and the idea would immediately be quashed. If, however, you presented a complicated, inefficient solution, it would be embraced as a new wonder system that would revolutionise the military.

In moulding the academy, the staff completely alienated the senior cadets. Whether by design or accident, we were made to feel like an unwanted link to the previous colleges. This may have been true, but it was hardly our fault.

The decrees started coming thick and fast. First, the name had to be settled on. ADFA was the one most commonly used up until this point. However, this was deemed unacceptable by a smiling lieutenant colonel who introduced himself to the class as Ron McDonald. 'We would all have to agree that calling this institution ADFA could cause some confusion with the Australian Dairy Farmers Association or the Australian Dried Fruits Association, so from now on we will hear no more ADFAs. This institution will be known as the Defence Force Academy.'

'Ron's obviously a busy man for a light colonel, if he has time to make high-powered decisions like this,' I breathed quietly to Archie and Jude.

In a fit of semantic generosity, Lieutenant Colonel McDonald decided a week later that we could drop the 'Force' and refer to the institution simply as the Defence Academy.

Lieutenant Colonel McDonald, who was the second in command of the Corps of Officer Cadets—COC or COOC, whichever takes your fancy—held the position of chief instructor.

Next came the decree that army cadets were not allowed to 'bash' their peaked caps, which was an army-wide fashion. Bashing of caps was an art form that allowed each cadet to have his cap slightly individualised depending on his tastes. To obtain a cap to bash, you had to invest $120 in an imported British woollen cap. You then moulded the wool when wet. Bashing your cap saved looking very undignified in the army-issue flat-peaked version, which was not attractive to the eye. Most army cadets simply ignored the non-bashing rule. I, however, went to the Quartermaster store and bought the biggest, flattest cap I could find and wore it with great apparent pride. To anyone in the army I looked ridiculous. However, I used to march around the area exhorting all who would listen to follow my example. Captain Steel, my divisional officer, confronted me.

'You look ridiculous in that cap. I believe you're trying to make a mockery of the situation.'

'Sir, I am only doing my best to set an example and comply with the dress standards of the academy and Lieutenant Colonel McDonald.'

Captain Steel looked at me suspiciously but my expression would have told him nothing. I thought I should have been applauded, not admonished. In my wildest fantasies I could imagine Lieutenant Colonel McDonald presenting me to the rest of the army cadets. 'Officer Cadet Sneyk looks like a million dollars when he walks around the area in his cap. Why can't the rest of you cadets do likewise?'

Then came the order that Second Year cadets would continue to clean the showers and toilets each morning. First Year cadets might be allowed to assist us later on in the year, when they were responsible enough. Well, that went down like a pork chop at a bar mitzvah. Despite the fact that I had complied with the staff rulings on the caps, I now found I was at extreme odds with the hierarchy. I certainly wasn't going to clean bathrooms two years in a row. What other reason was there for First Year cadets?

Navy, army and air force all do drill differently, so common style of drill needed to be adopted for the academy. Air force drill was chosen. This would have worked if the air force cadets had known their own service drill. Unfortunately, it appeared after our first lesson as a combined class that the air force had not been taught drill. That first drill lesson widened the divisions amongst us. The navy cadets shuffled around so as to not fall off the ship's sides, as apparently was their custom, while the army cadets found it hard to break the habits that the daily hour of drill at RMC had instilled in us. The air force cadets had enough trouble coordinating themselves to walk. The drill became a greater farce every day, and the ex-RMC cadets found it particularly frustrating, as only a month earlier we had participated in a graduation parade that Grenadier Guards couldn't have bettered. Eventually the drill sergeants realised that if they wanted to have a grand opening parade in three weeks time, as was planned, they would have to change a few movements. Modifications started to appear in the air force drill that had a distinctly RMC flavour. Hence, the academy now uses air force drill, modified, and the RMC influence is noticeable in small things to those of us who know.

SAME GAME, DIFFERENT RULES

By and large, the cadets fitted in well together. Army and navy quickly discovered they had much in common with alcohol abuse, womanising, practical jokes and a mistrust of the staff common to both groups. The air force were a little different, but even they occasionally let their hair down enough to allow themselves the luxury of wearing a loud tie.

Induction of the new wave of cadets soon began in earnest. The First Years arrived and so did the military staff, who appeared in the accommodation area at all hours of the evening. This really grated upon any goodwill the staff had left. The lines were our home, and while it had to be admitted the lines were owned by the defence force, unwanted guests in anyone's home cause tension. The staff's constant prowling was interpreted not as an attempt to correct unwanted behaviour, but as a lack of trust.

Females were another addition to the strange new life at the academy. We were happy to treat them like any other First Year, but that was not to be. One hundred and one rules were bought out to protect their innocence, although I often wondered if the defence force was sincere or just producing rules to cover their collective backside. If they were sincere, 40 First Year female cadets in an environment with 600 competitive males was a ludicrous idea. The female cadets really needed some senior class women to provide advice and support. This had not been organised when planning for the academy. I was always in trouble for swearing in front of them. I didn't do it on purpose. I just swear all the time. Everyone else could live with it, so I just guessed the young ladies would have to adjust. We all had to make adaptations in life, but I was stuffed if I would make adjustments for Fourthies, which was all they were to me.

FIFTEEN MINUTES OF FAME

The *Canberra Times* attempted at this time to bring allegations of bastardisation against the academy. It was a poor-cousin attempt to emulate the bastardisation scandal of several years before and grab national headlines. As far as that went it was a fizzer, although the staff certainly took it all seriously. One of the allegations made was that First Year academy cadets had been taken on midnight runs against their will. I had a little chuckle when I read that, but they didn't mention my name so I missed out on the infamy that was rightly mine.

I was still continuing my late night runs and had as a companion an army cadet a year ahead of me. Each evening we would leave at about 2130 hours and sprint up and down Mount Pleasant a few times before returning to the academy. A group of Fourthies approached me one evening wishing to join us on these excursions. It was an unusual request. Fourthies are normally so afraid to approach a senior class I vaguely wondered what I was doing wrong. I agreed, however, and four or five would join us each evening.

Next thing I knew I was on the mat before Captain Steel. I attempted to explain the circumstances but the conversation was rather one way. 'You do not appear to grasp the seriousness of your position,' Captain Steel threatened. 'Let me assure you if you are caught bastardising First Year cadets again, you're out.'

A ROOM WITH A VIEW

One day while walking through the corridors, I smelt a distinctive pungent aroma. I followed my nose upstairs and through the process of deduction I headed for the most likely source room. I tried the handle surreptitiously. As expected, the door was locked. I braced myself against the opposite wall and drove my boot into the flimsy panelling of the door. It burst inwards and I followed up behind it. I found my way through the thick air and grabbed my classmate by the throat, pushing him out across the window ledge until half his body was over the two-storey drop. The only thing preventing his fall was my grip and his eyes bulged at me in surprise. 'Staff don't give a shit about dope smoking, but I do,' I ground out passionately in his face. 'If I smell it around here again, I'll drop you next time.' I gave him a shove to add emphasis before dragging him inside, pushing him onto the floor and stalking out.

BATTLE OF WILLS

The Defence Academy was organised into squadrons, commanded by a major. Each squadron consisted of three divisions, each containing about 40 cadets and commanded by a captain. The divisions were numbered and my division was 33. The divisional officer was Captain Steel. A tallish well-groomed man, with a neatly clipped moustache and glasses, he was coldly professional. Captain

Steel individually interviewed each member of 33 Division. After the formalities of saluting had been put aside, I was indicated a seat.

Captain Steel had a list of questions in front of him. Name? Next of kin? The usual ones I had answered a million times for the army. I wondered why they asked these same questions all the time. Maybe they hoped you might forget what you said last time and then accuse you of lying.

'Do you have any loans? Debts?'

This was a new one. 'I'm sorry?'

Captain Steel repeated the question.

'I don't think that is any of your business, sir,' I responded after some thought.

'You are bordering on insolence, Officer Cadet Sneyk. Everything about you is my business. I am here to deliver value for money for the Australian taxpayer, and if you are in financial debt you may get into difficulties down the track. I want to avoid this by knowing now and anticipating any problems.'

'I still don't think this is any of your business but let me assure you, sir, if any creditors threaten to break my arm you will be the first to know.'

Captain Steel did not seem to know quite what to do, then looked at some notes which seemed to give him the inspiration to launch into a prepared speech.

For a start I had been bastardising the First Years and had brought discredit on the academy. I appeared generally to have a bad attitude, as demonstrated by me wearing that cap, and finally I was on a chief instructor's warning to be removed for 'weak academics' and another for 'officer qualities'.

It was my turn to look perplexed. Within two short weeks of being at the academy I'd suddenly been elevated from an average cadet to public enemy number one. I was nonplussed and politely inquired further into what exactly the chief instructor's warnings were and what they meant.

'All those who have failed an academic subject are automatically placed on a chief instructor's warning for weak academics. If your performance in academics does not improve after this you will accept the consequences.'

Captain Steel did not elaborate on what the consequences would be, either because he didn't know or because he expected me to use my fertile imagination and begin quaking in my boots.

'Sir, that subject I have failed, I wished to drop after mid-year exams at RMC. However, I was not allowed to do so by my company commander. This seems a little unfair as cadets who did drop subjects have exactly the same number of accredited units as I. Under your rules, they would not receive a warning.'

'You have failed a subject, Officer Cadet Sneyk, and policy is you will receive a warning,' was his uncompromising reply.

'I am being penalised for following directions, sir.' I glowered at Captain Steel.

'You are still on that warning. You failed a subject.'

'Sir, as my divisional officer, I request you make a representation to the chief instructor. This is unfair.' I knew I was pleading and that made me angry.

'I am here to represent the chief instructor and his policies first and foremost,' intoned Steel. 'I know his policy and do not need or wish to question it further.'

'Yes, sir,' I replied bitterly. 'May I ask what the officer quality warning is for?'

'All those who have received an academic warning have also received an officer qualities warning. Officers strive to achieve their best in everything they do. You have the capability of passing everything at university, otherwise you would not be here. Therefore it is obvious you have not tried your utmost, and you have thus been placed on a warning for lacking officer-like qualities.'

I could never fault logic like that, so I signed some official-looking documents that were held out to me and took my carbon copies before leaving.

Livid, I went up to see Salty, who was fast becoming a friend.

I appreciated his jocular carefree attitude. He had not yet had an interview with Captain Steel.

'Officer qualities,' I fumed. 'I've never heard anything like it. The man's an absolute clown.'

'Don't worry,' Salty soothed. 'The chief instructor's only a lieutenant colonel. Look, I've got warnings from the Chief of Naval Staff. Here, check these out.' He went straight to his bookshelf and pulled down three pieces of paper similar to mine signed by an admiral. 'It's all crap, Tommy. I'm still here. Who cares?'

I was still not happy. 'I think it's a joke. I'll just stick these to my door.'

Salty thought they looked rather decorative and did likewise with his. The bet was on. I could get more warnings than Salty.

A LINK FORMS

Due to the tri-service nature of the student body, military training at the academy had to be adjusted. Military training consisted of Common Military Training and Single Service Training.

The Common Military Training program ran through the year, with three or four periods a week on activities that were common to all three services. Military law, service writing, English expression, physical and recreational training, and academy drill. All very interesting for bureaucrats, not so much so if you wanted to become a soldier.

Single Service Training was generally arranged for the four weeks before or after the academic term. It was arranged by each service, depending on specific requirements. The military training wing at RMC was responsible for the training of army academy cadets. All it required was for us to walk back across the spur line and report to RMC.

After the induction of the First Years had begun in earnest, our class returned to Duntroon to begin our Single Service Training.

The class was divided into two, the usual format from the previous year. The divisions were obviously made with the rolls of the previous year's RMC companies. All ex-Kokoda, Beersheba and Tobruk Company cadets were in one half-class, while the other half-class consisted of ex-Romani, Gallipoli and Pozières cadets. This was as it had been the year before, except I was now on the roll with the ex-Romani, Gallipoli and Pozières cadets. It seemed to me likely that the roll book that had left me standing alone on a parade ground a year ago was still being used. I had no close friends amongst this half-class.

The military lectures we were subjected to were exceedingly boring and all the material had been covered in the previous year at Duntroon. I couldn't imagine why we were going over lessons we knew relatively well when it was obvious that there was so much more to learn. The fact that we'd covered it all before did not deter some classmates from asking a host of inane questions which in my opinion interfered with the more important TOC or lunchtime. It appeared to me that a large percentage of this class were attempting to get brownie points by asking questions.

I sat there in discomfort, one day, not knowing anyone well enough to be able to vent my frustration. Five minutes of precious TOC time were already gone and I was still listening to idiotic questions. Were they all mad? What kind of priorities did these people have? My eyes scrutinised the room. Intent faces leaned forward waiting for the pearls of wisdom to drop from the instructors' lips. The fact they had had exactly the same lesson only three months ago did not seem at all disconcerting to these people. My eyes eventually met another pair, and I instantly recognised the same impatience and disgust.

After everyone had finally quenched their desire for last year's information, we were released. I pushed my way outside and plonked down against the back of the building, my eyes closed, a clear sign that I didn't wish for a conversation. There was a shuffling sound near me. Without moving my head, I raised my eyes in what I hoped was a hostile manner. When I found myself staring into the other impatient eyes, I straightened slightly and moved a fraction in an invitation to sit.

'Exciting morning,' I tested.

'Hmmm,' was the reply. 'So many morons asking stupid questions when it's TOC time.'

He had a handful of biscuits and offered them across. Cream-filled, I noted with satisfaction. Nobody's fool. Must have knocked a few people aside to get a hold of these. I munched in silence for a while, and took a sip of his brew when he offered it.

'We haven't met,' he said friendlily. 'I'm Phil Newman.'

That made me a little bit more curious. Phil Newman was touted as the best runner in the class, and had recently been appointed commandant's personal assistant for army Second Year cadets. It was a prestigious position that more or less made him the senior army cadet in our class. His appointment had caused a lot of rumblings and I had the distinct impression he wasn't all that loved by the 'in' crowd. For once, I had abstained from having a bitch, because I didn't know him. Yet here he was.

'Tommy,' I held out my hand. I didn't tell him my last name. He probably already knew. If he didn't he could find out.

Phil and I became firm friends over the next few weeks. We lived fairly similar lifestyles and both spent a great deal of time in Sydney. We started driving there together, racing backwards and forwards late at night. We spent countless hours on these trips talking over our ideas about individual personalities and the system that controlled our lives.

COLD STEEL

Sergeant Lemon introduced himself to our class as follows:

'Listens in, youse peoples, what's the main killing weapon of the soldier?'

'A rifle?' one of us replied hopefully.

'No! No! No!' snapped Sergeant Lemon. 'Killing men, *killing*!'

'A tank?' offered a classmate.

'No!' yelled Lemon. 'I'm beginnin' to thinks that all youse peoples are thick.'

'A nuclear hand grenade?' cracked one member.

Sergeant Lemon's glare cut short the class's collective titter. 'It's the bayonet,' said Sergeant Lemon, triumphantly producing a fiercesome-looking weapon from nowhere and holding it before our eyes, daring us to challenge him. I looked at his demented expression and hoped nobody would.

'Forget these whizkids who think the next war's goin' to be won with nuclear weapons and technology cause it's not. You see. Cause it's goin' to be youse peoples on the ground with your bayonets just like it was at Gallipoli, see.'

This was all rather too much for me and I gave way to fits of laughter. The sergeant was obviously trying to enthuse us for the lesson on bayonet fighting that would follow. Unfortunately it was not quite the right pitch for his audience.

This sergeant was in charge of writing reports for our class. As the military training period finally drew to a close, reports were handed out to the individuals on their performance. Pinks were now rated from one to ten. Ninety per cent of our class had received less than five, and some had received a mighty zero. Sergeant Lemon explained it as follows. 'Overall, I'm not real happy with youse peoples. Some of yas show potential, but if I give ya a zero youse a waste of rations.'

Four out of ten made me a top performer, but it did not stop me from racing forward when given the opportunity to question the sergeant about the comments I had received. 'Member has a severe confidence problem'; I just wanted to know how he had found me out. Sergeant Lemon looked perplexed for a moment. 'Youse shows potential, but ya hesitated on top of that fence one day before jumpin' down. Youse gotta have more confidence than that.' And so came to an end our class's first Single Service Training period. When I joined the army I had never expected to be assessed on climbing fences, but life was full of surprises. I wasn't angry. It was too unreal to become upset over.

The stories of Sergeant Lemon's ranking system provided the class with much amusement at the bar. One classmate who scored zero received the following explanation: 'You're fucked. The reason why you're fucked is course youse knows nothin'. The reason youse knows nothin', is scause you arks no questions. And the reason why youse arks no questions is cause you're fucked. Got it?'

MANUFACTURING TRADITIONS

Back at the academy, the academic year started again and the grind of day to day life began in earnest. Much debate was entered into at the bar about what to call our First Year cadets. The 'class' system of RMC was dismantled and the academy called cadets by the year of training they were in. The navy felt that they should be called 'Grubs', as they had been at *Creswell*. We all felt there was much merit in the idea, because grubs was exactly what they were, but it just never rolled off the tongue. Even the navy had to admit that 'Fourthie' had the right ring to it. It had a derogatory tone implicit to it. Someone suggested 'Firstie', but was sorry as soon as he opened his mouth. I can't remember who won the debate, but First Year remained Fourthies in my time simply because there were more ex-Duntroon cadets than anyone else in the senior classes.

One RMC tradition that was embraced with open arms by our navy and air force classmates was One Thousand Days to Go. In fact when the navy Second Years found out the details of this tradition they wondered why they hadn't thought of it earlier. Obviously enough, One Thousand Days to Go meant a thousand days until graduation as an officer. This would fall somewhere in the first few months of your second year at the college. The whole idea was that your Fourthies should shout the Second Years drinks for the evening as a sign of gratitude for the help you had supposedly given them in their first few weeks. No Second Year ever really assisted a Fourthie, but when we were Fourthies we had been got, so it was now considered fair that we get someone else. I've seen all kinds of traditions come and go, but when your hip pocket is bruised as badly as it is on One Thousand Days to Go, the tradition is never forgotten.

One Thousand Days to Go was organised and Salty popped around beforehand. 'Ready for a big night, Tommy?' he asked in excitement. Salty was one of the main men for the navy in the drinking stakes and his belly was testament to his expertise.

'No. Actually, I might have a bit of a quiet one, not really in the mood. Find the whole occasion rather uncivilised, really,' I replied in my best imitation of a wet blanket. 'Besides the poor Fourthies probably couldn't afford it.'

'Crap, Tommy. I've heard army people say you're a bit of a drinker, but every time I ask you out on the juice you come up with an excuse.'

'Well, I am in training, Salts, but if you're trying to challenge the army never let it be said that we welch. You're on.'

And on it was. Despite my principles which didn't want me to do to my Fourthies that which had been done to me the year before—that is, have my then Third Class merrily drink their way through a fortnight of my wages—the pride of the army was at stake. Apparently I won this competition, although neither Salty nor I can remember the exact moment of triumph. My memory deserted me at 2200 hours although people assured me I was still firing on all four cylinders at 0400.

BATTLE LINES DRAWN

'Excuse me please, ladies and gentlemen. All army Second and Third Year cadets are to assemble outside the chief instructor's building at 0700 hours in dress of day . . . Please!'

I shook my head, half-opened my eyes and peered at my clock, placed strategically so I could see the time with minimum effort. 0620 glared at me. This was most uncivilised. I wondered what the caper was as I struggled out of bed. Surely not even these clowns would stuff the lads around on a Sunday morning. I jumped into a shower and slowly woke up. Must be trouble of some kind, but why only army? Better find a uniform and iron it up a bit. Not too well, though. With two classes on parade I'll definitely be able to hide in the middle somewhere.

We straggled down to the Headquarters area in small groups, still speculating on the unusual event of a Sunday parade. On arrival in the courtyard to the back of the chief instructor's building we were directed to fall into three ranks and stood at ease. At 0700 hours the chief instructor himself appeared and we were all called to attention. The lieutenant colonel then set off with the senior cadet in tow to do an inspection. A slight stirring went through the ranks as we all realised our dress left something to be desired. It was Sunday, after all.

'Chin strap needs more polish . . . Two show parades.'

'Shoes require more shine . . . Two show parades.'

'Stain on your shirt . . . Two extra drills.'

Down the line he went and no-one escaped unscathed. I was sorely tempted to point out to the chief instructor that he was making a jolly fool of himself, as he'd left his pocket undone in most untidy fashion. However, something told me this attempt at frivolity would be less than welcome.

After the theatrics of the inspection were over, we were treated to an explanation for the morning's activities.

'Try as I might not to single out any particular service for special attention, in the best interests of unity I find that I have to fight an uphill battle against certain elements of the cadet body who seem bent on resisting me every step of the way. Again, the ex-RMC cadets have come to my notice in a particularly disturbing manner. Last evening at the bar, members of the corps who have been identified as Second and Third Year army cadets have behaved in a most offensive fashion, standing on tables, smashing glasses and urinating on pot plants. All those who are responsible are to fall out to one side where they will be dealt with separately.'

An uncomfortable silence followed and no-one moved.

'All those who were present at the bar after 2200 hours when the incident took place are to fall out.'

Again there was silence and we all looked steadfastly to our front. I felt a little swelling of pride in my chest. Lieutenant Colonel McDonald was a graduate of the Officer Cadet School at Portsea and he constantly ran down Duntroon. His appointment was believed widely, both within the cadet body and the army, to be an attempt to break down the RMC mafia which had a stranglehold on the military system.

Well, I thought, you've singled out the RMC boys for a little rough stuff. A battle of wills was developing and you could feel it. The anger of the lieutenant colonel versus the collective pride and defiance of the old RMC. I felt certain we were quite capable of winning. The issue was not whether we were harbouring criminals in our ranks, the issue was Portsea versus RMC, and we all knew it. Time slipped away and we still hadn't moved half an hour later.

The lieutenant colonel sighed. 'If the culprits have not reported to me by 1600 hours, further action will follow.'

I walked away with Phil, Jude and Bluey. Discussion centred around the destruction of the bar and we were insulted, to put it mildly. It was not unknown for RMC cadets to wreck a bar when the service was slow or offensive, but to break up our own bar was just plainly silly. Urination in the facility was just as stupid as we'd all be back to drink there again. This was an insult of the highest order and there could be no mistake about that. Indignation was the feeling left in the ranks of army cadets, and rightly so as it turned out. The culprits were later discovered to be Third Year navy cadets. No apology was ever offered.

Three army classmates were thrown out of the academy for smoking marijuana. One of them was the fellow I'd assisted to get a better view from his window. However, I didn't see these events as a sign of any determination on the staff's behalf to eliminate drugs. They could have kicked out a hundred more cadets with no real effort. It was just a warning.

Many a stash was flushed as the boys hit the panic or toilet button. Suspicious looks were thrown as the cadets began to look for a traitor in our midst. I received some very hostile expressions, as my enmity with the three who had been thrown out was well known. I smiled my good mornings, enjoying the situation a good deal. I hadn't squealed. But I'd played my hand a year before, and now had nothing to say to the staff. I wasn't in the business of replying to the accusing stares. They could keep guessing. It was better that way.

Salty came to see me one night in my room and shut the door. 'Tommy, I'm not going to beat about the bush. Did you blow the whistle to the staff on the dope?'

What was his angle? 'That's not really anyone's business,' I said matter of factly.

'A lot of people think you spilt the beans. I'm asking you to say no, you did not. Then I'll spread the word for you amongst the corps. It could save a lot of grief.'

'Thanks, Salts,' I replied thoughtfully. 'I appreciate it. But I don't have to explain myself to anyone around here. My stance on the issue is well known and I'm stuffed if I'm going to justify myself to a bunch of dope-heads who I don't care two shits about.'

'Mate,' said Salts. 'I don't think you understand. There's a lot of really angry people out there. Not just dope-heads but people who think the code has been broken. I'm not talking a little bishing here, I'm talking physical violence.'

'I can take care of myself,' I said after a pause.

He was clearly exasperated. 'You can't, Tommy, not against the corps.'

Salty stared at me and I stared back. Salts finally stood to leave. 'Salts,' I said sincerely. 'I appreciate it.'

I couldn't take care of myself. Still, physical violence wasn't the corps' style and I'd gamble on that.

I don't know what Salts said to the dope-heads, but no-one bished or even threatened me. I owed him one. However, I sensed that I was on the outer and that I would never be trusted with corps business again.

Our forty-eighth, forty-ninth and fiftieth classmates were shown the door.

NO SURRENDER

Captain Steel called me to his office for an interview. I was perturbed as I was the only cadet in the division to be honoured so.

'I have your report from Duntroon on your efforts at military training. You have failed. I also note that, in an act of defiance, you have placed your instructor's warnings on your door along with Midshipman Salts. This is indicative of your attitude, which is a continuing bad example to the First Year cadets. This behaviour is going to change.' The captain's face was red by now, as his opening burst was said without drawing breath.

'Sir, that report from RMC is not worth the paper it's written on. Ninety per cent of the class failed and I have received no satisfactory explanation for my failure.' My thoughts flittered for a moment to Sergeant Lemon as I realised that he had finally found someone who would take him seriously. 'Furthermore, I feel you are misinterpreting the reasons why I put those warnings on my door. Rather than an act of defiance, they are placed in such a prominent position to motivate me constantly and remind me of what I am working towards . . . and that is to get off those warnings. It also has the effect of helping the First Year cadets. When they see what I've sunk too, they will strive even harder at academics to ensure they do not meet the same fate as myself and Midshipman Salts.' I was more than a little impressed with this reply, although I had trouble keeping the right look on my face. There is always a fine line between contrite and smug and I struggled to keep the correct expression.

Captain Steel appeared to be placated slightly. 'Well, those warnings should come down,' he huffed.

'Yes, sir.' I tried to sound enthusiastic. 'Now that I can see they can be misinterpreted, they'll come right down.'

Steel changed subject. 'What corps do you wish to go to *if* you graduate?'

'Infantry, sir!' I replied without hesitation.

'Infantry!' repeated Steel, changing in colour again. 'When I graduated, only the best went to Infantry.' He reached across to absent-mindedly polish the infantry badge on his cap. 'If this army ever lets you into *my* corps I'll resign,' he said bluntly.

Honesty was obviously the order of the day, so I saw no reason to hold back. I knew there was no-one else in the office but I still looked over my shoulder instinctively, to ensure there were no witnesses. Satisfied, I fixed him firmly in my gaze.

'You're a prick,' I said. Captain Steel's mouth began to move but no words came out.

I stood up and left.

ACADEMIC PAIN

I disciplined myself to attend academic lectures but beyond that my perseverance had run out.

I particularly disliked Business Management, which I had taken up in an effort to make up for my failed subject from the previous year. The senior lecturer for first year was a fellow named Jean-

Pierre Dupane, whose arrogance was considered by cadets to be a symptom of his national heritage. Dupane was without a doubt the most boring, disinterested lecturer I have ever clapped eyes on. While William Crick was ridiculous and slightly funny, Dupane was tragically uncharismatic. The only time he ever became animated was when he told the class the latest piece of advice he'd given the Minister for Industrial Relations, who I gather paid him as an adviser. This was an impressive boast until you had a close look at the nation's history of industrial strife. Interest glistened in his eyes when he held up his favourite book on business management, written by, you guessed it . . . himself.

Jean-Pierre saved the real fire for when he raved on endlessly about the cadets' lack of diligence and the large number who didn't attend lectures. This speech typically went for half an hour out of a 40-minute lecture, once a week. His arguments were faultless until you realised that he was talking to the same twenty or so faces who attended every lecture. It totally eluded him that you couldn't really convert an audience who was not there.

BED FELLOWS

I often used to talk to an ex-girlfriend of Bluey's on my social tours of the nightclubs of Canberra. Kathy was different from the type of girl I imagined Bluey with. She was pretty, though in a homely way, quiet and introverted. I sensed that, like me, she was forcing herself to socialise.

I found it very hard to come to terms with the concept of Kathy and Bluey. Bluey was self-confident, brash and insensitive, and he appeared to have nothing in common with Kathy. I never talked about Blue with her, although she was aware we were good friends.

One night Kathy was agitated and I sensed a need to talk.

'Do you want to go somewhere it's a little quieter?' I yelled over the cacophony of noise that was the Bin on a Friday night. She nodded.

I led her to a quiet coffee shop around the corner, ordered two cappuccinos and said nothing until they arrived. We'd talked often, but superficially, feeling each other out with carefully chosen words. Each question taking us a little further into each other's mind, yet we had only scratched the surface.

'I'm going to Sydney, Tommy,' Kathy said suddenly. There was a steely defiance in her voice that alerted me to inner turmoil. A battle had been fought and won, not by logic but simply by jumping. She'd made a decision and was telling me to reinforce that she was right. I was not surprised by the announcement, more by the tone of her voice. I looked at Kathy, trying to get inside her mind. 'I have to leave Canberra and start again.'

Suddenly there was emotion in her voice. She burst into tears and I held her hand. She cried for a long time but I said nothing. At the most joyful and most tragic times, words never conveyed enough.

'Blue raped me, Tom,' Kathy finally said as she composed herself and looked into my eyes. She was looking for a flicker of disbelief to cross my face or words of denial. I just looked back, I knew it was true.

'What are you going to do?' I asked. 'Can I help?'

'Nothing, Tommy.' There was an empty finality in her voice. 'We were on a date. I've thought about it and I couldn't handle the innuendo and bitchiness of court. It would not be worth it. It's done and so am I.'

Kathy started crying again and I could feel the tears welling up in my own eyes. I cried with her. For all of us. God would damn us all for our inaction and our lack of courage. Truth was truth, but Kathy was right. It would not be worth it for her. It was an almost hopeless struggle to try to get justice, and the system just didn't handle rape well. How could it? Rape was ugly, and date rape just blurred the lines. Date rape made something black, grey in the eyes of the law.

'You know what the hardest thing to come to terms with is?' Kathy continued. I could only stare in reply, but she didn't stop. 'It's senseless, completely senseless.'

I drove Kathy home and said goodbye. I never saw her again.

Her revelations in no way changed my pledge to assist Blue to graduation. My word was binding and I would be true to it. Surely Blue was innocent until proven guilty and I comforted myself with the thought. It was one of those little tricks of the mind that we use to justify our actions, or our lack of them. I recognised it as that and allowed it to comfort me anyway.

THE PAIN CONTINUES

Mid-year exams came and went. I passed everything marginally. There was an old RMC credo that I had adopted and held close: Fifty-one per cent, 1 per cent wasted effort; 49 per cent, a wasted year. The chief instructor was disturbed by this 'un-officer like' credo and had sent down many hundreds of decrees on the matter and not a few threats as well. Unfortunately Lieutenant Colonel McDonald's enthusiasm for excellence was undermined by people like William Crick and Jean-Pierre Dupane, who destroyed any desire to achieve.

By the criteria of the credo I had wasted 2 per cent effort in Management at the mid-year exams. This in my opinion was extreme overachievement. You can imagine my chagrin when I received a letter from Professor Dupane, who it appeared was worried about my marginal performance. He cordially invited me to make an appointment so that we could discuss any problems I was having with the course. If old Dupanesy had had a good-looking secretary this may have been tempting, but he didn't, so after toying with the note for a moment I threw it into the round filing cabinet I kept by the door for just such purposes.

The nerve of the man. Not content with boring me in lectures, he now wished to bore me one-to-one in his office. What did he think I was . . . a glutton for punishment?

A LESSON IN LEADERSHIP

After mid-year exams all those who were on chief instructor's warnings were called up for an interview with Lieutenant Colonel McDonald himself. I joined a queue that looked as if it contained half the cadets in the academy. Finally it was my turn and I walked into the chief instructor's office not really knowing what to expect.

'What are you doing here?' was the chief instructor's first question. I was slightly perplexed and hesitated before answering with a question.

'In what way do you mean, sir?'

'What are you doing here?' he repeated impatiently. Aha, I thought to myself, it's make the horrible little cadet confess his own sins time.

'Well, I gather that you have put me on an academic and an officer qualities warning,' I replied evenly.

'Why?' snapped the chief instructor.

'I really don't know why, sir. It's your warning.'

'Have you failed a subject?'

'No, sir.'

'Have you been charged?'

'No, sir.'

'Well why are you on an officer qualities warning?'

I stood there uncomfortably and the chief instructor glowered at me. 'You must know or have an idea,' he prompted.

'I have an idea, sir.'

'Well then, what is it?' The chief instructor was very excitable.

'I'd rather not say, sir.'

'Why not? What's the problem?'

'Well, sir, it would be disloyal for me to say any more.'

'Disloyal?'

'Yes, sir, we learnt about it in leadership. A person must be loyal to his superiors, sir.'

'Now! I want to know now why you are on these warnings.'

'Sir, simply I have a personality clash with my divisional officer.'

'Who is your divisional officer?'

'Captain Steel, sir.'

The chief instructor snorted derisively and instantly ripped up my warnings in front of my face, then dropped them in the bin.

'You can go,' he said after a long silence.

I wasn't sure if I had heard correctly so I stood rooted to the ground.

'Go,' said the chief instructor impatiently.

I saluted and withdrew hurriedly.

What a strange man the chief instructor was. I didn't tell him that the other half of the leadership lesson was on loyalty to your subordinates. My mind slipped back years to when Cadet McDonald should have been paying attention to that lesson. As far as I was concerned, Lieutenant Colonel McDonald had just done his first right thing. However, his behaviour appeared to be erratic and you can never really trust an erratic person.

TWO ANGRY BULLS

I was called down to an interview with Captain Steel. He was eating humble pie and I could sense it.

'I am not totally convinced that you are putting in 100 per cent effort, but I want to give you an opportunity to build up your performance from here. I intend letting you off the chief instructor's warnings' as an incentive after passing mid-year exams.'

'Yes, sir. I know.'

'You know?'

'Yes, sir. Lieutenant Colonel McDonald ripped the warnings up in front of me yesterday,' I said smugly.

Captain Steel turned a horrible shade of purple, picked up the telephone receiver and put it straight back down. There was a long silence, during which he did some very heavy breathing.

'The other matter I wish to talk about was your non-reply to an interview request with Professor Dupane.'

'Sir?' I said in a surprised and questioning tone. 'What interview request was that?'

'It was sent in the mail to you,' Steel said impatiently, 'two weeks back now.'

'No, sir, I haven't seen it. The internal mail system is very poor at present. I don't think they've quite ironed out all the glitches. Would Professor Dupane like to see me? I wonder what that could be about? Perhaps I should give him a call and see what time would be convenient.'

'Perhaps you should,' Captain Steel ground out. 'I'm now tutoring in the Management Department and I'll be taking a close interest in your progress.'

'I'm sure you will, sir.'

PULLED IN LINE

It was about this time that I started my favourite rebellious activity—non-shaving and non-ironing days. They were completely harmless but they did offer an element of excitement to an otherwise boring day. Ironing and starching of uniforms was of course mandatory, and so was shaving on a daily basis. The objective of my game was to attend all lectures and parades unshaven, or unironed, without getting charged. The truth was I was bored.

The whole day was spent dodging staff members and walking

around in large groups of people so as to be less conspicuous. Andy confronted me about my dress one day.

'Tommy, you haven't ironed that shirt! And look at those shoes. You look like you've been playing football in them. Come on, that's no example to set the Fourthies.'

Andy was immaculately turned out as always. Shoes shining, shirt crisply starched.

'Well, what example do I need to set for my peers, Andy? You seem to forget that Fourthies hold the rank of officer cadet and Second Years hold the rank of officer cadet, so they can do what they like and I'll do what I like.' I was fuming. 'There's one thing that seems to elude you, Andy. If you are such a great example and I am such a poor example, then you should not worry about my dress because no-one would follow an obviously bad example like me.'

'Look, Tommy, I'm not stupid. I can tell you're being sarcastic.'

'No, facetious maybe.'

'The point is your attitude isn't winning you any friends. I'm telling you this as a friend, in your own best interest. You are really alienating a lot of people. Look, I recently read *How to Win Friends and Influence People* and it's changed my life. I suggest you do the same. For example, let me tell you some of the techniques I've picked up. If I'm going up to talk to Adrian, I remember his pet fish's name is Oscar, so I'll ask Adrian about Oscar and he immediately sees that I'm interested in him and he likes me in return.'

'That's good, Andy.' I was enthralled. 'Go on.'

'Well, Tom, take for example your girlfriend Yvonne. If every time I see you I ask how Yvonne is going, you will respond to me more warmly,' Andy said triumphantly. 'I think you should try it.'

'I can see what you're saying and I do think you're interested, I'll remember that. Thanks, mate, I appreciate your time,'

I hoped I sounded sincere.

ALL AT SEA

Saturday morning parades were a constant source of amusement. At Duntroon I'd usually woken up at 0700 hours, twenty minutes before parade time, had a quick shave and dressed before racing down the hill with a minute or two to spare. Since coming to the academy I'd found it necessary to change my habits to accommodate the navy, or more particularly Salty.

Salts believed I was an alcoholic because of my habit of downing seven or eight drinks each evening. He pointed to this as proof that I was reliant on alcohol. Salts believed he was in control of his habit because he never drank mid-week. Of course he drank a bottle of bourbon on each of Friday, Saturday and Sunday nights. In truth, any impartial judge would have classified us both as alcoholics, but we both would have denied this strenuously.

Because of Salty's drinking habits, I always set my alarm an hour early on Saturday morning. I would get out of bed, walk past the laundry half-asleep, pull Salty's uniform out of the washing machine and put it into the drier before continuing down the corridor to the shower. Once in the shower, I turned the cold water on without even checking on Salty, who was usually curled up in the foetal position on the tiled floor. He would quiver once or twice and mumble 'Go away' before I turned the shower off and wrestled him into the upright position. I would then drag him into his room, sit him on the edge of his bed and then thrust a black coffee in his hand before going to retrieve his still damp uniform and attempt to iron it dry. Once all this was done, I would dress Salty myself and guide him down to parade.

Everyone in the army, navy and air force was issued a bayonet, a rifle and several magazines. Not Salty. He had a 'knife', a 'bangstick', and 'bullet holders'. One day before going on parade I pulled Salty's knife out of its scabbard and went to put it on his bangstick.

'Salts, this knife is hopeless, mate. It's rusty.'

'I'm going to get charged, aren't I?'

'Yes, Salts, I'd say at a guess you are.'

Salty then promptly grabbed his knife and wiped it between his legs. This took the most obvious rust off his knife. However, a big red streak of rust now contrasted nicely with the blue of his trousers.

The morning inspection was conducted with Salty standing pigeon-toed so the rust stained area couldn't be seen from the front. As the inspecting officer came around behind, Salty changed position so that he stood like a duck and the red stain was invisible from the rear. Living with the navy was never boring.

THE LAW OF THE CORPS

Friday nights were invariably spent in the Private Bin, drinking with the cadets you worked with all week. Why I spent some of the best days of my misspent youth in this particular pub cum nightclub is beyond me. As a norm I did not like talking to cadets after hours, but I just went to be seen. I never went with a group, as this would tie me down to a hard night's drinking, and I contented myself with moving from group to group, a can of Victoria Bitter in one hand, till I was bored.

One night while driving home, a car followed me all the way from town. In the rear-vision mirror I noted that the lights were similar to that of a Ford, so I realised it might be a police car. Meticulously, I drove back to the academy at 60 km/h the whole way, coming to a dead standstill at every stop sign. It was late but this car stayed at a constant distance, never getting closer or further behind.

I watched the vehicle even more closely as it passed under a set of street lights and I noticed it was a panel van. Perhaps it was the early hour, but my mind was not functioning. It's not a police car at all, I thought as I left Russell and went the back way into the academy over the side of Mount Pleasant. The accelerator went through the fire wall as I attempted to make up for all the restraint I had demonstrated earlier.

As I prepared to enter into the academy, a blue light behind me warned me all was not well. I came to a halt and so did a police paddy wagon. Not real clever of me, I thought.

I pulled out my licence and held it for the approaching police officer.

'Have you been drinking?' The policeman asked as he approached.

'Yes officer, but I am not over the limit.' My tone was meticulously courteous.

'Do you realise you were doing 145 in a 70 zone?'

'Yes, officer.'

'Can I see your licence.' There was a pause as he peered at it by torchlight. It still showed my address as Beersheba Company, RMC.

'Do you still belong to Beersheba Company?' asked the policeman.

'Yes, officer.' I didn't feel like explaining the ins and outs of the academy at 0300 hours.

'That's interesting, I used to live there too,' he said. 'Have a good night.' And he was gone.

Thank God for failed cadets, I thought. It was good to see that even ex-members of RMC remembered the law of the corps went above all others.

CONFUSION

I walked past Andy on the way to a lecture. 'How's Yvonne going?' he asked in his usual polite manner.

'Yvonne?' I replied. 'Oh, you mean Archie's girlfriend. Haven't seen her in a while. Why don't you ask Archie?'

Andy wore a puzzled expression before quickly changing the subject.

A CRY FOR HELP

'Simon, I need to borrow your essay tonight,' I said with a smile. 'I haven't started yet, mate, and I just need to see what direction to take.'

'I've told you a hundred times, no. Do you understand? No.' Simon used his arms to emphasise his position. He was getting frustrated, and I was being particularly persistent.

'I'm up the creek without your help,' I said, unabashed.

'No', yelled Simon and he walked quickly away.

Jude waited for Simon to disappear before he spoke.

'You've already got my essay, Tommy. You don't need his.'

'Yes I do,' I said. 'Haven't you noticed that Simon never gets involved in our study parties? He thinks it's academic misconduct. I just want to broaden his mind. He's a very moral man, old Simon, a true Christian. He goes to church every Sunday you know.'

'You're a bastard, Tommy,' said Jude.

'I'll take that as a compliment.'

A CONTACT WITH A DISAPPEARING SOUL

I stepped outside into the cold Canberra night and instantly felt the numbing cold on my face. A chill ran through me and I involuntarily shivered as the wintry air seeped through my gloves and the rugby jersey. Just as the cold numbed my face, it galvanised my mind, which had been going through the routine of making an essay. It wouldn't be a good essay. The Geography lecturer wanted fifteen hundred words in the morning, so that was exactly what he would get. Five pages of nothing. I deliberately made my writing scratchy. If I had to torture myself to write an essay, I might as well get revenge on the marker.

What did people do before lycra? I wondered as I started running stiffly, to get circulation into my legs, which were co-cooned in the warmth of the material. The air was motionless and I cut my way through the heavy fog as I headed up the hill. It was already three in the morning and I needed to clear the dull throb in my head.

As the lights of the academy disappeared behind me, the grey swirl closed in. I shortened my stride as I powered up the steep slope with choppy steps, and my feet hit the metre or so of bitumen I could see in front of me with satisfying thumps. I enjoyed concentrating on my stride as my body automatically registered where I was. I'd been here a thousand times before.

Watch for those little potholes ahead. Not much danger of twisting an ankle. Still, you never know. There they are, underfoot, right on cue. There's a couple of raised sections of bitumen ahead. Roots growing underneath the road. That's them.

Little bit of a bend to the right up here. Oops, almost missed it.

Now a little steeper.

Further to the right.

It flattens out a little here and we're at the end.

I peered through the black and grey and found an old cannon that I knew was there. I climbed on top and faced out over Canberra with one leg over each side of the barrel. I couldn't see a thing. I couldn't even see the muzzle some feet in front of me.

This is the only country in the world where I can climb over a national memorial, I thought. It's special, I love it.

If the women of Canberra could only see me now. I looked at the barrel between my legs. Impressive.

I jumped off the gun, placed my feet on a low sandstone wall to the front of the gun and my hands on the ground two feet below. I extended my body and commenced push-ups, struggling to 50 before stopping.

Slowly, I stood back up and looked around. I stretched and flexed the muscles in my back and arms. Well I guess that's it, time to roll back down the hill. I dived back into the cold dark vapour. I closed my eyes and lengthened my stride. No need to look. I could do this blind.

It's getting a little steeper, round to the left, now straight. A bit more to the left up here. Not yet though, a little bit further . . .

I hit the guard rail with a thump, went over the side, and fell, rolling down the hill in a tangle of arms and limbs till I eventually stopped.

I lay still. Listening to the silence. The noiselessness was eerie and I moved a hand in front of my face. Nothing. I touched my nose to confirm that it was still there, then started running through a checklist. Legs, arms, stomach, head. No unusual pain, I must be okay.

My cheeks were cool and I could feel a warm line of liquid running down one of them. I touched the cheek and felt a small stream drip on to my finger. I put the finger into my mouth to confirm what it was. Blood.

Laughter echoed through the bushes. I knew it was mine. So they think these runs are madness? Never. I've just proved I'm alive.

SATISFACTION

It was 0340 hours when I knocked on Simon's door. I had finished the essay and the run, but I hadn't completed work yet.

'Simon, open up buddy, it's Tommy,' I called.

The door opened a crack and I looked at Simon's sleep-laden eyes. I was covered in blood still and I hoped this would gain extra sympathy. 'Mate, I need that essay of yours or I'm screwed.'

Simon went to slam the door.

'Simon, for a mate you can't turn your back. I've hurt myself on a run trying to stay awake. You have to help,' I pleaded.

He sighed heavily, disappeared for a moment and returned with his essay. He held it out reluctantly. 'Don't get caught, Tommy. I don't want to get thrown out for academic misconduct.'

'Hey mate. Me? I'm an expert. Let me tell you about all my methods of plagiarism. Change the tense. Alter the order of the paragraphs. Change the subject and the predicates around. It's a cinch,' I said with a smile. 'I appreciate this,' I threw over my shoulder as I disappeared down the corridor.

So I was wrong. I always thought Simon had high ideals, but it was only a fear of being caught. Such a poor motivation. And from a Christian too. What was the world coming too?

ALL FOR ONE

Bluey was losing direction. He spent most of his days sleeping and his nights womanising or attempting to. Blue was not in love, whatever that meant to Blue, and that was his problem. He needed to be in love and to feel loved. The military staff were putting the acid on him for his lack of performance at academics, his non-attendance and poor attitude. None of this made any difference to Blue, who was in bed every time I stopped around to see him.

He was a moody kind of character, whose priorities often appeared to me to be confused. Probably because they were. I note this with some amusement, as I was somewhat confused myself. Suffice to say, I considered Bluey to be more confused. I took around Geography work for Blue, but he wouldn't even bother getting out of bed. He had two essays overdue, the lecturers were baying for blood, yet they remained unstarted. I spoke to Archie and Squizzy and both agreed he was not going to make it. He was on the slide out the door. Try as I did, I could not motivate Blue. Eventually the only thing to do was to write his Geography and Philosophy essays for him. I was not in the least enthused, as I could barely stomach my own study. However, he passed and stayed afloat long enough to fall in love and get back with the team.

CASUALTIES MOUNT

I sat in a corner stall of the Ainslie Hotel with Blue, Phil and Jude. The conversation centred around work. I didn't say overly much. Most of it had been said before, so I analysed the pattern on the nasty looking maroon carpet, stared at the black vinyl chairs and the wood veneer booths.

What side of human nature was appealed to by this mismatch of bad taste? Yet the Ainslie had character. In any other town it would have been kitsch, but in the sterile world of Canberra it was interesting.

I played with the steak on my plate. It was curious, I thought, but they were the best steaks in the world when it was a Sunday lunch here with a girl. On a Friday night with the lads it was just another piece of meat. I sipped at a schooner of Reschs. Reschs always tasted good as long as it came in a schooner. You either drank enough to relax, or enough to forget—the end result was more or less the same. A pleasant feeling of nothing. I was drinking more and more lately.

My mind roamed, but I kept my eyes vacantly on whoever happened to be chairing the conversation within our little group. I concentrated on Jude for a moment. He was talking animatedly and his eyes met mine, just for a second. He knew I wasn't concentrating. It struck me for the thousandth time that talk was cheap, yet that was the best any of us could offer. I wanted a revolution with academics and military staff being put to the sword.

I refocused my attention across the room and watched Freddie. He had just resigned and a group of his friends were having farewell drinks with him. I didn't know any of them well, most of them did too much dope. I didn't dislike them for that, I just didn't understand how they reconciled it with being an officer in my army. I'd never had an argument with any one of them about it. There weren't any arguments. I know it was out of fashion, but the subject was black and white, at least as far as the army went. Well, it was supposed to be. I guess that's why I had thought I would like the army, and now found I didn't. The army was supposed to make life simple, but all it did was hide the complex issues so it would appear simple.

I drained my glass, said, 'My shout' and stood up to buy another round. It wasn't, but I was restless and bored and you never expect any arguments on a call like that. Besides, they could only have said something to my retreating back.

I stood at the bar, stretched my legs and enjoyed the change of perspective.

Freddie turned from the bar with his hands clasped around three schooners. The top layers of beer were dripping down the side onto his fingertips. I winked and smiled.

'I need to speak to you before I go,' Freddie said in passing.

'No worries, mate. I'll have a yarn later.'

I didn't like farewells. My childhood was full of them and I knew that 'later' could easily be interpreted as not at all. I already knew that I would conveniently forget.

When I returned to the group I finished off my schooner in a couple of large gulps. 'Well, if you'll excuse me I'll get going.' I didn't invite anyone to join me. Jude would go back to the college, he had a long-term girlfriend in Sydney and didn't go out in Canberra. Phil would go back to his room and get up early to start training. Bluey would go around to his girlfriend's place and do whatever they did. My mind didn't connect him with making love. Blue always called it love, but it was just a power game. He always found his own power attractive for a while. Me, I thought, I'll go out and drink too much just for a change.

I threaded my way through people and out the door and gulped down a few mouthfuls of fresh air. Maybe I'll surprise myself and just go home. I started to form a mental picture of me doing that when my thoughts were interrupted.

'Tommy, wait on.' Freddie stuck his head around the corner of the door, disappeared inside for a moment, then reappeared.

'Tommy, I needed to see you away from them. They don't understand. Everything you've ever said about Duntroon and the academy is true. It finally came to me and that's why I've resigned.'

'Good for you, mate. It's a courageous move. I hear you're going to pursue photography.'

'Yeah, I think I could be good at it. What do you think?'

'You'll do it if you want to.' I nodded my head in agreement with myself, then held out my hand and shook his warmly.

Freddie returned my gaze. 'Tommy, I'm leaving because I know this is all just shit. You know this is shit but you still stay. Why?'

I looked at him long and hard. 'I don't know why . . . look after yourself,' and I left. Now I knew what I would do. I'd go into town and get absolutely ripped for a change.

I walked with my shoulders hunched, hands in pockets. Was it just that I didn't have the courage to resign?

Freddie was the fifty-first member of our class to leave.

EASY OPTIONS—NOT BEST OPTION

I'd often return to my room after lectures to find a note saying the adjutant had called and wished for me to return the call. I couldn't imagine what he wanted to speak to me about, but decided it could only be bad, so I ignored the messages. Each of the messages was ripped off my door and thrown in the bin. He could get lost as far as I was concerned.

One Friday afternoon while strolling through the academy, I walked past a captain who I saluted smartly. This captain eyed my name tag. 'Stop,' he cried. 'Sneyk, I've been looking for you.'

'Me, sir?' I was all innocence.

'Yes, you. Do you own that eyesore up in the car park, sitting on bricks with no engine, that looks like a prop from a Mad Max movie?'

'Yes, sir,' I was wary.

'Get rid of it. If it's still there on Monday you will be charged. The academy is under constant public scrutiny. Do you know what that wreck does for first impressions?' There was no anger in the captain's voice, just a glint in his eyes.

'Not a lot sir. It will be gone.' I promised. It was not an unreasonable request and I had the weekend to comply with his wishes.

The best course of action was to call the tip and arrange to dump it there, so I went back to the barracks and called. It was closed for the weekend. This was not good. I spoke to Phil and Jude and their news was not good. The car in question was a body that I owned for spare parts, and it was slowly being cannibalised to keep my other vehicle roadworthy. I was not mechanical, so Jude and Phil did the work while I acted as drink boy.

'That car has the problem of having no steering,' Jude informed me. 'Even if we get it back on four wheels it's going to have to be dragged around every corner to get wherever we take it. Of course the best spot would be the anti-armour range. Then we'll get a chance to shoot at it with some rockets a little later.'

'That's a fair way,' Phil said. 'We might have to take it some-where closer.'

A towing frame was hired, spare wheels were borrowed and the body numbers were beaten out so that it could never be traced back to me. A big V8 was borrowed to drag it around corners.

Down to the bar we went to think things over. My suggestion finally won out because it was the easiest. 'Drop it in the old Molonglo River!'

It was raining cats and dogs as we drove down to the Molonglo at 0300 hours for the launching of my first boat. It was a failure, the boat sank. Then for a quick getaway. There is no God. The getaway car wouldn't start. We sat there, not knowing whether to laugh or cry. We cursed and shouted. Cars lights came and went on the distant highway. We hoped no-one would see us.

Finally the car started and we felt much happier. No charge on Monday.

A QUALITY CALLED LEADERSHIP

I was sitting in the back of the lecture theatre with Phil, Bluey and Squizzy watching Andy organise the parade state and handover to a staff member for the umpteenth time in the last few months. It was not really Andy's place to conduct this ritual, as a duty student was appointed for such purposes. However, every time I turned around Andy was up the front being noticed. I was not the only one who was aware of the emergence of Andy out of the shadows.

Blue nodding his head in Andy's direction. 'What do you think his caper is?'

'He's just having a crawl,' suggested Squizzy.

'Yeah, probably,' I said, unconvinced. I knew how his mind worked, he'd given me a very good insight. 'But who really cares? He's saving me doing anything. Good luck to him.'

CORRUPTION

At the end of Second Year, all of those who were finishing off their sub-majors in Philosophy were invited to a dinner with the academic lecturers. I had initially wanted to do a major in Philosophy but I couldn't motivate myself to the subject after the previous year's episodes. I was in a festive mood. I had achieved three passes in my second-year academic subjects, although 'achieve' is probably the wrong word. All of my marks in my two Geography subjects and Philosophy were between 50 and 54 per cent. I considered myself a fine judge of minimum requirements.

I'd failed Management by three marks, but I'd never seriously thought I would pass after Captain Steel had joined the department. And Jean-Pierre Dupane had definitely had his nose out of joint when I'd finally made it to his morning tea. Despite my sincere apologies and my concern over the academy's mailing system, I gained the distinct impression he'd heard it all before and was less than impressed.

At the dinner I seated myself next to Sue, who was a tutor in the department. She was a wonderful lady and everyone adored her. Like most tutors, she was not involved in the politicking that was evident in most academics' actions. Tutors generally were more reasonable people because they had not yet invested all that much of their life in academics and did not feel the need to protect their own position so staunchly, or backstab to achieve the next promotion. She was a homely looking mother figure who had a pleasant demeanour and always gave high-quality instruction.

We engaged in deep conversation about the college and academics. Sue surprised me by asking what kind of a person Andy was.

'He's a bit personality deficient, a quiet little geek who keeps to himself,' I replied in a straightforward manner.

'Well the military seem to have a very high opinion of him as a leader,' Sue said. 'They have gone to great lengths to ensure he passes.'

'Meaning?'

'Come on, Tom, you're not stupid. You know the pressure the military put on the academic staff.'

'Yes I do. But that's no reason to give in to their demands,' I pointed out. 'You only undermine your own credibility.'

'I agree.' Sue was her usual patient self. 'But it's a very persuasive argument, that cadets are career soldiers, and it is senseless to ruin a potentially good military career just because someone fails an academic subject.'

'Yes, but it's only a matter of opinion whether Andy's going to have a good military career. I guarantee I know him better than any staff member and in my opinion he's a bit of a nonentity who you really oughtn't pay too much attention to. Not quite Napoleon, but he tries hard to be liked.'

Sue was not to be put off. 'The military staff seem to think differently. Most of the academics think much as you do, but the military give the impression he is one of the great leaders of our time.'

I thought about it a little more. 'He has his good points from their point of view,' I said at last and we left it at that.

A TEST

Cryptic Challenge was a quick-decision exercise conducted in adverse conditions at the end of second year. It was carried out in sections with navy, air force and army cadets mixed in together. The idea was to identify potential leaders from the cadet body for our final year at the academy before returning to RMC for a fourth year of purely military study.

Adverse conditions is a clinical way of saying the military staff will push you till you break. I liked these kind of exercises because they uncovered selfish individuals who in my opinion flourished in day-to-day academy life.

The exercise started at 0200 when we were woken in the barracks. After twenty minutes of frantic packing and pulling on of uniforms, we assembled and ordered into the back of waiting trucks. The canvas flap was shut behind us and we lay in complete darkness on our packs, not knowing where we were going.

'What the hell's happening?' I recognised the voice of Salts.

'Doesn't matter. They're just trying to disorientate and confuse us. Army shit mate. Go to sleep. All you need to worry about is time. In a week this will be over, and if you catch a couple of hours rack, it'll be a week minus two hours.'

A short while later the trucks jolted to a stop and the flap of canvas was thrown up. The steady thud of helicopter blades could be heard as we piled out. We were immediately ordered into groups and allocated an aircraft.

I tried to switch off, though it was more difficult in a chopper. The aircraft shook and pulsed with an excitement that is infectious. I could see a glow on the horizon where the sun was due to emerge, and beneath my feet the coastal escarpment could be distinguished in the dark. The aircraft continued towards the coast before losing height and hovering for us to jump out. We landed in waist deep sludge and I held my rifle over my head as we waded as a group to high ground. The outline of a soldier was visible on this knoll. He, we presumed, was our directing staff.

He handed each of us a piece of map with all names obliterated.

'You're at grid reference 956 271. The section is to find a downed airman who is suspected to be injured in the vicinity of grid 934 243. You are to assist the downed airman to grid 921 236 where an air medical evacuation is to occur at 1400 hours. If you are late you will be required to complete the evacuation of the airman yourselves. Midshipman Salts is the leader for this activity.'

None of us army cadets expected Salts to be able to navigate, but he would have been marked down by the directing staff if this was discovered as a weakness. So we naturally provided surreptitious assistance to aid Salts in navigating us to the location of the downed airman.

It was no surprise to any of us that the airman, when found, had mythical spine and leg injuries. We improvised a stretcher and proceeded to carry him cross country. Despite the weight, I noted with satisfaction that we might just make the evacuation point on time.

About 500 metres short of our objective I heard the distant whir of helicopter blades. I looked at my watch—the chopper was ten minutes early.

Fireman's carry was quicker though less energy efficient than the stretcher, so I threw the airman over my shoulder. We sprinted down the road and I was gasping for breath about 100 metres short when we saw the helicopters rise into the air, pilots waving.

'Shit,' said Salts.

Phil looked at me and didn't say a word. It was going to be a long week.

I shifted the casualty on my shoulder, ensuring that I bounced him a little bit, and drove my upper arm into his groin. He winced, to my satisfaction. If we had to carry him for a while longer, he might as well suffer.

After three days tempers amongst my section were becoming frayed and I found the whole exercise totally amusing. I was fitter than everyone else and I didn't find it a hardship at all, although section mates were obviously struggling as they reached physical exhaustion.

I kept my own counsel walking down the rear with Salty, who lacked stamina. Still, he battled on and I chatted to him, telling jokes and occasionally having a giggle as people up front began to argue with each other. Salty never complained and my respect for these sailors who had to take part in what was basically an army exercise knew no bounds.

MATESHIP

Archie failed a subject at the end of the year and was allowed to repeat second year. The Musketeers were down to Bluey, Squizzy and myself. Archie had become introverted during the year and spent most of his time on sick parade. He had chronic fatigue syndrome. I'd visited Archie hundreds of times during the year. But he didn't even know where my room was.

Archie was in a program of self-pity. He had no interests any more. He didn't play rugby or do karate, which he'd loved with a passion. He didn't write poetry.

Another nine classmates were removed from the academy.

Year Three

TO LEAD TO EXCEL

At the beginning of our class's third year the leaders amongst us were formally identified by the staff by the awarding of rank. Eighty-eight cadets of the original class were left. I became an under officer and took command of the newly formed E or Echo Section, 33 Division. Andy was identified as the senior cadet of our class.

The induction of the junior cadets was the first task of the year. Selected senior class cadets were placed in charge of induction groups of ten to fifteen newly arrived Fourthies. I had been selected to lead a group. This was a dubious honour, I remarked to Jude and Phil, considering the heights to which Andy had recently risen. Perhaps the selection process was not all it was cracked up to be. Phil and Jude were working in the Supply store, which was considered to be a menial task. This was a far cry from Phil's heyday of commandant's personal assistant and Jude's year as the class senior, but they figured they'd met me since then.

At the prescribed time I moved down to the Central Administration building to pick up my new group of Fourthies. Their youth startled me as I assembled my small knot of juniors and they looked at me all eyes and expectant expressions. They were strangers, outsiders, invading my world. Their freshness and keenness exuded from every pore and I found myself resenting their naivety. They wore their dreams and hopes on their sleeves as a rebuke to us

cynical old hands. The openness of their minds and their willing-
ness to please gave me a power over them which I could feel. My
mischievous nature begged me to let it loose and give it free reign.
I could feel the corrupting pull of power and I could also sense
the possibilities. Take this power and use it wisely. Produce think-
ers, questioners. Don't taint them like yourself. Give them the
opportunity to be.

I watched for a long moment, knowing what to do but baulk-
ing at it.

'Pick up your gear and follow me,' I said, barely recognising
my voice.

One of the group looked hopelessly at a mountain of baggage and
then back at me, clearly not daring to ask for help. I walked across,
picked up the two largest pieces of luggage without saying a word
and walked up the hill towards 33 Division at a furious pace.

SO HARD TO PLEASE

The next five days were spent taking my induction group from
one area of the academy to another. First down to the supply point
for the issue of uniforms and clothes, next to the hospital for
needles. The activities had a familiar ring to them.

I took a great deal of pride in my induction group and I harassed
them until they looked like Grenadier Guards. I even took the
trouble to reintroduce my uniform to starch and found an old tin
of Nugget left over from Fourth Class. I was quite shocked to
realise this was only the second tin of boot polish I'd used in two
years in the army. I'd raced through the first tin in four weeks but
had noted with satisfaction that the second tin might see me
through to graduation. Military intellectuals seem to believe in the
correlation between shiny shoes and good leadership. I had long
since decided that this was tenuous at best.

'It's good to see you setting an example for the Fourthies, but who polished your shoes?' asked Andy in an obvious barb.

'No-one Andy.' I could barely restrain myself. 'You make the mistake of assuming that, because I don't polish my shoes, I can't. It's just that I don't find the activity as sexually exciting as you do.'

You might think I am being nasty here, but Andy was one of a large group of people whose face took on a glazed expression as they rubbed their shoes in the circular motion required for spit-polishing. I hoped he didn't waste all his libido on his shoes, but I suspected he did.

'Don't worry, Andy,' I continued 'I'll stop bogging shortly. After the first five weeks the Fourthies can make their own decision on which way they wish to go . . . super soldier like yourself or lowly soul like me.'

Generally, I was harder on my induction group than the other leaders. I did my best to eliminate activities that I regarded as senseless. My role, as I saw it, was to teach the Fourthies skills necessary to survive, which meant they learn how to iron and march as well as, and preferably better than, everyone else. The choice to use those skills later was theirs, but I felt the responsibility to give them that choice.

One of my Fourthies, a navy cadet, annoyed me no end. He was a real little sycophant and I hated grovellers, not least because they appeared to do so well in the military. I took an instant dislike to his obvious and stupid questions and to his pestering behaviour so I waited for an opportunity to cut him down to size. Squizzy now sported an almost shaved head and a demeanour that scared the Fourthies near to death. My induction group were getting their haircut when inspiration struck.

'You know Under Officer Taylor don't you?' I asked the Fourthie innocently. I knew damn well the annoying fellow did. Squizzy growled at him at every opportunity.

'Yes, Under Officer,' was the eager reply.

'I tell you what, when you get your haircut, get one just like Under Officer Taylor. I'm sure he'd be impressed with your look.'

The navy cadet appeared a minute later with his new haircut. I was most pleased, and assured the Fourthie that Under Officer Taylor would be likewise impressed.

When I next saw Squizzy I told him what I'd done and suggested he finish off the day's work by telling my favourite Fourthie he was a navy poof and had no right to insult the army or a senior cadet by getting a haircut that no-one in the navy was tough enough to wear. Squizzy was impressed and readily agreed.

I bought Squizzy a drink down the bar an hour later after he had reduced my Fourthie to tears.

AN EXERCISE IN BOREDOM

After a week and a half of induction the Fourthies went to Club Med to finish their training and we returned to Duntroon for three weeks of military work. Salty and our classmates in the navy went on a cruise of the South Pacific in a destroyer and our air force classmates learnt how to fly solo.

Exercise Monte Cassino was one of the funnies inflicted upon our class that no-one else in the history of army officer training in this country will have the honour of going through.

Monte Cassino was where the acronym LBE entered the class language. The LBE was a 'low budget exercise' specifically designed to teach nothing. Under the new Training Management Program adopted on the opening of the academy, at the end of the three years we were to be at the trained soldier level. The problem was that under the old RMC system, everything they intended teaching us in the first three years at the academy had been taught in our year at Duntroon.

Originally the military staff hoped to be able to press on and teach us material already taught. However, when they were confronted with 80 pairs of eyes, either closed or completely vacant, they took the hint and came up with something new. No resources were allocated for any interesting training, so a 'modified' program was developed, which was limited by a lack of everything except cadets. The aim Captain Steel developed for this resource-limited training was apparently to give cadets an idea of how boring war could be.

The class was driven out to Tallaganda State Forest and told to dig into a defensive position. We were supposed to dig down to 'stage three', which requires sleeping bays with overhead protection to be dug out to the front of your foxhole. This is where we struck our first problem. No funds were allocated for stores such as corrugated iron and sandbags, which are essential parts of the construction technique. We were told to improvise, adapt, and overcome. We rapidly discovered that the reason the ingenious Australian digger from World Wars I and II and Korea used corrugated iron to support the ton or so of dirt on his foxhole roof was because fallen limbs of trees don't do the job quite as well.

After the charade of digging in for two days was over, we settled into the task of seeing how boring war could be. The days were spent on our back like lounge lizards, playing cards and making brews. Curiously the staff objected to us playing cards although they had no better suggestions for what we were supposed to do.

After three days of sitting around doing nothing my section went on a patrol. This included a one and a half kilometre walk before sitting on a hill. There was nothing to do and I decided nothing was going to happen because the ever present military staff promptly went to sleep. I took a map and went for a bit of a walk. Others slept. Goose decided to take a blunt machete and chop down the largest gum tree in the area. After four hours of solid work it came down with an almighty thud. This woke the sleeping staff member, who wanted to know what was happening. He accepted our assurances that a kangaroo was crashing around in the undergrowth, pulled his hat over his eyes and went back to sleep.

After our night on this patrol it was back to the main defensive position, where I settled back in for a number of days. I was roped into a regular card evening with Phil, Bluey, Squizzy and Jude where we honed to fine precision our skills at black bitch and five hundred.

One night I was called aside and told I was in command of a one-half platoon fighting patrol the next day. I was given my orders, which included clearing five hills of enemy. Odds-on we would get ambushed on one of these hills, probably the steepest, so I went back to have a chat with the boys. I sat down and organised my plan for the coming patrol, going over my ideas with Phil and Jude. We formulated a circuitous approach to each hill, which would hopefully confuse the enemy, if indeed there were any. It's not that I am cynical, it's just that we didn't have anything else, so why should we have enemy.

After some discussion Jude was moved to call me a hypocrite. 'You laugh at everything and everyone around here. Now you're in charge you suddenly get interested. What makes you so sure anyone's going to be interested in playing this game tomorrow?'

'I've never put down soldiering, Jude,' I replied after a moment's thought. 'I only put down idiots and idiot ideas. They'll follow me, don't you worry. If only because they're competitive, because they still want to win and I'm going to offer them victory. It's called leadership, in case you've forgotten.'

'You are one arrogant bastard,' Jude said with a shake of the head.

Next morning the patrol headed off in high spirits, sure that we would successfully confront any enemy. Misleading location reports were sent by the radio operator, for the enemy was sure to be monitoring the frequency, and we approached each hill as planned.

On our third hill we struck it lucky. My one-half platoon was in extended file and we caught the enemy from the rear while they waited in ambush. The fire fight was brief before the enemy melted away. I quickly ensured no-one had gone berserk and fired their allocation of twenty blank rounds for the exercise on the one contact.

As the reorganisation was winding up we received a radio message to investigate enemy activity about three and half kilometres away. My patrol was allowed 45 minutes to be in the new area and we would have to rush. Against that, I felt certain we would be ambushed. Not intending to fall into the transparent trap being set by the directing staff, I formed the one-half platoon into single file so we could move at a half-run and we headed off to the designated location by a circuitous route. Again, false location reports were sent to confuse the enemy.

On arrival in the area designated, my lead scout spotted a Land Rover which obviously belonged to the enemy. We approached it cautiously. No enemy were in sight so I set an ambush and waited for their return. After giving my orders, Goose, the woodcutter, suggested that he wait in the back of the Rover and spring the ambush by jumping out and letting loose with an M16. This appealed to me. It was totally untenable from a military point of view but it would be great for everyone's morale.

The ambush went off with a bang when Goose jumped out of the Land Rover in front of four enemy, M16 blazing. We all laughed at their astonished expressions from our position in the rocks.

'Who's in charge of this rock show?' The voice rang out above the medley of rifle fire. I stood, paused and hurried in the direction of a red-faced Captain Steel.

'I am, sir,' I announced unabashed.

'You don't spring an ambush by putting a man in the killing ground. Your men are totally out of control, running around like mad things. You have not been where your location states indicate you are.'

'I must have been lost,' I lied, staring Captain Steel directly in the eyes.

Captain Steel's chest heaved and he snorted several times. I strode away.

Another couple of instructive days followed, in which we learnt more about how boring war could be. The culmination of Monte Cassino was an attack in strength by the enemy on our position, followed by our withdrawal. The withdrawal must have been due to the lack of ammunition, or the lack of interest. No-one had much of either. I was now company runner and had the job of passing messages to the platoon and section commanders.

As I went from section to section passing the word to withdraw I came across Frog, a classmate whose jumpiness and constant worrying about minor issues had alienated him from the class. Frog asked me to ensure the rest of his section knew to withdraw. This was a ridiculous request. If every section commander had asked me to do likewise I'd have had to visit something like 50 foxholes. I was about to tell him to take a running jump when inspiration hit.

'Oh . . . Okay,' I said. 'No worries, mate.'

I went to each of the foxholes in Frog's section. 'You are the counter-penetration force. Leave your packs here and follow Frog.'

Off they went, Frog leading, pack on. The rest of the section following, minus packs.

About a kilometre down the road Simon, who was in Frog's section, realised they were too far back for counter-penetration. He turned to Sergeant Lemon, the nearest member of the directing staff. 'We appear to have left our packs behind, Sergeant. When can we go and pick them up?'

Sergeant Lemon's eyes bulged and fixed on Frog, who was walking along unsuspectingly, pack swinging jauntily from side to side.

I poked Jude in the ribs. 'Is that a good bish or what?'

'It's amusing, but everyone else in the section now has to walk extra kilometres to pick up their packs. You've bished them too.'

'Who cares?' I replied. 'They need the exercise.'

Jude shook his head.

It was great to return to the academy and talk to our classmates in the air force, who were enthused after completing their first solo flight. Our classmates in the navy had adventures from the Pacific nations to recount. My fellow army cadets and I just had Exercise Monte Cassino to dwell on. I had learnt a lot. Not so much about the boredom of war, but about more relevant matters. Goose the Machete Murderer and ambush initiator extraordinaire put in a service transfer to the air force. His loss was a blow to the morale of the whole class. Others, too, talked about leaving.

WALK OF THE WARRIORS

The staff had organised a night navigation as a finale to the field training. We were divided into groups of six to trudge around the Majura Range complex for several hours. Phil was in my group, which was a small consolation. I also had Andy, Simon, Frog and Tiger. Tiger Joe O'Reilly was a fiery fellow of Irish descent who earned his nickname because of his ferocious spirit and aggressive love of all things to do with the army. We did not get on. He probably thought I was a cynic, and I thought he was a robot who unquestioningly did the military staff's bidding.

The exercise was non-tactical, which was a major bonus. This meant we could use roads and paths that we avoided in a tactical environment. It was especially good news around Majura Range, which was covered in old barbed wire entanglements, half filled-in foxholes and tank traps. I didn't intend breaking a leg in the line of duty and nor did Phil.

We were dropped off at our start point by a Land Rover. The red tail-lights quickly disappeared in a haze of dust as the hard-working engine ground its way up through the gears. There was one compass in the group and Tiger had it. If we had one machine-gun, one hand grenade and one shoulder-launched missile, he would have had them all as well. That was Tiger. We each carried our own maps marked with checkpoints that were dispersed over a twelve kilometre range. Tiger Joe volunteered to navigate to the first checkpoint and immediately headed off across country.

'Hang on a minute,' I called out to the fast disappearing section. 'If we head up the road and around the corner a little bit, the first checkpoint's only just off the track.'

'Be serious,' Andy snorted impatiently.

'I'm being very serious. Why screw around out there tripping down holes when we can meander down the road? Look at your map. All the checkpoints are just off the road, so the lazy staff member who set the course up could drive around it to place out the markers. We can be equally lazy and follow the roads.'

'Tommy . . . for goodness sake, pretend you are in the army,' said Simon. 'You're not a civilian in uniform. There's an enemy out there.'

'Guys, the directing staff said this is a non-tactical exercise. There is no enemy, so let's just go down the road.'

'I agree with Tommy,' said Phil. 'We'll be finished in no time if we stick to the roads.'

'Jamie, you're very quiet.' I used Frog's first name for a change. 'You're a sensible dude. You reckon we should walk down the road don't you, Jim?'

I used all my manipulative powers. Jim wasn't a sensible fellow, in fact far from it, but you never know your luck. The pressure was on Frog and you could feel the weight of the world pressing down on him. Which way would he jump?

'Oh . . . Um. I really don't think we should walk down the road,' he quavered.

'You're a dickhead, Frog. Do you understand that? I don't know why I had any kind of faith in you because you're a loser. God put you on this planet to screw me around. You are a complete knuckle.'

'It's okay, Tommy, relax,' said Phil. He placed a hand on my shoulder. 'We'll let them lead us around the paddock and we'll just walk behind waiting for them to find any holes for us.'

We followed behind the group, chatting away loudly. I was determined to show them I was having a jolly good time. Every now and then a curse would float back as someone fell down an unexpected hole or caught his foot in barbed wire. Then there was a thud and rattle in front of us, followed by a muffled curse.

'Can someone give me a hand? I'm caught,' muttered Tiger Joe.

I stood on Tiger Joe's back and walked across the barbed wire unhindered.

'Shit, Tommy. Watch out!' he yelped.

'No, you watch out. I don't want to trip down any holes myself. You get back up the front there and find me a few more holes, will you.'

I stood over Tiger Joe with a smile on my face while Andy helped to extricate him from the entanglement. It was a shame, I thought, that Tiger Joe couldn't see my smile in the dark.

'Do you realise that cadets always whinge about being stuffed around by the staff,' I said. 'But what's really funny is that every chance we get we stuff ourselves around.'

'Give it a rest, Tommy. Don't you ever give up?' snapped Andy.

'Never, Andy. Never.'

We walked on in silence. I'd said my piece. It was time to let them think.

When we finally reached our first checkpoint the group gathered together and Tiger Joe attempted to hand over the compass to someone else. Indecision crept over the group and no-one appeared to be willing to navigate the next leg.

'I'll navigate,' I volunteered after a long silence. 'However, we'll be walking straight down the roads.'

Silence was my only answer, so off I set and the others followed.

'People always fight laziness,' I said to Phil matter-of-factly. I also ensured my comment was loud enough for all to hear. I liked rubbing salt into wounds. 'Why do they continually delude themselves that they are busy beavers, when all they want to do is take the path of least resistance.'

I handed the compass over to Simon at the next checkpoint. Now that we had broken through the mental barrier, everyone quite happily navigated by the roads. In fact the whole exercise became a total waste of time, but we played by the rules.

We were the first group into the finishing checkpoint, so we stretched out on the ground to wait for the trucks to take us back to the academy. The air had become chilly and I pulled out a jumper and a jacket that I kept in my patrol equipment. I checked that Phil had brought a jumper and jacket as well and unnecessarily repeated a cadet creed: 'When in doubt, rack out.' Then I promptly fell asleep.

Just before dawn, the coldest part of the morning, I woke up with a start. I've been left behind, was my first startled thought. However, when I sat up quickly I saw myself surrounded by 80 other sleeping bodies.

I suddenly needed to go to the toilet, so I pulled on my boots and went for a short walk before watering an unsuspecting bush. A shiver ran through my body and my core temperature seemed to drop two or three degrees. I could be awarded my first doctorate for my thesis on this little-documented subject, I thought with a smile before trudging back to my sleeping position. Interesting that we are still here. I'll lay 50 dollars that there's been a screw-up and the staff forgot to book transport, or 50 dollars that tomorrow we are going to play a game. I stretched it out to more likely 60–40 in favour of the games before nodding back off to sleep.

In the morning 80 disoriented cadets were blinking at each other in surprise. A buzz of conversation immediately started and I racked my brain to come up with a plausibly ridiculous rumour to spread. My brain failed me. I grabbed Phil and we went off to find Bluey, Squizzy and Jude. Phil had brought some cards and I thought we might squeeze in some five hundred before breakfast.

We'd just settled into our first hand when we were interrupted by Captain Steel. 'Due to the recent rain the trucks have not been able to make it through to pick us up. Get your gear and follow me. We'll meet them three or four kilometres down the track.'

We looked at each other and shrugged. The explanation didn't ring true, but the five of us moved in silence down the track indicated for 30 minutes. Our spirits were quite high and most knots of cadets chatted as they walked down the track.

When we stomped into a small clearing there was a group of instructors, rather than the expected trucks. We were gathered centrally and all was finally revealed. 'Welcome to your introduction to survival training. This course will introduce you to survival techniques and will continue indefinitely.'

I shifted my gaze around the class and the perky faces of just a minute before had all stopped smiling. Depression swept the group in a wave. I could feel it. I grinned and shuffled around the group to where Tiger Joe was standing.

'You're not smiling, Tiger Joe,' I whispered mischievously. 'How war-ry. A challenge we can finally get our teeth into. This should be great fun.'

I beamed at him, patted him on the back and moved on.

PLEASE SIR, CAN I HAVE SOME MORE?

The drink and chocolate machines which were located in each building were placed out of bounds to Fourthies by the cadet hierarchy. I sought Andy and Simon out and questioned them aggressively on the issue.

'Discipline is too lax,' was Andy's nonsensical reply. 'The Fourthies have too many luxuries and the senior class must regain control. They lack respect and we must establish our authority. It's all a part of the process of breaking the junior class to the one level and building them back up with the correct values.'

Somehow, I had expected better from my class. We weren't like those who had gone before. I'd firmly believed that as a group we would not repeat the continuous petty sniping that had characterised our time as Fourthies. It was disillusioning to realise that, as a group, we had grown as a likeness to our senior class.

'Have you ever considered that we don't do a particularly good job of building people up once we have broken them down? In fact, if we do build people back up, why do we forget to put back in vital ingredients like compassion and integrity?'

Silence reigned. I wouldn't get an answer. 'You're megalomaniacs and morons,' I snapped out. 'They don't lack respect because of the corrupting powers of chocolate, but because you're a dick. My Fourthies will be using the machines.'

I stormed off.

I'VE ALWAYS LIKED THE BEACH

Enrolments began for my final year of academics. At this stage my degree was well set. I had my Philosophy sub-major completed and intended finishing off my Geography major and sub-major. Don't assume I'm a mad keen geographer. I was mostly keen about the fact that I kept passing with no effort.

The only problem I had with my degree was the issue of a first-year subject. I had failed History, then Management, and had no real desire to repeat either. Both departments had funny ideas about study and work to which I no longer fully subscribed. On top of that I had the distinct impression that my name was mud in the Management Department. After much procrastination I eventually decided to do Oceanography. This might seem a strange choice for a potential army officer. However, I had been seasick when near the water from a young age and was very interested in the subject. Furthermore, after considerable research I couldn't find one person in the navy who'd ever failed Oceanography. Salty assured me that if I achieved that dubious honour I would be the first ever. Oceanography could only be Geography with a layer of salt water on top, some forests taken out and a bit of seaweed thrown in. I could handle that.

A PEST TO BE ERADICATED

My army classmates and I were not pleased to see Toad reappear at the beginning of the year as a First Year cadet. His unprecedented return came as a real surprise, as most of us had consigned this sorry figure a very small part of our memory.

The usual rumours were flying around the corps about his return, but I didn't have much faith in any of them. I usually invented half the rumours myself when I was bored and I knew it would only take one other bored cadet out of the 600 to produce the other half.

I moved through the rabbit warren of the academy's buildings, taking the direct route across the grass rather than the paths which curved prettily between buildings. It was quicker that way. It was also illegal, as we had to use the paths. Well the answer was simple—they could make the paths straight. I wasn't going to walk in circles for anyone. In fact the whole matter was an affront to the entire Corps. Didn't they think we had better things to do? Places to go, people to meet. Of course someone could argue that the curved paths were aesthetically pleasing. This was a defence force, a killing machine, yet it seemed aesthetics ruled over ruthless efficiency. Curved paths were definitely the thin edge of the wedge. What would be next? Where would they stop? Toad was back! There would no doubt be a cogent explanation for his return. I smiled. The boys bished him out the first time. He would be got again.

In the distance, I saw a major I knew by our common interest in running. 'Good morning, sir,' I called out and threw a salute. It was a lazy salute but I imitated the recoil some hands get when they whip up to the peak of the cap before coming to a dead stop. It was not so much recoil as a friendly wave. I cut across the grass and the major stopped to allow me to catch up.

'I just saw Toad,' I said. 'Interesting to see him back in the junior class now that we are seniors.' I hadn't seen Toad at all but it initiated contact.

'Yes, a long story, that,' the major muttered a trifle resignedly. He was a soldier, not a bureaucrat, and I knew he hated the academy.

'Well it could be a short and messy return. There are a number of upset people. I don't know who made the decision to let him back, but they are going to be responsible for murder.'

The major looked at me seriously. 'Look, Tommy, no staff here wanted to let Toad back. It's just that he had some good solicitors who argued that he had never signed anything to say he was required to pass military or academic subjects. He has the army over a barrel.'

'What a load of crap. He knew the rules and he lost.'

The major shrugged. 'I guess he couldn't face being a failure when he returned home.'

'Well I guess that's his mistake,' I noted sadly. 'He shouldn't have come back.'

A PACT

The bishing started on Toad almost immediately. I just ignored him. He was pathetic, but I made sure everyone knew why he was back.

The staff passed a message to our class that we were to stop bishing Toad. They didn't want him to have any excuses when he was thrown out next time. The implication was that the staff would take care of him.

A FALLING OUT BETWEEN ALLIES

Bluey was incensed.

'Toad's going, all right,' he said, 'but he's going to get compensation for a knee he reckons was stuffed-up here in training. The man hasn't done any work to stuff his knee up since he arrived, fat lazy ball of slime that he is. He can always walk to the chocolate machine without difficulty. We should have bished him out. There's no justice in this. At least when the corps do something, they do it right.'

I patted Bluey on the shoulder and shrugged.

Bluey led a delegation of classmates who went to see Toad on his last night in the academy, to let him know that they didn't think he should return again. I was reliably informed that perhaps there was something wrong with his knee after all.

RACING AT LAST

We assembled on the start line and I looked across at the competition. I wasn't worried about Phil. He was in a different class and I didn't have the training to allow my stocky frame a chance of competing with his diminutive athletic figure. The RMC runners were tall and lean; they looked like class athletes. A careful check on their best times this summer suggested that I was out of my league as they had run sixteen to my seventeen minutes. I looked at the navy and air force athletes and discounted them immediately. This wasn't their field. Distance running was an army domain.

The gun went and I tucked myself in behind the leaders. I wanted a feel for the other athletes and that was the place to get it. Phil sat off my right shoulder, having a look around for a lap or two, as was his habit. He was just gauging the competition and would shortly branch out on his own. The two RMC runners set a good pace and I was more than content to leave things go, when on lap three a navy cadet went past at a hectic pace. I looked at Phil and he looked at me. The same questions were going through our minds.

How good is this runner?'

Can he keep the pace up?

If he can't, what the hell is he doing?

Phil accelerated and the Duntroon cadets followed. I picked my pace up but made no attempt to chase as yet. I'd let the chains be broken. I had confidence in my ability to re-establish them when the time was right. Let them think I was a spent force. It would make my comeback a harder psychological blow to them. No-one else attempted to follow and I knew it was now a five-man race. The academy crowd came to life two laps later as Phil took the lead. Although he was still in front of me, I knew our navy friend had shot his bolt. I focused to my front, concentrating on the RMC cadets. A four-man race now. The RMC athletes had settled into a rhythm and looked content to run for second and third. Thirty metres separated us as I picked up my pace again. I bore down on them relentlessly and steeled myself for the mental battle which would ensue. On lap seven I rejoined the RMC runners and slotted myself in behind them. The academy crowd was chanting 'Tommy, Tommy' in encouragement and I waved in response.

First of all I contented myself with flicking the heels of the runner immediately in front. I flicked them ever so lightly and when he turned to look daggers at me, I smiled. 'Tommy, Tommy,' yelled the crowd and I began to enjoy myself. This was the payback for those long cold midnight moments spent running around the lake. 'Tommy, Tommy.' I breathed in gasps, feigning exhaustion. 'Tommy, Tommy.' I pulled out and cut in between the two RMC runners, causing the second to break stride and the first to look at the jostling behind. I smiled. 'Tommy, Tommy.' Time to go—a good long burst that will break their hearts. I swung wide as we entered the straight. This broke the chain. First one fell away behind me, then the other. The crowd went crazy as I pulled ahead.

I could see Phil in front and knew that that was where he would stay. We came home, one–two for the academy.

For seventeen short minutes I had belonged. The academy and I had united in purpose for a brief moment in time. I wished the moment would last.

BABYSITTING

After the athletics was over, a function was held in the mess for cadets and their visiting guests. I acquainted myself with a colonel whose son was a particularly unruly Fourthie in my division.

'The young fellow needs discipline,' the colonel said of his son, 'and this is just the place to give it to him.'

'In what way, sir?' I asked curiously.

'You know, the military will give the young fellow the discipline to see him successfully on his way in life.'

'Is that so!' I was becoming belligerent. 'Well let me tell you that at twenty years of age I don't see my role as babysitting an eighteen-year-old child. I suggest if there were a few more responsible parents around I wouldn't have to give certain individuals the attention that their father should have provided. I find your attitude to be an insult to these institutions, sir.'

The colonel looked at me, rage evident, before racing off to talk earnestly with Captain Steel.

A BOLSHIE BASTARD

Echo section became an enclave of equality, free living and dissent. Revolutionary posters were purchased from a Marxist bookshop in Redfern and they adorned the corridors. Captain Steel derisively called my section 'Little Russia'. He never realised I took it as a compliment. Card games and port parties were the most regular activities conducted outside of sleeping, but the section worked well. Everyone was relatively happy and there were no major problems with academic failure. I became firm friends with my Fourthies, who were fine fellows, and the only rule I kept was 'no bullshit'. Many of my classmates confronted me about my easy-going section.

'The authority of the senior class is being undermined by your attitude to the Fourthies,' Simon told me. 'You must have more strict discipline.'

'But why?' I asked innocently. 'We are all officer cadets, surely we should stick together.'

'We are under officers, Tommy, with authority over these people.'

'No. You will notice that we are all officer cadets. The "under officer" part is made up by the staff to divide and conquer us.' I could almost picture myself storming the Bastille.

'You're childish, Tommy.' Simon sounded frustrated and angry.

'Me, never,' I mocked and walked on, sticking my thumb in my mouth in imitation of a two-year-old.

I was being childish, but I was sick of the us versus them attitude the senior cadets had for juniors. Surely my peers must recognise that it was cadet versus military staff, cadet versus academic staff, academic staff versus military staff, and that the only thing that gave the academics and military the winning edge was that the cadets had been divided and conquered. We were young and keen and hell-bent on grabbing a little power ourselves. That power was grabbed at the expense of junior cadets.

A CONSPIRACY OF SILENCE

The corps regularly held parties in the mess, and it was at one of these that I had the pleasure of meeting Blue's new girlfriend. She filled the room with a radiant glow and I felt compelled to meet her, although I had earlier decided never to meet another one of Bluey's girls. I didn't want to deal with what they would tell me when they joined the long list of exes. I didn't want to get close any more. The less I knew, the less I saw, the better.

Bluey was by himself and I sensed he was looking for friends, as he called out to me in an obvious invitation to join him. Blue was by now a much hated man in the corps. He was aloof with his classmates, and arrogant and bullying to his subordinates. People didn't understand him and feared what they didn't understand. Blue didn't need friends and I understood that. Probably because, after all this time, I was beginning to understand that I didn't really need them either. What Blue needed now was someone to pretend to be his friend, so this beautiful girl wouldn't think there was anything wrong with him. Most people thought it was normal to have friends and were suspicious of individuals without any. I understood that and so did Bluey. I think that's why he and Squizzy spent so much time together. Girls admired the bosom-buddy relationships men had and it was essential for Blue and Squizzy to demonstrate this myth lived on. Now Blue wanted to involve me in the myth.

I weaved across to them. Well past tipsy, I was deep into the philosophical stage. I slurred my introduction to an exceptionally polite lady. Her name was Mary and I sensed she was new to cadets. I said many uncomplimentary things about my fellow cadets and the girls who hung around them. It was an attempt to warn her off, but she returned my sarcasm with polite smiles and nods. She did not take any of my openings, to challenge what most people would have considered outrageously dangerous statements, bordering on insulting.

Mary mightn't have been provoked, but it wasn't because she didn't hear. I could tell she was listening carefully, although probably she did not wish to show offence.

Eventually, I said my goodbyes and left. She might be starry-eyed and innocent now, but I had an idea that would change. What was I supposed to do? Take her arm and whisper your new boyfriend's a rapist? I have no proof but trust me. Was that too

155

harsh? Was that the truth? Had I really had that conversation with Kathy? Or was it just my imagination? I didn't know any more.

Not knowing what to do, I stumbled off and drank myself into another mind-numbing stupor.

BUREAUCRACY

Physical and recreational training at Academy had turned into more recreation than training. I attended my designated classes but was gaining no benefit. Lessons included how to play tennis and squash, all good fun but of no value to my physical development. In fact I found the whole system of physical training frustrating.

The head of the Physical Training section, Squadron Leader 'Ned' Kelly, was rumoured to be experimenting with the physical fitness program to gain data for the thesis that was part of his postgraduate course. Whatever the reason, the program was disjointed and the cause of much frustration for both the other instructors and the cadets.

One day an army corporal instructor who appeared particularly frustrated with the prescribed course took us for our programmed lessons in tennis. No balls or racquets were in sight as we surveyed the tennis court. Instead, a nasty array of hand held weights could be seen.

'Today's lesson is tennis,' the corporal said with a broad grin on his face. 'Tennis circuits.'

I smiled from ear to ear. At long last a session that you could get your teeth into. The lesson was conducted at a furious pace, with the weights being thrown around in complete disregard for the courts. At completion I could barely raise my arms.

The corporal gathered us around into a tiny huddle. 'Well done, men. Good effort,' he began.

Almost immediately, Hong, a Singaporean classmate, brought up his lunch. The corporal continued unflustered. 'As I said, well done . . . As for you,' he pointed to Hong, 'that will teach you for not eating rice at lunch, so count the carrots.'

ANTI-SOCIAL BEHAVIOUR

Andy banned playing cards in recreation rooms. He considered cards to be an anti-social activity, as the rowdy players prevented people from watching television in peace.

A DINOSAUR

Jude looked at me. I was laughing. Proud as punch.

'How's that for no wasted effort?' I asked with a smile. My latest exam results included a mark of 50 per cent.

'Tommy, grow up,' he said. 'In case you haven't noticed, the game has changed. You're the only 50 per cent man around here now. Everyone's playing a different game. It's called crawling and licking up to the staff. Part of which is actually doing work.'

I looked at Jude. He was right of course, but it was a bitter pill to swallow. 'Lighten up, Jude. I don't crawl to staff. I don't need their help.'

Jude shook his head. 'You have to play the numbers. I taught you that. Go with the flow, that's where your best odds are, that's where you get your best returns. Right now, crawling will get you exceptional returns.'

THE DRUNK IN THE CORNER

Mid-year exams came and went and I passed all my subjects, barely. This was of no real consequence to me as I lounged in the leather mess chairs, drink in hand, watching the world go past. I drank too much, but this was preferable to the alternative.

'I'm a corrupt little bastard,' I reflected to Phil. Blue, Phil, Squizzy and I sat there. 'I couldn't give two brass razoos for this place, but here I am, lounging here with drink in hand watching these deluded fools walk past. Here, watch this.'

I sat up a little straighter as Andy neared.

'Andy, you megalomaniac knucklehead,' I called with a broad grin on my face. 'Been getting a few kicks screwing the Fourthies around this week? Must make you feel real good, buddy!'

'Tommy,' said Andy whimsically, 'if I didn't know you so well I'd think you were serious. Sometimes you're a hard man to work out. Such a kidder.'

'But Andy, I'm deadly serious. I hate your ignorant two-faced butt.' All traces of my smile had gone.

'There you go again.' Andy laughed, shrugging off my comments. 'Always mucking around.'

'But I'm not!' I yelled to him as he disappeared down the stairs. 'You're an arsehole.'

I looked at the others, shrugged 'what can I say?' and took another swig.

NO SEX PLEASE—WE'RE BRITISH!

Going out with a female cadet was banned. It was threatened that you would be immediately removed if caught. Fraternisation, as it was known, had been a major problem with the senior class of the previous year. A meeting was held and Andy and Simon, with some of the other senior cadet appointments, stood up to lay down our class policy.

'We must all stick together as a group and resist temptation,' Andy lectured. 'If we can do this and have a clean year we'll have set a standard for other senior years to follow.'

'It's all right for him,' I grumbled to Blue. 'He's discovered the true sexual pleasures of spit-polishing. What about the rest of us poor souls?'

'Shut up!' snapped Bluey. 'This is serious.'

'Get real,' I snapped back. 'You've not been a moral bastion. You've dabbled a little in the pleasures of the flesh. Last I heard you were going to marry your little cadet friend.'

'Okay, so I was joking.' Bluey grinned at me sheepishly.

'Look at these posturing clowns. Why don't I ask them all to stop smoking dope and do the army a real favour?' I went to stand.

Blue put his hand on mine. 'Don't, Tommy.' He looked deeply into my eyes. I relaxed into my previous posture.

Fraternisation was a major issue. Rumours were always flying about hot new couples. The fact that it was forbidden by both academy law and our class's high ideals made the subject even more fascinating. At the opening of the academy I had been a moral crusader on the subject. I had since decided that it was reasonably natural for girls and boys to screw each other. Certainly, it appeared to be better for your mental health than spit-polishing, although with spit-polishing you never had to worry about foreplay. You could just pick your shoes up and go for it.

Being a weak man, I had succumbed to temptation and started seeing a Fourthie. I felt sure that this relationship could be kept secret and no-one would ever know. This of course is theoretically possible, but it is a very hard thing to achieve. I had already noticed that males are bigger gossips and bitches than females and decided to use this in my overall plan. Rumours were always easily started, so I began a campaign spreading a whole heap of harmless but amusing ones that would keep people gossiping for weeks. I would engage people in conversation and would then drop a confidential 'Don't tell anyone, but . . .'

Sure fire, never misses. There is nothing a cadet likes more than to show his knowledge of what's happening around him.

The next thing to do if you intend to fraternise is to go to restaurants and pubs the cadets never frequent. This tactic has one flaw. Every other cadet who is fraternising or stealing a mate's girlfriend is busy romancing in the same place. The most obscure and distant pub in Canberra probably has two fraternising cadets looking deeply into each other's eyes right now. The only problem is when you and your girl walk in and make it four. That is most definitely a crowd.

My particular bubble burst one Sunday morning when Phil came to get me to go pistol shooting. I'd arranged this the day before and, come 0700, there was a knock on my door.

'Get up, Tommy. Time to go shooting.' A pause. Silence is his only answer.

'I know you're in there you drunk, so get up, let's go.'

No more knocks. Life is looking good. Then Phil, who is a persistent type, tries to climb through my window.

'This is not a good idea,' I protest loudly. 'Phil, don't come in that window. Phil! Do not come in that window.'

A mad dash to slam the window fails, and my best friend is standing in front of me, a huge grin on his face.

'You're right, Tommy, this is not a good idea.' He leaves.

Immediately carry out the damage control drill. Pull on your trousers, chase after your best friend and try to appeal to his good nature. This works best if none of those harmless rumours you made up earlier are about him.

AMBUSHED IN THE MOST UNLIKELY AREA

Although I was physically very fit, I had been unable to pass my Defence Academy Physical Training test. The academy had, of course, introduced a test that was unique to the defence force. It was different from all three services' tests and was the brainchild of the head of Physical Training. This test included not only the traditional run, heaves and sit-ups, but flexibility tests, fat tests and jump tests.

I'd never passed a physical test since arriving almost two years earlier. Firstly because the pass marks always changed and no-one really knew quite what they were; secondly, because no-one told me to; and finally, because the fact that I had such good natural endurance meant I was unlikely to have the explosive muscle development required for passing the jump test.

As the year drew to a close the message was passed that cadets who had not passed the physical test would not be graduating. Phil and I were both prominent failures and were invited down for a special audience with Squadron Leader Kelly.

We were ushered into a modern office and left to stand on a worn patch of carpet facing a seated squadron leader. Two vacant chairs were behind my back. Aha! So it's going to be like that, I thought. The symbolism of not being invited to sit was obvious in the military. So I'm supposed to feel like a bad boy, you fat arse, I thought as I surveyed the rotund figure and ruddy complexion of a man whose greatest exertion was getting out of bed in the morning.

'You have both been good performers at physical training,' said the squadron leader. 'However, I am worried by your continual failure of the test here at the academy. The jump test, isn't it? You will obviously have to put in more effort.'

'Surely, sir,' I replied, speaking for both of us, 'if Officer Cadet Newman or I were capable of passing this jump test, we would have done so in our numerous attempts over the last two years. All the effort in the world won't help me to pass that test because I believe, for myself, it is physiologically impossible.'

'It is not impossible,' the squadron leader spat in annoyance, 'and we will organise a training program to help you achieve the required standard.'

'Sir, I train for sit-ups by doing sit-ups. I train for push-ups by doing push-ups. I train for running by running around the lake. I would gladly hop around the lake if I could see it doing me any good, but I fear I would only look ridiculous. Both Officer Cadet Newman and I do the five kilometres run faster than anyone else in the academy. I'm sure with your education in physical training you realise we both have slow-twitch muscle development rather than fast-twitch. We have high endurance but little capacity to jump. This test is beyond my capacity.'

Phil nodded in agreement. I was becoming annoyed with the so-called expert who knew next to nothing about physical training.

'We conduct this test for a reason,' Squadron Leader Kelly huffily pronounced. 'Perhaps surprisingly, long-distance runners were amongst the first to fall out on the march during the Falkland's War. This is due to the almost exclusive development of one type of muscle group.'

'I have read on this matter too, sir,' I continued unabashed. 'While some people found the study findings surprising, I most certainly do not. If you read a little more closely, you no doubt noted that most distance runners have a small body weight, so a full pack of equipment is more of an imposition upon them than a heavier man. Secondly, it was noted that the runner's low body fat percentage would have been critical to endurance in such a cold climate. All of which is irrelevant here. As you can see, I have a heavy frame for a distance runner and a very high percentage of body fat. I'll walk any member of the academy into the ground with a pack on my back, and so will Officer Cadet Newman.'

I was about to continue when a movement caught my eye. Unseen to Kelly, several of the physical training instructors were outside the door making signs of encouragement and a few rude ones as well. I couldn't contain myself and burst into laughter. The corporals and sergeants immediately disappeared from view and I was left in front of an angry bull who was turning a bright shade of purple. Snorting noises were coming out his nose and his eyes had the look of death.

'Stop laughing at me or I'll get up from behind this desk and sit you on your arse,' he spat with rage.

Poor old Phil was shuffling around uncomfortably while I struggled to gain composure. 'None of this solves our problem, sir,' he chimed in. 'Perhaps we should organise another test.' His suggestion calmed the situation.

Still glaring at me, Squadron Leader Kelly indicated for us to follow him into the Physical Training instructor's office where he'd organise a retest right now. When we entered the office the instructors who had been gathered outside his door moments before were casually reading papers.

Kelly approached the first corporal. 'I want you to conduct a test right now for Officer Cadets Newman and Sneyk.'

The corporal lowered his newspaper and peered over the top for a second before replying. 'No, I'm busy,' he said, then raised the paper and continued to read.

There was a long silence before a sergeant in the corner volunteered to conduct the tests.

'Good,' blustered Kelly. 'Let me know the results.' Then he beat a hasty retreat.

The sergeant took us downstairs into the gym. Phil did a jump that looked no higher than his previous efforts and was passed. Then it was my turn, 'Well done. Pass,' said the sergeant.

'No it's not,' I said. 'That's barely 40 centimetres.'

The sergeant looked at me and shrugged. I watched him to ensure he placed an 'F' by my name.

'We'll arrange another time,' he said hopefully.

'Yeah, another time,' I replied.

We both knew there was not going to be another time. I looked at Phil as we walked out of the gym.

'I'll never be a graduate now,' I observed frankly.

'Don't worry about that crap,' he said. 'They carried on the same way last year but everyone graduated.'

'No, I think I'm going to be different somehow.'

NO MORE EFFORT

I was sitting at the bar late one Tuesday night, Scotch in hand, reading the papers. The duty officer, a Flight Lieutenant Tymms, walked in with a new naval lieutenant. All was quiet as exams were nigh and most cadets liked to pretend they were studying. I had given up pretending long ago. There was a world to learn about, and I liked reading papers.

'G'day, sir, how's it going?' I greeted him amicably.

'Good, Tommy. Yourself?' replied the flight lieutenant. He was a good bloke but was always in trouble. It was just that he liked other officers' wives more than his own.

'Not too bad. It'd be better if I was somewhere else, but that's life.'

'Didn't shave today, Tommy?'

'Nah, couldn't give a rats,' I said. 'My face needed a rest, and so did my uniform, so I didn't iron it either.'

The naval lieutenant's jaw had now hit the ground as he eyed me up and down in disbelief.

'Must move on. See you later,' said Tymms.

'See you later, sir. Have a good night.'

THE CHARADE

I slouched in the Rec Room with Phil, debating whether to go for a run, when Captain Steel sat down beside me. I wanted to leave immediately but felt that would be too obviously rude. We had settled into an uneasy truce and I didn't need to open up old sores.

Captain Steel was particularly conversational and wanted to discuss the terrible problem of fraternisation. I had absolutely no problems with being a hypocrite.

'I don't know why the staff don't identify those cadets who are fraternising and throw them out. The rules are clear enough.'

'This is true, Tom,' the captain said. 'But it's not as easy as you would think.'

'The rules are black and white, sir, and it undermines the staff's authority when this is not done.'

Being the friend he was, Phil excused himself and walked out of the room to have a loud and obvious coughing fit.

'He's picked up a terrible chill,' I remarked quickly. 'Running at this time of year can be awfully bad for your sinuses.'

Captain Steel glanced at me suspiciously.

'Anyway sir, we must go for a run. Excuse me.'

ALL FOR ONE

My last Geography assignment was a team effort between groups of three. I teamed up with Squizzy and Jude. The assignment was worth half of our year's marks. I required at least 50 per cent to pass the year.

The three of us had done a large amount of background work and, to bring the whole exercise together, we divided the written submission into distinct parts. Each of us was allocated a section. Four days before the assignment was due, we would meet and produce a final copy.

On the day allocated, Squizzy did not have his work ready, but he assured Jude and me it would be by the next morning. It wasn't. Nor was it ready the next. On the morning the assignment was due, we again visited Squizzy. Again no work had been completed. I turned and left with Jude, to massage our much reduced assignment together. I didn't say a word and haven't spoken to Squizzy since.

In my eyes, the Musketeers had now been reduced to me and Bluey. Squizzy's lack of interest in the assignment was due to the fact that he already had enough marks to pass the year. Jude and

I needed this assignment to pass, but I did not feel anger or malice or disappointment, just emptiness.

A frantic two hours was spent on the computer terminal and we left the computer building with our final draft with three minutes to spare before the deadline.

NO TASTE FOR THE FIGHT

I found it difficult to study for my last exams. I did not care for the military. I could not graduate from the academy, as I had not passed Physical Training. I had no respect for the academics who I thought were a bunch of posturing hypocrites. The class had disintegrated as a unit and the incident with Squizzy was indicative of the loss of ideals that we were all grappling with. I did not like myself. I lived in all this wrong and did nothing, while I tried to believe that I was different from the others. That I was better. I tried to believe in myself and my actions, but I knew there was no self. Caught up in circumstances that were changing me, I hadn't fought back. I just contented myself with being anti-social, drinking, and mocking everyone. The only thing I really enjoyed was making the farce of this cloistered world bigger than it actually was.

Geography exams came and went. I had a good feel for bare passes at this stage and was confident of a marginal decision falling in my favour. Oceanography was harder. I had achieved an unprecedented 58 per cent mid-year and knew that 42 per cent in the final exam would scrape me home for a pass. This made me cocky as well as ambivalent, a fatal cocktail.

Jude and Phil were having their twenty-first birthdays in Sydney the night of my last exam. I was to leave directly after Oceanography and meet them at a restaurant in Liverpool. The only problem was that, being a Friday, I would be caught in all the Canberra traffic heading to Sydney. This was almost an unbearable thought to a regular traveller on the Federal Highway. An endless stream of public servants doddering down the road in the aimless manner they brought to everything they did.

To avoid this scenario, I devised a cunning plan. An hour of furious work in the exam would just about swing the 42 per cent required, allowing me to leave two hours early and miss all the traffic.

I followed my plan to the letter and on the first chime of my watch I stood up, happy with what I had achieved. Giving the person overseeing proceedings my sweetest and most ingratiating smile, I left. The old bat's eyes were boring into my back and I could feel the reproving look on her face—a mixture of loathing and pity that they reserve for truants like me. As I moved through the door I saw her look at her watch and mark the time on my paper. That would ruin me if my work was on the down side, but it all added spice to life.

REINFORCEMENTS

Military training for our last month at the Defence Academy was to be a joint exercise between the remnants of our class and the RMC cadets on the eighteen-month non-degree course who would join us at the start of our final year. Most of the RMC cadets on this exercise had spent only six months in the army, although there were ex-soldiers interspersed amongst them who gave them much needed experience. They reminded me of myself two and a half years before. Very serious about my military career and very naive.

Administratively, the exercise which was known as Samachon was a disaster. I started the exercise with four water bottles and received another supply of water mid-week. Thus I was given eight litres of water for seven days of walking in 30 degree heat with packs on from 0600 to 1800 hours. Eight litres of water a day would have been barely adequate. Eight litres for the week was dangerous and negligent.

On the other hand, I had so much blank ammunition I did not know what to do with it. Every day, instead of the expected water resupply we'd receive 200 rounds of blank ammunition. This was fine but I was lucky to expend 20 or 30 rounds in a day. When my personal supply reached 1200 rounds I decided enough was enough. I waited until the directing staff weren't looking, then picked out a bag of 60 rounds and kicked it into the nearest bush, raising my hands in mock celebration of a goal. One of my new classmates came over to me on a halt, a concerned look on his face. 'You can't do that with the ammunition,' he whispered tensely. 'We might need it.'

'Do you really think so?' I didn't whisper. Mock surprise was in my tone as I lifted up a log and dropped two more bags of ammunition underneath it before placing it carefully back down.

'You know it really is terrible stuff and makes rifles awfully dirty. I couldn't have that, because then I might have to clean it.'

My new friend looked at me in bewilderment before moving away. I don't think he wanted to listen to any more.

The most interesting part of this bush trip was the fact that our class went into the field with female cadets for the first time. What an education this would be. In my section was a particularly temperamental child who lost her temper at the slightest provocation. As we patrolled in relatively thick country, our rifles frequently got caught in the foliage. The simple thing to do was to stop and remove it, but not my fat little friend. She would throw a tantrum, kicking and flailing around in a most unbecoming frenzy before moving on.

If I had done this I'd have had a boot from the directing staff up my backside so quickly I wouldn't have seen it coming. Not our lady, though. Extraordinarily, the directing staff ignored her antics.

One night while on gun picket with her, she tapped me on the shoulder. 'Do you mind if I have a cigarette, Tommy?' she asked.

I didn't like her calling me Tommy. That was for friends, of which she was definitely not one. 'I couldn't care less,' I replied irritably.

Immediately I heard the distinctive noise given by a waterproof match being struck. This was the last apparatus anyone should have used if trying to have a sly smoke at night. They flare up in an uncontrollable fashion, casting light everywhere.

'What are you doing?' I whispered urgently.

'Havin' a fag,' was the nonplussed reply.

At that moment the match caught, illuminating the whole area while she waved it in the air before lighting her fag. I lay in darkness, listening to her inane chatter.

During a quick halt the next day our young lady started thrashing around on the ground and making the most frightful noises. I immediately raced across, thinking she'd been bitten by a snake, which were numerous in the area.

'What's wrong?' I asked, eyeing the nearby undergrowth.

'Ants,' she wailed. 'I've sat in an ants' nest.'

I was now thoroughly annoyed with my new female classmate. However, determined not to get angry, I decided to get even.

Our young female had no idea of how to operate the machine-gun and I found myself clearing all the stoppages during one attack. The clapped-out M60 was being a bitch and our whole assault was held up while I took charge of the gun and cleared the fouled breach. Then inspiration struck. I cleared the gun and put a burst through it to show it was cleared from obstruction, but as I handed it back I slipped on the safety catch. After the last couple of minutes' antics the directing staff were now quite close. My female friend pulled frantically on the trigger and nothing happened. She tried to cock the weapon and found she couldn't.

'Get that gun back into action,' yelled the directing staff. 'You're holding up the whole assault.'

'I can't. It's broken,' she whined, hitting the gun hopelessly.

The directing staff came across, had a quick look at the gun, placed the safety catch on repetition and placed a burst through the gun. He reviled her in no uncertain terms. I was pleased. She was reduced to tears. I smiled.

I received an average report for the exercise. 'You're leaving the academy and all that academic wimp stuff behind,' was the directing staff's comment, 'so you'd better start switching on, because you're coming to the real army now. We want decisiveness and commitment and I'm not totally convinced you have it.'

It starts again, I thought.

NEW TRADITIONS

The usual post-exercise refurbishment of stores took place on return to Duntroon. As a finale to the whole activity, a dining-in night had been organised to assist the new-found team spirit of the RMC class and the academy. On paper it was a sound idea, but it lacked something in the translation to reality.

The timings for the activities were, to put it mildly, a wee bit tight. The dining-in night was scheduled to start at 1900 for 1930. At 1845 the rest of the class and I were still at the Quartermaster store trying to hand back weapons. 'Not clean enough.' 'Too much oil.' 'Not enough oil.' The Quartermaster store staff were carrying on with their usual performance.

At 1857 one of RMC's staff took the bit between his teeth and decided that the commandant couldn't be kept waiting for dinner, so we were released to do a mad split back to the academy. I burst into my section full of bad manners and language. I called out to Wang, who was one of my Fourthies, to set up an ironing board and to see if he could find a mess kit somewhere in my room. I headed for the showers, undressing as I went, and tried unsuccessfully to wash off ten days of dirt and camouflage cream in a quick shower. I burst out of the shower and headed for the ironing board, only to see Wang putting the finishing creases to my outfit.

A good Fourthie is worth his weight in gold. I threw him a thank you over my shoulder as I ran out the door, still doing up buttons.

The familiar cadet mess was now unrecognisable after renovations. It was lighter, and not as oppressive.

When I looked at the seating plan I found I'd been placed in a corner far away from the head table. This, I was informed by a new-found friend, Whitie, was no coincidence. Whitie was seated opposite me and suggested that all fun-lovers had been placed in the corner to ensure the night started off on the right note. This was organisation that I could appreciate and we tossed down a few more dry sherries in anticipation of a good evening.

I became rather rowdy as the night wore on and the alcohol started to take its effect. Towards the close of the evening Whitie slowed down the volume of alcohol he was consuming. He informed me that he and the rest of the RMC class were required to do a fifteen-kilometre battle walk, with packs, the following morning.

What could I say? It wasn't my fault RMC staff couldn't run a bath. I informed Whitie, in the interests of class spirit, that it was his duty to continue on his primary task . . . which was to get drunk. At this I was interrupted by a major on my left who said it was fine for me to suggest drinking all night, but no doubt I'd be wrapped up in my sheets when the RMC class headed out in the morning. I couldn't recall inviting this clot into the conversation. I'd studiously ignored him all night.

'When I went to RMC,' I slurred, 'cadets were quite capable of talking for themselves. Not only that, they could do a little drinking and back up the next day for a trivial fifteen-kilometre route march.' I invited the major to accompany me into town, continue drinking till dawn and then race the fifteen kilometres. I didn't see any point in walking.

'That sounds like a challenge to me,' the major blustered.

'Make of it what you like.' I was undaunted. 'The only question is, are you man enough to take me on?'

Out of the corner of my eye I could see Jude was making an

effort to indicate that I should look closely at the badges the major was wearing.

'So,' I continued, 'a little gentleman's wager would not go astray for our race tomorrow, although the odds would have to take into account any advantages that you might have, for example, if you were in infantry. After all, walking like a mule would then be your whole reason for existence and I would most definitely be disadvantaged.'

The major looked down at his lapel badges, which were the distinctive winged-dagger shape of the Special Air Service Regiment. The Australian Army's most elite unit.

'I suppose you could call it infantry,' he said regally, falling right into the trap.

'Yes that's right, it's only infantry, and don't you forget it.' The major glared at me and I returned the glare before shifting my position so my back was to him. I continued my conversation with Whitie.

Later in the evening, as the port was passed, I noticed people going out of their way to ensure the decanter did not touch the table. I poured myself a glass, plonked the decanter onto the table and flicked it along the polished wood to the major.

'The port isn't allowed to touch the table at RMC,' a short-course cadet informed me in a low voice.

'Isn't it?' I said loudly in surprise. 'That's curious, because when I was at Duntroon it was.'

A perplexed and worried look creased my friend's face before he replied inspirationally, 'It must be a new tradition then.'

'A *new tradition* sounds a little incongruous, don't you think?'

A blank expression was my only response. Half in the mood to give an English lesson, I began to open my mouth but then closed it.

I'LL MEET YOUR 50 AND RAISE ANOTHER 50

Our exam marks were posted the next day, and although I passed Geography the impossible had happened. I failed Oceanography with 46 per cent. I should have cared but I didn't. I knew a month before that I couldn't graduate from the academy.

'Situation no change,' I said to an attempt at condolences being offered by Jude. I strolled down to Headquarters to see what they had planned.

I was finally presented with a document signed by the commandant. I thanked the staff politely and went back to read it in detail. When I had read it through for the third time I still hadn't gleaned anything. 'Concentrate, stupid,' I said and I re-read it sentence by sentence, taking long pauses to assimilate all the information. I read as follows:

To: Officer Cadet T.A. Sneyk
Australian Defence Force Academy

Well I had to admit that was me.

NOTICE TO SHOW CAUSE WHY YOU SHOULD NOT BE REMOVED FROM THE AUSTRALIAN DEFENCE FORCE ACADEMY

So you want to get rid of me, do you?

TAKE NOTICE That I, Major General A.J. Knight, the Commandant, Australian Defence Force Academy, DO HEREBY CALL UPON YOU TO SHOW CAUSE why you should not be removed from the Academy on the following grounds:
a.   Since commencing studies at the Australian Defence Force Academy you have failed to make satisfactory progress in your Arts degree. Your year three results were:
   (1) Geography 3A   Pass
   (2) Geography 3B   Pass
   (3) Oceanography   Fail

Well, I know all this. Poor old General Knight, still the handicapped engineer. Wordy but you've really said nothing.

b.   You have not demonstrated the necessary aptitude to complete your degree in three years.

I can't really argue with that. They ain't going to give me a degree.

c.   I am not prepared to grant you a repeat third year next year.

My, aren't we being presumptuous. I never said I wanted one. You can bash the academy, I just want out of here.

d.   At the Chief Instructor's Training Board of Review on 3 December, you were raised for special mention.

I'll bet I was. I'd have loved to have been a fly on the wall for that performance. The night of the long knives would have looked like a kiddies' picnic. Ned Kelly and Captain Steel would have had the Tommy Sneyk voodoo doll jumping a merry dance.

After reviewing your performance I have formed the opinion that you are unlikely to succeed in your academic studies and I therefore intend that you be removed from the Australian Defence Force Academy.

I couldn't agree more. My bags are packed. Let's get out of here and back to RMC.

YOU ARE HEREBY INFORMED that you have seven days from the date upon which this Notice is served upon you in which to show cause in relation to the action proposed to be taken against you.
Signed: A.J. Knight, Major General, Commandant.

I'm sure I can beat all that. This doesn't seem overly difficult, but there's no mention of RMC. I wonder if they've got a bed booked for me across there?

I wandered back down to Headquarters to clarify a few points. I was bluntly informed that there was no intention that I be sent to RMC with my class. I either win the 'show cause' and spend another year at the Defence Academy or be thrown out of the army.

'I have no intention of spending another year here doing a first-year subject. I have better things to do with my life, so you see I can't really show cause. What are my options, sir?'

'You'll have to resign, that's all,' Captain Steel said in a matter-of-fact way.

'Fine, sir. Then I resign. I'll be back with the documentation shortly.'

I returned to my room and tossed a resignation together before returning to Headquarters. No-one seemed willing to take my resignation and eventually I tossed it on a desk and left. I had the distinct impression that everyone had fought their show cause before, and no-one was quite prepared for me to resign. I, however, had had enough. I had no interest in the academy's brand of academics, nor their physical fitness tests, nor the illustrious military staff.

NO ANSWERS

I canvassed around the academic departments to get an appeal put in on my behalf to the University Board. The requirement for an Arts degree at the academy was 66 credit points, which I had. A major and two sub-majors and a science subject which I had also completed. The only stumbling block was the last degree rule that required me to have three fields of study. As my major and sub-majors only came from two departments, I needed a third subject or a recommendation from a head of department to vary the degree rules in my case. Eventually I browbeat enough people in the Geography Department to get a case put forward at the next Academic Board.

At the same time a lecturer who was sympathetic brought sharply into focus rumours I had heard. Other members of my class had failed subjects, only to be given an assignment or worksheet to complete over the weekend. Some of these students who had marks down as low as 30 per cent had then been passed and given a degree. Of course the three or four cadets accorded this 'academic consideration' were considered to be stars by the military staff and I had no doubt where the pressure for this illegal assistance had come from.

It was time to have a chat with the chief instructor and leave the little people behind. I wrote a minute, not a very good one, so I could refer to it if I was stuck for words and snuck upstairs in the Headquarters building and headed for the 'out of bounds' chief instructor's office. I had no business being there, other than my hunch that the chief instructor didn't see the academy from my perspective. I was on my way to set him straight.

Fortunately for me, I had to go through the executive officer's rooms before I could get at the chief instructor. The executive officer was a man I had never seen before. In fact up until this moment I never knew he existed. He treated my intrusion with cordiality and showed interest when all I had received before was indifference. I explained my background to him briefly, and told him how some cadets received worksheets while others like myself received nothing. What I wanted to know was why this occurred and how I could make myself eligible for the same treatment.

The executive officer assured me he would take the matter to the chief instructor and some sort of explanation would be forth-coming. I thanked him very much and left. I felt I had met a rare individual who wasn't ensconced in the filth that tainted all our lives.

Graduation came and went. I said my farewells for what I expected to be the last time. I still had my resignation in and was refusing to show cause to stay at the academy. As with all the others on show cause, I stayed around to find out what the future held. Not that I had much to say to the others. They were all fighting tooth and nail to stay at the academy. I was completely, utterly desolate as a human being. I had cheated, I had lied, I had bastardised, I had condoned drugs and rape by my silence. I was empty. As a human being I had nothing but contempt for the military staff, the academics, my fellow cadets, the padres. It was a barren world, but I saved most of that loathing for myself.

I spent a lot of my time with a naval classmate, Pete, who I regarded as an innocent in this house of horrors. He was a victim of the military staff, who despised him. I know why they hated him and harassed him. They saw in him a dreamer who still dared to dream. This scared them because they recognised what they had lost. To an empty soul, his simple presence was a threat.

Peter was tearing himself apart trying to reach an understanding of why he could do no right. In his simple, honest, straightforward way he did not understand that there was no requirement for real integrity in the military.

The pair of us drank many a bottle of port together over the next couple of days, and it was he who eventually convinced me to write a reply to my show cause. I allowed myself to be persuaded, as the military weren't accepting my resignation and there was bugger-all else to do. I dictated as Pete furiously typed. The end result was sarcastic and insubordinate, but neither of us broke into a grin. It wasn't as funny as it was grim. It was the truth, and it was sad. The only problem was that it lacked evidence.

Once again, I was a man with a mission, and I was on old ground as I strode down into the Headquarters area to rake a little mud. There was no sense of elation or the mischievous, just a sense of familiarity as my mind sharpened itself for the impending competition. I knew it was the first time I'd really challenged my mind in three years and the feeling of being alive came home.

I picked up my personal file which contained every report written on me since joining the army. The staff member who handed it to me looked at me curiously, but when my eyes met hers she hurriedly looked away.

At the Academic Administration building they dealt with hundreds of cadets and had no reason to know me. 'Hello, I'm Officer Cadet Sneyk and I've come to see the university secretary,' I said to the lady at reception.

'I know who you are,' was the disapproving reply. 'Wait here and I'll let him know you've arrived.'

I was quickly shown into the office of the secretary. I didn't have to explain my story in any depth. That, it seemed, had been done for me by the executive officer. I received studied indifference and no cooperation. When I stood to leave, a sarcastic 'Thanks' was all I could manage.

'You know why I don't like you,' he said. I didn't answer.

'Because you are at a university with great facilities, the best student/lecturer ratio in the country, everything is paid for, you don't have any of the pressures that a normal university student has, and you throw this amazing opportunity away.'

I stared and the silence grew between us. 'You hold that thought,' I sneered. 'It has been amazing and an *education*, so maybe you and I are not so far apart after all.'

The people on the front desk stopped a whispered conversation as I went past. I waved but didn't smile. The academy had always been a zoo but I'd never considered myself bad enough to be its prize exhibit.

As I walked across the main courtyard two officers looked in my direction and I heard distinctly, 'That's Sneyk there' floating across. I pulled myself up a little taller and put an added spring in my step. I'm not out yet, you bastards, I thought.

I went down to the Physical Training section and had a good long talk to the corporals and sergeants. We had a coffee and swapped a few pleasantries before I came to the business side of the visit.

'There is no Physical Training report from last year on my personal file. I need to find that report for the Board of Studies. If it's a good one, I can pooh-pooh any failure this year.'

'If it's not on your personal file I can't think where it would be,' was the flat answer from the sergeant. 'But I'll tell you what. If you go down to the Headquarters after lunch, I'll see if I can find those reports in the meantime.'

We both knew that if they were not on my personal file they didn't exist.

After lunch I returned to have a look at my personal file. The missing documents had magically appeared. They were exactly what I wanted. An Olympic athlete would not have received a more glowing report. I phoned the Physical Training instructors and left a message of thanks.

I went back to my room to pick up some port and headed off to see Pete, feeling as if the pieces were coming together. On my door was a message for me to see a Professor Goldbert in the History Department the next morning. I didn't know much about the man, other than he'd lectured to me some years before and I vaguely remember his lectures had been interesting, a rarity at the academy. My initial reaction was to throw the message in file thirteen and forget it, like Professor Dupane's. However, I took the time to have a look at the university handbook and check out my suitor. Professor Goldbert was the deputy rector of the University College. I was impressed. I found it interesting that he had not used his title when leaving the message. Either he assumed I knew who he was, or maybe he just didn't use his title. That was different. Most people in the military couldn't wait to impress the hell out of others with their title.

The next morning I turned up at his office at the appointed time. The deputy rector's office was comfortable. The furniture and decorations clashed, but they only looked quaint in his presence. Professor Goldbert made a favourable impression. I was politely offered a seat, which I took formally. I did not expect any favours from academy staff, least of all from the deputy rector, so I waited cautiously for the professor to speak. He appraised me for a long period. This was not a battle of wills as yet, but neither of us wished to give any ground at the start. There was no defiance in my return stare, just a statement that I was strong.

'Your academic appeal has been knocked back, unfortunately,' the professor said at last.

'Oh, that is disappointing.' I was neither disappointed nor surprised. My appeal had been an option and I had used it, nothing more. 'May I ask on what grounds?'

'To award you a degree on the grounds of your appeal would

179

have set a precedent that others would surely follow, so the university has chosen to reject it.'

'And my chances of receiving academic consideration in the form of a post exam or a worksheet?' I asked with no display of emotion.

'These are against the University College policy.'

'Yet I know that does not prevent it from happening,' I replied evenly.

'In exceptional circumstances it may have occurred.'

'Yes, exceptional,' I intoned with no hint of sarcasm.

'I have studied at some length the problems relating to your degree, and I am sure you will have no problems completing it next year.'

'Unfortunately, at this stage of my military career there will be no next year. In any case, I have no desire to spend a whole year of my life doing one academic subject.'

'Hmm, I'm sure we could make arrangements in certain departments, like History for example, for that subject to be completed in six months,' Professor Goldbert replied generously.

'I lost interest in history when I did it in Fourth Class at RMC and I doubt that even the thought of achieving my degree would restore my interest. Sir, if I may be so bold,' I continued uncertainly, 'I have no interest in academics in this institution. In fact I take it as good luck that I have survived here as long as I have. I do not intend spending another minute of my life here. My only desire is to graduate with my class from RMC in a year's time. What I need is for the academics to stop screwing me so that can happen.'

'It is not the academics who are *screwing* you, but certain elements in the military who you seem to have put offside . . . a certain squadron leader, for example, does not seem to like you at all. Unfortunately for you he has the ear of the commandant and is whispering in it all kinds of nasty things.'

'I have that fat chump covered,' I replied. 'However, I do need something to tie up some loose ends from the academic point of view.'

'Well, I fail to see how I can help,' the professor said.

'The point is, sir, that I received barely enough marks at school to enter this institution. What I require is a piece of paper from someone in the university saying that, considering my lowly marks at school, I must have put in a lot of hard work to achieve what I have so far at the college.'

'I haven't known you over the past three years, so I can't say that. But I can word around it saying that you've achieved very good results indeed, considering your HSC marks.' Professor Goldbert was catching on.

'Thank you very much, sir. That would be appreciated,' I said with no hint of triumph in my voice.

I stood to leave and was half out the door when the deputy rector said, 'You're not as stupid as you would have some people think.'

I turned and looked at him for a long moment.

FAREWELL

Pete and I massaged the last pieces into my show cause the following night. He assured me that it was customary to state that 'I wish to be an officer in the Australian Regular Army.' This disturbed me because I didn't. I just wanted to win, to show that I could. After much debate I finally relented, as Pete was getting frustrated. He didn't understand that what I wanted was to graduate with my class; the fact that I would be an officer at the end of it all was purely incidental at this stage.

After a two-day wait I was finally recommended for transfer to RMC. I prepared to go on Christmas leave, while Pete still fought to stay on in the services. His two brothers had arrived and were now offering support but I felt I was leaving with a battle half-finished.

I had my exit interview with the chief instructor.

'Good luck,' he said, shaking my hand.

'Yeah,' I replied. 'And meanwhile this place still goes on graduating druggies, while screwing decent people like Midshipman Peter Stuart.'

'Merry Christmas to you too.' He smiled. 'You've maintained your dignity when many others have lost theirs. Keep that and you'll never lose. You'll do well across in the army.'

'I doubt that,' I replied as I left.

Dignity? I thought as I left the building and walked into the sunshine. Wrong choice of words. Noble ideals have nothing to do with this business.

I smiled and revelled in the strangeness of the sensation as I felt the tension run out of my body and dissipate into the air. It was, I realised with a shock, the first time I'd smiled in several weeks. I'd never picked Sergeant Boots for a philosopher, but he was right, people don't like smiling around here. Well, you bastards, you have my soul but not my smile. I put my hand to my face and traced the outline of my mouth with my fingers. Reinforcing that it was real.

Thirty-three classmates resigned or were removed.

Year Four

KNOWLEDGE PROMOTES STRENGTH

This was to be my class's final year at the college, and in terms of the old RMC it was to be our First Class. Fifty-four of us had made it this far. It was difficult to believe that we had climbed our way from Fourth Class, especially since the demigod status that used to accompany the final year of training had disappeared. The new RMC consisted of an eighteen-month course, with three classes of six months duration each. With twelve months of the course to complete, we would not be First Class for another six months. Enduring another six months under the heel of a group of cadets who were given First Class status, yet had for the most part been in the army for only twelve months, was exceptionally difficult to take.

Our senior class were mostly younger than the survivors from our first year, and they were less mature both in mind and in their understanding of the vagaries of the military system. Their behaviour was reminiscent of our own when Fourthies and, hard as we tried to suppress it, resentment often flared. Like Fourthies, our senior class were keen to obey every whim of the military staff; we were less so. We had long since learnt to ignore trivial instructions or those that did not meet with our approval. We collectively wore a blank expression on our face, careful to show neither agreement nor disagreement before continuing to do as we had always done. If ever questioned about our non-compliance to new orders, we always pleaded a misinterpretation of the new rules and promised sincerely to get it right henceforth.

One week, we were to have a name tag on our parade pullover. A week later, all our uniforms were to have a name tag on them, except ceremonial dress of the day. The next week we were not to wear name tags on parade, so thus they had to be taken off parade pullovers. On it went. Trivial decisions eroding enthusiasm. Unfortunately, our senior class had not been exposed to this stupidity long enough to lose the desire to please. They also wanted us to feel the same, and that's where most of the ill-will began.

The year before our arrival at the new Duntroon, the term 'Baker' had been coined. It referred to the half-baked nature of the eighteen-months cadets, as opposed to those who had done the four-year course who were well done. The Bakers, our senior class, were the most uninspired group of potential officers I had laid eyes on. They lacked charisma and flair and spent most nights watching videos or spit-polishing shoes. There were of course three or four stand-out rebels who were always in trouble, but they were a lonely group who were ostracised by the majority, for fear of their being thrown out by association. Fear was now the dominant emotion amongst the cadets at Duntroon. The staff wielded the axe of doom with a heavy hand and cadets had been thrown out for trivial misdemeanours. Fear is an insidious emotion, that can be felt. It caresses you when you least expect it and sends a shiver through your soul.

The Baker was a product of the new 'course mentality' that had taken over the college. RMC was now just an eighteen-month long army course that required passing. The idea was to attend your lectures, pass your tests, and at the end you would wake up one morning with the rank of lieutenant pinned on.

I'd returned to RMC with no illusions. I'd taken all of my personal property home to Tasmania and returned only with some civilian clothes for the Bin and my running gear. I restricted my belongings so that when I was asked to leave I could walk up to my room, pack a suitcase and do exactly that. I had no false hopes about my chances of finishing as I drove into the car park. I was tired of the game. What I hoped for above all else was that I would be left alone and allowed to stay reasonably fit and get on with doing my job. This was a forlorn hope, and I knew it, but I clung to it because it was all I had. My soul was tired and I had little fight left.

A SLACK TIME

Barely a month had passed before we were on our class's first exercise, known as Timor. Exercise Timor was designed to assess cadets under adverse conditions. Food was reduced and one day's worth of rations was supplied for the first five days. A range of difficult tasks and deadlines was set in the mountainous country of the southern New South Wales coast. During the rare sunny moments we looked with awe at the contrasting colours of the deep blue Pacific Ocean and the grey-greens of the native bushes. Golden sands formed the framing interface and gave stark contrast.

The class was divided into sections, with the mandatory directing staff allocated. The section I was with had the overweight Sergeant Slack. The same height as me and with a bundle of untidy straw for hair, he had a sickly pale complexion with a contrasting red scar on his left cheek.

It rapidly became apparent that the main impediment to our progress as a group was not the lack of food or the heavy loads, but this cream puff who was assessing us. This slob of a staff member slowed us down with his frequent stops as he gasped for breath. Although some of my classmates were finding the going difficult, it infuriated me that this sergeant would be writing reports on our performance. What was really required was for us to write a report on the sergeant's deficiencies.

Each major hill we came to, Sergeant Slack fell towards the rear of the group, face as red as a beetroot. You could see him wilting under the weight of his pack and I was agitated as I matched him step for step, always walking beside him, so he would see my disdainful eyes watching him every time he looked up. Eventually I'd had enough and decided to make my opinion of him a little clearer.

'It's a nice view across to the ocean, Sergeant, but there's no need to stop and look at it every ten metres or so. We'll all stop and have a look when we get to the top. The view will still be there . . .'

'Try and keep up with the rest of us, Sergeant. We've slowed down already for you . . .'

He seethed at every barb, and his little red scar would twitch angrily at me. This only broadened the grin which I made no attempt to conceal.

Simon looked across with a worried expression before walking beside me. 'Ease up, Tommy, he's not a happy camper.'

'Screw him,' I whispered back. 'He's an incompetent semi-illiterate powder puff. What's he going to do to us? Make us all walk another twenty kilometres for laughing at him? Not likely.'

I looked back. 'Almost there, Sergeant, you can do it,' I yelled in encouragement.

For assessment purposes we all rotated through the position of section commander and before long it was my turn to put on the corporal's stripes and lead the section. I immediately made preparations to move to the next checkpoint, twelve kilometres distant.

'You won't start now,' the sergeant smugly interrupted. 'I think we'll do a little night navigation. You can start the next leg at 0300.'

'Sergeant, this is my command. There is no requirement to walk in the dark. We have plenty of time and doing so in this terrain could only be dangerous. Someone will twist an ankle or break a leg. It's just not worth it.'

'You don't appear to have heard me, Staff Cadet Sneyk.' Sergeant

Slack was barely able to conceal his glee. 'You will start the next leg at 0300 hours, or don't you think you can navigate at night?'

'That's not the issue, Sergeant,' I calmly replied, hands on hips.

'0300 hours,' repeated the sergeant.

'Fine, Sergeant.' I was angry but too proud to show it, and I thought for a long moment before adding, 'The going should be fairly slow. You might be able to keep up.'

At 0245 hours I woke the section and they started to pack up in the pouring rain. As was the custom, I woke up the directing staff last. This kept them one step behind for the start of the day. Everyone was nearly ready to go when the sergeant poked his head out from under his sleeping bag and croaked wearily, 'It will probably be a little bit dangerous in the wet. Tell the men to go back to sleep.' I glowered through the darkness as I thought about tearing the sergeant out of bed. Eventually I calmed myself.

'Back into your farters. We won't be leaving till the morning.'

'Hutchie up, rack out buddy.'

No-one grumbled, although they were all soaked to the skin and the sleeping bags they had to climb into were now wet too.

'What about radio picket, and what time's Reveille?' asked Simon. They were good questions. Radio picket was mandatory for safety and a start time was the usual practice.

'Don't worry about that, I'll get you up in the morning. Rack out, mate.'

I stood in the rain and waited until the sounds of movement had died away before unpacking my own gear. There had not been one murmur of dissent and I felt proud of my classmates for a totally professional display. I was the cause of them being stuffed around. I knew it. They knew it. I was sorry about that, but I wouldn't have done a thing differently.

I was woken up in the morning by a shake from Simon. 'Tommy, get up. The sergeant is hopping mad and looking for you.'

'Really? Why doesn't that surprise me?' I stood up casually, stretched out slowly and brushed my wet hair back with my hands. The sergeant came barrelling up, scar red with rage.

'Why haven't we left yet?' he yelled accusingly. 'The sun has been up for hours.'

'So it has.' I glanced at my watch. 'When you cancelled our little walk last night, you didn't give me a time to leave this morning, so I presumed you'd wake me up when you were ready. After all, you do appear to be running this show.'

'Everyone will be ready to leave in ten minutes,' he directed me under his breath. 'You don't appear to think very well, Staff Cadet Sneyk, and I'll reflect that in your report.'

'On the contrary, Sergeant, I think too much.' I turned my back to him and packed up my sleeping bag.

THE WASH-UP

Another three classmates resigned.

BROKEN HEARTS CLUB

I stood in a corner with Tiger Joe, watching the world go by. Expediency makes for strange bedfellows, I thought. This time last year we were at loggerheads, but things were different now. I took a sip of beer. It was warm and bitter. The beer was always warm now. I had it in my hand because people expected it there. I didn't want to explain that I didn't need drink any more.

The crush of the crowd moved by, people pushing and shoving in an inch of space trying to get to the bar. Trying to get away from the bar. Trying to get out the door and escape the crush. Trying to get in the door and join the crush.

Tiger Joe was drunk. He'd been doing that a lot lately. I didn't ever say anything to him about his problem, I didn't know him well enough. Besides, I'd been there myself. Not as badly, I thought.

Well, maybe I just saw myself through rose-coloured glasses. Who cares? Joe could drink with me.

'I love her, you know,' said Tiger Joe.

'Yeah, I know, Joe,' I said. His eyes were following a shapely blonde who was pushing past, but I knew she wasn't the one he was talking about.

'I love her so much it hurts,' he continued.

I nodded. What could I say? I knew the feeling, but I'd managed to get over it and decided it wasn't love after all.

Tiger's hand clutched at my arm. 'No, Tommy, I mean it really hurts in here,' he said, thumping his chest. 'It aches and aches and it doesn't stop.'

I grabbed Joe by both arms and looked him square in the eye.

'I know, believe me I know, but my knowing doesn't help you. Only you helps you . . . You are alone. We, all of us, are alone.'

Tiger Joe stared back at me. I thought he was sobbing at first, but then I realised he was gasping for air. Short violent gasps like he was having a fit. 'Breath deep, Joe. Slow down,' I yelled at him. Tiger Joe continued to gasp and I realised he was choking. Choking on hurt from a love that would never be returned.

I grabbed him by the collar and pushed my way through the crowd, pulling him behind me. When we finally reached the street, I held Joe against the wall. He was still choking. I slapped him hard across the face. He calmed down, slowly. I took Joe's beer can which he still held and hurled it into the gutter, narrowly missing two pedestrians who were in the wrong place. I was about to apologise when the bigger of the two opened his mouth.

'Watch out, you idiot,' he snapped angrily.

I was two inches taller than him, I rounded fully and yelled, 'Fuck off!' placing emphasis on each word. 'It's not worth your life.'

The smaller of the two grabbed his mate by the arm. 'Let's go, he's just a drunk.' They scuttled away.

I turned to Tiger Joe cheerily. 'Home, James,' I said in an

attempt to cheer myself up as I grabbed a sobbing Tiger Joe around the shoulders and led him to my car.

We didn't say anything on the way back to Duntroon. Joe was thinking and I thought about him thinking. I hoped he would draw the right conclusions, though I didn't put much store in that.

I took him to his room and put him to bed. He was breathing normally now. 'See you in the morning, pal,' I said as I walked out the door.

'Tom . . . Thanks,' Joe mumbled. I held up a thumb in a signal that all was well, then turned to leave. 'Tommy, I could never work you out. I guess you must have hated my guts for being so regimental in my approach.'

'No, mate, I envied you.'

I went up to my room, changed, and went for a run.

On the way back, I stopped at Tiger Joe's room. He was sleeping soundly. I lay awake for hours.

MISSING LINKS

I walked with Phil to the start of the 5000 metres at the Inter-Service College Athletics Meeting.

'Let's make it one–two for old time's sake,' said Phil. There was no doubt in his mind that the only issue was who would come second to him. I wondered for a moment if he knew what it was like starting a race you couldn't win.

'We'll see.' I glanced towards the two academy runners who I knew would be my main opposition. 'I wouldn't want to get too cocky, but I'll give them something to think about.'

The race started slowly. The academy runners sat off Phil, not wanting to make the pace too fast at the beginning. They obviously wanted to hang around and try to out-sprint Phil at the end. Popular rumour had it that he was not a good sprinter, and if you were with him at the end you would win. I'd never seen anyone run with him to the end of a race, so I didn't know if it was true or not. It was a good rumour, though.

Well that's not going to happen, I thought. Let's make this a four-man race and stop mucking around. I went straight to the lead with Phil tucked in close behind. Almost immediately we dropped the navy and air force runners. That's more like it, I thought, as I steadied my pace after another three laps and moved clear to let Phil go around. The academy runners went to follow and I increased my pace again, just so they would have to jostle and break rhythm. That accomplished, I tucked myself in behind and relaxed, letting the academy runners set the pace.

On lap eight, one of the academy runners drifted rearwards. Far enough rearwards to know he would not be back. The chain was broken. It was now a three man race. Well, let's pick up the pace, I thought as I waited till I was in front of RMC's supporters before moving past. Not a whimper of encouragement came my way. The academy started chanting 'Grayee, Grayee' in encouragement to their runner. Grayee came at me again and I let him pass. You deserve it, I thought. Why should I hurt myself for these arseholes sitting in the stand? I cruised home in third. I ran for me, not RMC. Today third was fine. I would never belong. That used to worry me, but not any more. The chains were being stretched.

My scorn was only increased by the congratulations that were heaped on me. Morons. They might have provided some kind of support during the race.

INTO THE FRAY

I stood by the indoor barbecue in the Ainslie Hotel, beer in hand, watching the steak sizzle. Over in the corner I watched Jim and a group of First Class from the eighteen-month course drinking with a drill sergeant who most people liked. I'd never really had an opinion, but now I did. He was a fool.

Instructors and cadets didn't mix socially. That was the rule; it was clear cut, black and white. There were good reasons why it existed, but that was not part of the debate. The rule existed, and the sergeant should stand by it just like every other petty law he'd stood by and expected us to obey. That was his duty. Staff were at Duntroon to enforce the laws. Cadets were there to flaunt the stupid ones.

Jim should have known better, we'd been to school together. All of the First Class should have known better, but Jim especially. I expected better of people I knew. The others were just Bakers, but Jim, well we'd been to school together for six months before I'd moved again, but schoolmates we had been and that made all the difference in my mind.

A new Fourthie walked in, dressed in shorts and thongs. Not a very smart move. He was not supposed to be in town dressed like that, but if he did he definitely shouldn't have come here. He was a dickhead and he deserved to get in the shit, but it wouldn't be from me. I didn't talk to Fourthies any more. I didn't care what kind of officers they made. That was the army's problem. Shorts and thongs didn't make the man. What did I care?

The drill sergeant spoke to Jim, who stood up and walked across to the Fourthie. A discussion started and the Fourthie turned to leave. Phil was returning from the bar, hands full of beer glasses when he stopped to join in. I left my steak where it was, I liked it burnt, and walked across. The Fourthie was not happy. 'He's going to charge me, when he's dressed in jeans, which is illegal too,' he whined.

'Sad story,' I butted in. 'What are you trying to say? That this is hypocritical? Get used to it. You screwed up. Sod off.'

I waited till he was gone, looked at Phil and shrugged. 'You can't help idiots, my friend. Let's find out what Jim's story is.' I waited for Jim to get up and head for the toilet before intercepting.

'G'day, Jim.'

'G'day, Tommy. What's happening?'

'That's what I was going to ask. Not real cool you charging someone for illegal dress when you're dressed illegally too.'

'The sergeant told me to charge him, Tommy. I didn't really have a lot of choice.'

'You have all the choices you want. Tell the sergeant to take a jump. What's he going to do, go and complain to the commanding officer? He shouldn't be here drinking with the lads, just like he shouldn't be rooting that female cadet in your class. He hasn't a leg to stand on.'

'When a sergeant tells me to do something, I do it.'

'You'll make a fine officer then.' Jim stared back at me. He wasn't going to change his position. 'You're a loser, Jim. If you want to look a fool just so you can crawl to a sergeant, so be it. You've changed, Jim. I liked the old James better.' I had my fork, which I still carried, pointing threateningly at his nose. I brandished it every now and then to add emphasis to my words.

The drill sergeant, who had been listening, moved across. 'Who the hell do you think you are, talking to one of the senior cadets like that?'

'Sneyk . . . Thomas Sneyk.' I did not add the customary 'Sergeant' on the end. He could make what he liked out of that.

'I suggest you tread real carefully,' spat the sergeant.

I glared back at him.

Phil touched me on the shoulder. 'Let's go, mate.'

I went back to my steak reluctantly.

THE FALLEN ANGEL

Andy had been having a torrid time since our arrival back at Duntroon. The staff seemed to be going out of their way to knock him down a peg or two. This didn't worry me in the slightest. Good luck to them.

The only thing that amused me was that the staff had been

entirely responsible for creating his present nature by constantly praising him to the point where he thought his shit didn't stink. If Andy had been a little more worldly he might not have let the good press go to his head, but he was really very naive. I'd been watching Andy closely. He had come to rely on constant positive feedback from the staff, and now that it was not forthcoming he quickly became withdrawn and unhappy.

I decided the staff were deliberately chopping a tall poppy to bring him back down to earth. After all you couldn't have cadets thinking they were good. I did not believe for one moment that the staff would let such a star wallow for too long. They just wanted to put him in his place before appointing him to another powerful position in the cadet hierarchy. This was military leadership at its best.

Andy came up to me outside a lecture room between lessons. He shuffled undecidedly before eventually sitting down. The captain instructor had just unnecessarily ridiculed one of Andy's questions in front of the whole class.

'Tommy, I just want you to know that I have often thought your outbursts have been unnecessary, but now I get the picture. I see now what you're saying.'

'I don't say anything, Andy,' I replied evenly. 'I just hang shit on this place.' I stared at Andy, daring him to go on.

Finally he patted me on the back and left.

Phil, who had watched the exchange, walked across. 'What did he want?'

'Wanted to tell me I've been right for the past three years and the staff really are bad people because they don't like him any more.'

'My, my, things have changed.'

'No they haven't. He only told me so he could feel good by giving me permission to be what I already am. He hasn't changed. He still thinks his opinion counts to lowly sorts like me. Patronising idiot.'

TOOTHLESS TIGER

'Poor old Tiger Joe, he's one half of a screwed-up dude,' I confided to Phil. 'He's hitting a quart of a bottle of vodka first-up each morning.'

'Don't believe all the shit you hear. It's probably just crap.'

I was surprised at Phil's ambivalence. 'It's not crap, I had a yarn to him yesterday morning to check it out. He wasn't real lucid and the fumes almost asphyxiated me.' Phil looked unconvinced so I continued. 'He's a fucked unit, make no mistake. Between the army and that woman they've really twisted him up. Look at him. His war-ry mates don't understand him any more and he just bumbles around by himself or drinks himself senseless. They have a term for what he is, and that's an alcoholic. Let's go and have a yarn. It'll cheer him up a little.'

HOW TO MAKE A KING

The next field exercise for the class was offensive operations and was called Buna. The section I operated with had a Special Air Service Regiment sergeant for a directing staff. We all took turns doing section attacks, of which most were relatively disastrous. My attempt at killing the enemy went smoothly and the sergeant, who was spare with words, grunted 'Good.'

My section was full of people I mistrusted and I kept to myself. I had no time for the sycophantic behaviour they adopted for the benefit of the sergeant, only to revert back to their lazy selves when his back was turned.

Eventually section operations finished and we formed into a platoon for the next part of the exercise. The directing staff gathered in a huddle and the sergeant returned to tell me I would be first platoon commander.

'Don't worry about it, Tommy. You'll do well, trust me.'

I did. My platoon attack happened in exactly the same place as my previous section attack. The enemy machine-gun opened up when the platoon was in exactly the same position as when I was commanding the section. Not unpredictably, it went well. So that's how you make top cadet, I thought. Another way of making top cadet was never to be rotated through a command appointment during these field exercises. Having already been identified as rising stars from the previous year at the academy, Simon and Andy were never rotated through a platoon commander's position on this exercise or any other. The staff pinpointed people like myself so we would hopefully fail and give them the opportunity to throw us out. This time, thanks to a certain sergeant, I had done well.

IN THE TRENCHES

I shuffled around the blackness of my section area for the hundredth time. I purposely kept my feet low to the ground so that I could feel any undulations. I could hear the rhythmic fall of picks as they bounced off rock, and every now and then I could see a spark of metal. The noise echoed through the night and the odd flicker of light flared as someone checked out the depth of their trench. Normally I would have been unimpressed by the poor discipline, but the scenario we had been presented with had given the enemy as 400 kilometres away. Well, if the enemy were that far away then they weren't going to see the flicker of a torch.

The cobra, a petrol-driven jackhammer, roared into life again. It had stopped for a refuel. My section had our platoon's cobra and it was the only one I'd heard in operation for the last three hours. The fact that I couldn't hear the others told me that the other platoons had gone to bed. That annoyed me. The lazy bastards had their priority of work, just as I did, and they were supposed to have their foxholes to the depth of a man's shoulders within the first 24 hours. They would not have achieved this yet, as the hard rocky soil around Canberra had to be picked at, centimetre by centimetre.

'How are you going, Carlo?' I asked a shadow in the black.

'We're pretty well down. It's a bitch, though, struck some huge rocks, but the worst of that seems to be over. Can't see bugger-all, though.'

'Yeah, dark night,' I agreed. 'The cobra should run out of juice in about fifteen minutes, we'll rack out then. We're doing well. Keep going, you'll get the word shortly.'

I shuffled on, feeling for any obstacle or inconsistencies in my path. The night was freezing and the sweat under my jumper was cooling to a chill. The ground was soft and damp. Countless boots marching in the one area would soon churn it into a bog. I heard the noises of digging before I saw anyone. Finally I stopped only a pace away from some faint shapes.

'Phil?'

'Yeah, mate.'

'We'll keep going till the juice in the cobra runs out again. I think we'll get soldiers Casio, Timex and Seiko on to the gun picket, what do you think?' This method of doing gun picket allowed everyone to sleep. The electronic alarms were set to wake the section in the morning, ten minutes before the directing staff. As my second in command, and the person responsible for the gun picket list, Phil would share any wrath that came my way if we were caught by the staff with the gun unmanned.

'Too easy, mate,' he said. It never occurred to me that the answer would be any different.

'No worries. See you for breakfast.'

'Tommy,' a voice next to Phil whispered urgently. I couldn't see the figure. 'What if we're caught?'

'I'll be in the shit. Relax. You sound like my mother. I'll wear it.'

The concern was not about doing the wrong thing; it was about the consequences of being caught. He was only worried about his own skin. Another fine officer in the making. I'll break the laws as long as I don't have to share responsibility. What a college! Myself, I broke the rules because it gave me a feeling of independence, and I could kid myself I was different. The others followed if they thought they could be shielded from the blame. I wondered what kind of officers we'd make.

The next morning was one of the coldest I've spent on the planet. My hands froze to a creaking standstill and the still morning air burnt my cheeks numb. I stopped at Phil's pit and climbed in beside him for a chat. 'Cold, mate,' I said.

'Bloody freezing,' he agreed.

'Sleep well, Simmo?' I managed, as a way of showing interest.

'Not much. I froze, but it's okay.'

'Good. We'll start work straight after stand-down,' I said to Phil. 'That should get everyone warm, and we'll do morning routine a little later when the sun comes out and starts to give off some warmth.'

'Shaving?' asked Phil.

One of RMC's inviolable standing orders in the field was that everyone must be shaved by 0730 hours. A practical instructor from the Special Air Service had at one time tried to get the rule changed so that we only had to shave every second day while in the jungle to prevent rash, but he'd been quickly silenced. We were to shave every morning by 0730 hours and that was that. No arguments. It was written down, and it had to be obeyed. Facts like rashes were never allowed to cloud an issue at Duntroon.

'I'm just going to apply my camouflage cream a bit more thickly until I have my shave about 1000 hours. The others can follow suit or have a shave now.'

Several hours later Phil and I sat in a quiet copse to the rear of the section. There was a huge tin mug of coffee being passed between us and our faces were covered in shaving cream.

'It's still frigging cold,' I muttered. 'I wish they'd put RMC in a more salubrious climate. The Gold Coast would be just about right. Women and sun, what a combination.'

'They reckon it was minus 16 this morning,' Phil said.

I looked up to see a major heading our way.

'Morning sir,' I smiled cheerily. I liked this soldier. 'Pull up a chair, sir.' I indicated a piece of ground.

The major looked haggard, he always did, but he had a smile on his face. It was always there too. Sometimes I felt it was there to prevent him strangling some idiot, at other times to help him cope with RMC. I liked his smile. Some people thought he was ineffectual and a trifle mad, but they just saw a smile. They didn't see the reasons for it.

'Don't mind if I do. That's a good idea.' He indicated the shaving water. 'May I join you?'

'Sure,' said Phil. 'The water's a little cool now. We'll just whip up another batch. Brew?' Phil offered the communal coffee mug.

'Bit of a nip in the air,' I added conversationally.

'Certainly is. Too cold for shaving earlier,' said the major. 'Not a bad brew,' he complimented.

'Sweet and white like my women,' I smiled.

The major nodded in the direction of my section, working down the hill. 'How's everyone?'

'Good,' said Phil. 'They've still got smiles on their faces and are working well.'

'If you're happy and you know it, clap your hands,' I called to the nearest pair of diggers.

They looked around for a moment, spied us in the bush and with broad grins on their faces both held up a finger.

'Screw you too.' I gave a thumbs-up sign.

'They're still with us,' I continued to the major. 'You'll also notice that these foxholes are down deeper than any others in the company. These boys have worked longer and harder than anyone else.'

That evening it began to rain. All of our fighting bays were deep enough bar one pit where the digging was almost solid rock. We had still achieved more than any other section in the company. During the day three of my soldiers had helped do some digging for another section. They came back complaining bitterly. The other cadets didn't do any work and spent most of the day having brews. I immediately decided that my soldiers wouldn't work anywhere else. They should not be penalised for working hard.

I had six of our shelters strung together to form a large circus type tent to cover a foxhole that still required work. It was raised high so that picks could be swung underneath and it spread far enough so two men could work and the rest of the section gather around. I rotated my men through the following tasks. Two men dug. Two men had to make brews and ensure that the stream of coffee was endless. The remaining four had to gossip.

Morale was high and the boys enjoyed their new tasks. They rightly reaped the rewards of their hard work.

Andy came down. He was acting as platoon sergeant.

'Tommy, yours is the first section down. I need to send your soldiers across to help the other platoons.'

'All my men are busy,' I said without moving from my reclined position. 'You'll have to get men from somewhere else.'

'Tommy, all your soldiers are lounging around here. I want four of them,' he persisted.

'The other platoons have been lounging around since we arrived. Now my men are having a rest.'

Andy looked annoyed and perplexed. 'That fire, you can see it for miles,' he blustered, trying to change the subject. 'Put it out.'

'No. There's no enemy threat. I'm not going to fuck the boys around needlessly. Instead of annoying me I suggest you go and make the other platoons and sections do some work. Spend your time a little bit more constructively.'

'Tommy, you leave me no option but to tell the directing staff.'

'Good,' I replied. 'Tell them that you can't make the other sections do any work, so you'd rather take the easy option and drive the only decent soldiers around here into the ground.'

Andy was becoming irate. 'I'm not joking.'

202

'Ooh . . . Ah . . . You're a dobbah,' I said in fair imitation of a five-year-old. A titter went through my section.

'Come here,' Andy said tersely before disappearing up the track.

I followed into the darkness. My night vision was temporarily ruined by our fire and I fully expected to feel a fist hit me in the face. I was pushing Andy and I knew it. We barely tolerated each other at the best of times. I tensed myself and clenched my fists, ready to retaliate.

'Play the game, Tommy,' Andy hissed from out of the darkness.

'No game, Andy. Head off. Annoy someone else.' I moved to one side to ensure I wouldn't be silhouetted by the fire at my back. No need to make myself too easy a target.

'You're leaving me with no option, Tommy. I'll . . . What the hell are you doing?'

'A piss. I need to do one.'

'You're doing it on my boot,' Andy bellowed.

'Am I?'

Andy turned and left. 'You disgust me,' he threw over his shoulder.

AMBUSHED

I lay in the bitter cold, feeling the rain pelting down into my clothing. Drops of water formed in puddles on my shoulder before running in rivulets down my spine. Chills trembled through my body. They made me want to scratch, but I knew this would be a waste of effort. So I just lay still. There was a canopy of trees overhead but they made no difference. The rain drove through. I could barely feel the rifle, which was numb in my hands. We'd lain here unmoving since 1700 hours. The only noise was the rain. The eyes looked at nothing. There was no light to see by. I'd tried to see my hand earlier but it had touched my nose before I realised it wasn't visible. Almost 0400 hours and it wouldn't be light for another two and a half hours. Eleven hours of lying still. What a bitch of a night. What a bitch of an ambush. Where was the enemy? I wriggled my toes and felt them slide in my boots, they'd been wet now for three or four days. There'll be a few pissed-off people about, no doubt. It never occurred to me that I should be one of them, I just lay there. I had a job and it would be done, that was all. I just tuned out. I sang songs to myself and I ran them through my mind until I was sure they were word perfect. I did this for every song I knew. When I was finished I started the process again.

Tiger Joe went missing that night. He'd finally had enough. He'd been in another ambush that night and by 0400 hours he could take no more. He took off his webbing, left his rifle and pack behind and started walking. We all worried. He wasn't sharp enough to survive in the bush any more. He was too far gone. God help them find him alive, he doesn't deserve this, none of it.

The class breathed a collective sigh of relief when they found him stumbling down a track. They flew him back to RMC by helicopter and I never saw him again. None of us saw him again. Three and a half years of mateship, forced on us by the military, counted for nought to them in the end. He just disappeared by the time we returned from bush. We never had the opportunity to tell him it was all right, that it wasn't his fault. That he was our brother. That we understood. The military he'd loved so much wouldn't allow him that. They were so busy being clever and making sure he wouldn't influence anyone else they forgot one thing. He was a human being who'd given the army his youth . . . life.

GOOD INTELLIGENCE IS VITAL TO THE SUCCESSFUL COMMANDER

A friend of Phil's had left the exam greens from the previous year behind. The greens were the actual exam questions and the discovery of these documents in a cadet's possession would secure an immediate ejection from the college. Basically, the greens didn't change from year to year and you could take a fair punt that if you had the previous year's greens you'd have at least 90 per cent of questions covered.

Phil used to have special study sessions with the greens for selected guests, behind closed doors. I didn't attend. Jude thought that this was indicative of my self-destructive attitude. He thought I had become so lazy that I couldn't even be bothered helping myself to easy marks.

I didn't contradict him on his beliefs. He might have been right. I didn't know any more. It was one answer, and if that's what he believed then it was valid.

On one occasion a new exam was introduced. Instead of the usual 95 per cent pass rate, only about 40 per cent passed. I smiled to myself. No-one said a word but it was obvious that Phil's study group was not the only one in operation around Duntroon.

It was curious, I thought, how times had changed. Suspicions and rifts now ran deep within the corps. The days when it had openly shared a secret had gone. Purges by the staff meant that mistrust was rampant and we all kept our illegal activities close to our chest.

LESSONS TO BE LEARNT

The lecture room was stale. It smelt of 140 bodies. The air was rancid. The room sloped upwards from the front and the seats were typically inappropriate for the venue. Someone thought they should be designed rigidly for good posture and an attentive sitting position. This made it extremely difficult for the slumped occupants, who lounged disinterestedly around the room trying to get comfortable. The seats had swivel tables attached that could be folded to the side when not in use. Mine was not in use, I didn't bother pretending that it was. Most everyone else was pretending.

The two captains who were giving the lecture were trying to put on a snappy performance. They'd obviously put in a lot of work and had a chipper look on their faces, pleased no doubt that the lecture was going so smoothly. There were a few affected expressions of interest but they did not fool me. The lecturers, however, were undeterred. It was after lunch and I had indigestion, something the Cadets' Mess always gave me. I always ate too quickly when I was tense. I ate quickly at Duntroon.

The sun was shining outside and it was a warm day. We are an ignorant bunch of savages, I decided. Why couldn't we adopt a more civilised routine? One that included a siesta. A sleep now would be just perfect.

The lesson was on leadership. We'd had the same lecture at least three times in the last three years, but I guess it was one of those subjects you could never know enough about. We were covering the part about loyalty to your subordinates again. Déjà vu . . . an amazing phenomenon. I wearily put my hand in the air. There were a few points I hadn't cleared up the first three times I'd had the lesson.

'Yes, Staff Cadet Sneyk?'

'This part about loyalty to subordinates I don't quite fully understand. Surely cadets are subordinates to the staff here at RMC, but we don't get any loyalty from our superiors.'

'The situation is different in training institutions like RMC,' said one of the captains.

I nodded my head as if I'd suddenly been enlightened, 'Oh that clears it up. I've always made the mistake of applying leadership universally to all situations, but now I see what you're saying.'

The lesson droned on and I settled back down into my uncomfortable position. No-one had woken up yet.

'Thus the importance of organisation can be seen. Your soldiers will not respect you if they are unnecessarily put out by your poor organisational abilities. If the men do not receive a meal because you failed to organise it, you are upsetting your soldiers unnecessarily in matters that count to them.'

Up went my hand again.

'Yes, Staff Cadet Sneyk?'

'How come cadets are always getting stuffed around here at RMC, due to bad organisation?'

'Such as?' inquired the captain.

'Well the other day when we were out on Majura Range, it was minus 4 degrees Celsius, we'd been freezing all day, and someone sent us cold cordial to drink. Perhaps a coffee or tea might have been more thoughtful.'

'It's very difficult to organise everything smoothly in such a large place as Duntroon.'

'I don't think I understand,' I mused. 'Surely in large institutions like RMC, your organisation should be at its best.'

'Yes, that's true,' said the captain. 'But it's a valuable learning tool for yourself, because once you understand how upsetting poor organisation can be, you'll realise how frustrating it can be for your men and you will not repeat the same mistakes.'

'I never realised there was a plan to it,' I said innocently. 'Now I know it's being done on purpose, I'll be able to accept things more easily. When stuff-ups happen I'll just think of the valuable lesson that is being demonstrated to me.'

I looked at Phil, who was sitting on my left, and shrugged my shoulders.

BISHING THE NEW WAY

The senior class organised for RMC to go and bish the academy. They were very proud of their efforts as they had written up orders and had sought approval from the military staff. If they stayed within set bounds, the staff said they wouldn't get into trouble.

A group of them gleefully explained this to me and that orders for the whole company would be given in the Rec Room at 1900 hours.

'You morons,' I snapped. 'I don't believe how stupid you are. You don't telegraph the fact that you're going to bish someone by telling the staff, and you certainly don't give orders. You simply go and do it. Just make sure you don't get caught, that's all.'

'But the staff organised it. It's good for morale,' exclaimed an indignant senior class cadet.

'It's a dumb idea. Personally, I'd rather get some sleep. Count me out.'

The next morning I wandered across to the academy. The staff had given the senior class such pathetic targets most cadets at the academy didn't even know they'd been bished. Zipper heads can't get anything right, I thought.

I went to bed with my alarm set for the early hours. I thought of giving orders for my impending bish but couldn't concentrate well enough at 0300. I then thought of calling the staff and asking if they'd give me permission, but it was so early I decided against it. I pulled on an academy tracksuit and a balaclava, picked up a sack of flour I had bought and staggered out the door. I strew flour through the Cadets' Mess and continued through Battalion Headquarters. At 0309 hours I climbed back into bed.

The next day the corps was full of talk about the Academy bish on RMC. 'Well, what do you expect?' I said. 'You bish them and of course they're going to bish you right back.' Foolish, they had a lot to learn.

ANOTHER DAY OF LECTURES

The padre sat at the head of the circle and our chairs were gathered around him. The spiritual leader and his flock.

'That concludes this presentation on the My Lai massacre,' said the padre. 'I want to emphasise in closing that as commanders you are under no obligation to follow an unlawful order. The defence "I was following orders" by Lieutenant Calley was not accepted by the US government, just as that same defence was rejected at the Nuremberg war trials at the close of World War II. You have a responsibility as commanders to do what is morally right. Are there any points or questions?'

'I think that when you are talking about My Lai and World War II these events probably occur because the soldiers involved are conscripts and not professionals,' Andy suggested. 'I think, given our professional training, it would be impossible for similar events to occur.'

There was silence as everyone thought about Andy's statement. Enough was enough.

'Give us a break, Andy,' I said. 'Your soldiers would have machine-gunned all the villagers to death, the old padre here would have been tossing in hand grenades to ensure that no-one was left alive and Lieutenant Andy would use the "I didn't know" defence. Half this room, padre included, would have done exactly what Lieutenant Calley did. You don't have to be naive all your life.'

Andy turned a bright shade of red and stood shaking his finger in my direction.

'And you don't have to be an arsehole all of yours,' he yelled. 'You apologise to the padre and the rest of the class . . . You have no right to say such things.'

I laughed. The padre and the rest of the room watched.

BOARD OF STUDIES

With a month to go in Second Class, the Board of Studies sat. The Board of Studies was a forum of staff which assessed the progress of each cadet. How the process actually worked I cannot say, as it happened behind closed doors. A certain mystique surrounded the

209

board, as cadets who had been identified as unsuitable officer material began to disappear soon after it sat. An unfavourable mention at the board secured you a counselling interview. An interview with the director of military art was very serious, only one very small step away from an interview with the commandant. And an interview with the commandant almost inevitably led to removal.

Previous to this Board of Studies at RMC and then the academy, those who were required for interview were informed either by note or through the chain of command. At the new RMC, however, the staff had a new way of notifying cadets.

The whole class was paraded in front of 'Panic Palace', where the adjutant read a list of names in alphabetical order and the level of interview they were to receive. Divide and conquer. Keep the fear going. 'Adams—Director of Military Art; Anstay—Commandant; Barnes—Director of Military Art . . .' and on it went. On this occasion eight classmates and I were singled out to see the director of military art.

The parade outside Panic Palace was obviously designed for maximum psychological effect. It was humiliating and unnecessary. And of course it flies in the face of a basic principle of leadership: never demean a subordinate in front of his or her peers. There is no doubt in my mind, however, that the staff at RMC were giving me, for my own benefit, a practical display in poor leadership so that I would never make the same mistake when it was my turn to command.

Although the idea behind the parade was immediately apparent to me, what I did not understand as clearly was why my name had been read out. I had not failed an exam, yet some members of the class who had failed as many as five had not been named. The fact that some of these cadets were females, or toadies, or both was instantly noted and improved my sense of humour not at all.

At the appointed hour, I duly appeared outside the door of the director of military art.

I remember waiting outside the office and appreciating the

pleasant attitude of the personal assistant who went out of her way to be friendly. A point of interest was the colonel's olive green vinyl door with brass studs. It was as if the poor fellow had gone on a scavenger hunt through a bad taste bazaar. This I found rather amusing and I had trouble concealing a smile as I walked through the hallowed arch. As I explained when answering the inevitable questions from my classmates, 'I really couldn't take anyone very seriously with a door like that.'

The interview centred around the fact that I was happy to produce marginal results. It appeared to the director of military art that I picked and chose from the syllabus, deciding myself what was and wasn't important. I was to understand that everything being taught was valuable to a young officer, otherwise it wouldn't be taught. Furthermore staff interpreted me to have a bad attitude problem. I was a noted individual who incited trouble by my behaviour which consistently bordered on the insubordinate. I was to change my attitude, and that really was it.

At this point I felt moved to point out that my bad attitude was due mainly to blatant double standards. The fact that some cadets had failed one exam, and were now in front of the commandant to be thrown out, while others had failed up to five and were allowed to continue was the most immediate and obvious example.

I was thrown out of the office by a livid colonel.

THE NEW QB

Queen's Birthday was still a Duntroon tradition. I froze to death in dress blues in June, in front of 60 people. These were mainly the girlfriends or family of people like myself, people who could remember a true QB. The day was a sad reminder of how few true links this place had with the RMC I had joined. The drill was atrocious by old RMC standards. The Bakers didn't see the point in having a QB parade and they put in no effort. Their big moment was to be graduation, in a few days time. I trudged off the parade ground in disgust. Bluey, Phil and Jude gathered to share a bottle of port in my room, to remember the days when QB meant acceptance into the corps for a Fourthie struggling for recognition in a strange world.

Our Baker senior class had their graduation a week later. Just as they saw no point in QB, I saw no point in their graduation. I took great delight in having sloppy drill. I didn't think of the ball afterwards as a graduation, it was more of a good riddance party.

'Goodbye,' I'd say. 'Hope I never see you again,' I'd add with a smile on my face. They would clap me on the back in turn.

'Never stop joking, do you, Tommy?'

'Never,' I would agree.

After I'd had my fun, and shaken hands with the four or so good guys, I decided it was time to sleaze. I returned to a blonde who appeared amused by my earlier rantings and decided on one last fling. The festivities began to wind up at RMC, but more work needed to be done, so I adjourned to the Bin. This was expressly forbidden, as only graduates were allowed to be in town after midnight. We partied on quite happily until 0500 hours, when a flustered apparition materialised before my eyes. It was the adjutant, resplendent in mess kit and drunk as a skunk. 'Get back to the college,' he leered at me 'and come and see me in the morning.'

'Yes sir,' I replied, more in pity than in anger. The adjutant really was a sad sight. At least I hadn't bothered to walk around town drunk in uniform, and nor had the other eight or so classmates who I could see. We had all changed. I had a quick emergency session with Sid, a lunatic from New Zealand.

'Two minutes out the front. Get your lady and we'll share a taxi.'

I was rudely awoken by a knock on my door at about 0800 hours. 'Adjutant wants to see you,' floated through the door.

'Yeah, okay,' was my disinterested reply.

'Now, Tommy.'

I rolled over and stood up with an effort. I organised someone to drive the girl home, found someone else to iron my uniform and had a shower to wake up.

Outside the adjutant's office was a small knot of Fourthies who had been caught out in town. They were distressed as they were to be charged for the offence.

'No dramas,' I announced with bravado. 'Seven days confined to barracks absolute max. More like three.'

I rapped on the adjutant's door and walked in without waiting for an answer. I gave my best parade-ground salute, which I'm told is abysmal, and announced myself.

'Staff Cadet Sneyk reporting as requested, sir.'

'You were out in town last night?'

'Yes, sir.'

'You will be charged for being absent.'

'Yes, sir.'

'Who else was with you?'

'Excuse me, sir?' I inquired.

'Who else was with you?' snapped the adjutant.

'Why, a lady sir.' I was a trifle amused that the adjutant was still looking decidedly seedy. 'You know as a gentlemen I couldn't say any more, and I am sure as a gentlemen you wouldn't ask any more.'

'You know what I mean. From the corps. Who else was with you?'

'Well, sir, that's a little difficult to say. You know how it is? Sometimes you lose your memory entirely.'

He looked at me long and hard. 'You may go,' he muttered finally, 'but you're still getting charged.'

'Of course, sir.'

I was almost out the door when the adjutant's eyes lit up. Divine inspiration had struck.

'I know who was with you,' he said triumphantly. 'That black shit, what's his name . . . Taranui. You get him and tell him to get his fat black arse down here now.'

I went up to Sid's room and knocked before sticking my nose around the corner. The fat black arse was naked and sticking cutely out from under the doona. Another body lay beside him. 'Sid, can I see you outside?' After a little shaking I took him out into the corridor and explained the situation.

Messages were now being sent around RMC telling all those who were in the Bin this morning to report to the adjutant. He had no takers. I'd already spread the word about his drunken loss of memory.

I was certain that all those Fourthies who were getting charged would get off lightly if two of the miscreants handed themselves in. One of them was Andy and the other was Simon. Both had taken up a senior appointment within the Corps of Cadets for our last six months at Duntroon. If they were 'caught' by the adjutant I felt sure that the others would forego the indignity of being confined to barracks. The staff could hardly so visibly punish two of the corps' most senior cadets. The biggest punishment Andy would receive would be a fine, and the rest of us would also only receive a fine once the precedent was set.

I spent my morning talking to people from all over the college. I told them about the drunken adjutant, about the charge Sid and I and the Fourthies would receive after owning up. The only thing I found slightly disappointing was the fact that Andy and Simon didn't have the integrity to go down and see the adjutant.

The story was an easy sell. The drunken adjutant part was the kind of scandalous behaviour cadets liked to hear about staff and the story spread like wildfire. Before long, I had a whole host of indignant cadets joining me in conversation about the lack of integrity of certain supposedly high-principled peers. By mid-afternoon Andy and Simon had an attack of conscience and handed themselves in. The whole affair blew over rather quickly after that and I was awarded a $50 fine, along with everyone else.

A PROMOTION

I was now entitled to wear corporals' stripes as a member of the senior class. I never wore them. I didn't see any point in sewing them on to a perfectly good uniform and ruining it.

By wearing rank I would became part of the hierarchy of oppression. This I would not do.

A PAINLESS OPERATION

'You big girl, Tommy. Always thought you were a bit strange,' Frog called to me at TOC.

I turned my back and ignored him. He was not a significant faction leader in our class. In fact he was the kind of friendless jerk who enjoyed abuse because it told him he existed. He and everyone else would understand the disdain conveyed by my turned back.

'I wonder what his story is?' I asked Bluey. 'Maybe someone hasn't punched him this week and he's getting cocky.'

'Who cares what's going on his tiny brain?' said Blue. 'No-one will ever know, I'm sure.'

After the morning lectures were complete, Bug Buchanan sat down next to me at lunch. I looked across to Phil, who didn't say a word, and then turned my attention to Bug. Phil's silence was unusual and I knew there must be something behind it. Bug was a nice chap, but very serious about his military destiny. We weren't enemies but we weren't friends. We had just lived together for the last four years and we were comfortable with the fact that we had nothing to say to each other.

'I'm really mad about this situation, Tommy. What do you think?'

I found this rather amusing, as I'd never imagined Bug being mad about anything. In fact I generally didn't think about him.

'Well you know me, Bug. I don't really think a lot at all. Far be it for me to have an opinion.'

'But it's an insult and slanderous and dishonest, and they've made us a part of it.' The words rushed out of Bug's mouth in a torrent.

'There's a lot of dishonesty at Duntroon. Which particular issue are you unhappy about?'

Bug looked at me long and hard, and I returned the compliment with a smile. 'You don't know, do you? I thought everybody knew.'

'I've never known much. I'm sure you must have noticed, I'm not everybody.' I liked the frustrating nature of this conversation, with a bit of luck I wouldn't have to talk to Bug for another four years. He bored me.

Bug reached into his pocket and pulled out a folded piece of paper—an advertisement for the Defence Academy. 'This is from a Sydney magazine,' he explained. I recognised the photo to be of the previous year's cross-country race. 'That girl there is you,' Bug said, indicating a not-so-pretty redhead. 'And this girl here is me.'

'Well I have to say you're a lot prettier than me, but I'm winning,' I noted, unimpressed.

'Tommy, can't you ever be serious?'

'But I am serious. Look, I'm winning and that ponytail . . . cobber, that is you.'

Bug looked at me in annoyance, but he pressed on. 'My father first noticed this and has made a little bit of noise. Apparently the explanation from Defence Recruiting is that they wanted to use this photograph. However, there were no women in it so they had it retouched and there we are.'

'So?' I leaned forward.

'So what are we going to do about it?'

'You've obviously thought about it. What do you want to do?'

'I want to take them to court and extract an official apology, maybe some compensation.' Bug's hand waved in agitation.

'Well they can keep the apology, but I must admit the compensation could help my indignant soul,' I smiled wanly.

The whole affair had obviously upset Bug, and I'm sure my attitude was annoying him, but considering other issues I'd confronted this was small fry.

'It's going to cost money, Tommy. I've spoken to a good solicitor. Up to ten grand each with no assurance of success.'

'Okay, Bug, count me in. I never miss a chance to screw the defence force.'

'You won't back out on me, will you?'

I looked at Bug for a long time before continuing to eat.

'Okay, Tommy, fine.' He stood up and left.

'What do you make of that?' Phil asked.

'Not much. I'm surprised to see such fire in the man,' I observed. 'I'll be even more surprised to see him go through with it. The staff will put some acid on him, and goodie two shoes will crack.'

'What if he does, though? What about the money? He's probably got a rich little daddy to back him up.'

'It's only money. I'll get it from a bank. Don't worry about it.'

APOLOGIES

Three days later a letter arrived from Defence Recruiting, signed by an apologetic Commodore Gulliver. He had spelt my rank incorrectly, as well as my first and second name. The man was obviously incompetent and his letter had 'I don't give a damn' written all over it. I was now very interested in court proceedings. I looked forward to returning the compliment and causing Commodore Gulliver some embarrassment.

My interest became even greater when I saw the secretary of Bug's chosen solicitor. I had to hand it to Bug, this was fun, and I never would have dreamed this caper up by myself.

217

CAPER OVER

Bug was found with a female cadet in his room and disappeared a few days later. Thrown out for fraternisation. Another member of our class was gone. Bug was not interested in the legal proceedings any longer and I didn't press it. He was fighting to get back into RMC on the strength of his immaculate record and he didn't need to be branded a troublemaker. I never did fix Commodore Gulliver up for that letter and I was sorry about that. It was actions like his, that were thoughtless and careless, that made the defence force so hard to live with.

POINT SCORING

We were all gathered in the mess, sipping on sherries, looking a million dollars in dress blues. I stood with Bluey and Phil, eyeing the gathered throng. I hated occasions like this. The food was average, the wines horrible and the company . . . well, apart from my close circle of friends I considered it to be terrible. Everyone mindful of a chance to impress would be busy romancing some staff member for the benefit of his or her long-term military career. I considered it all to be terribly un-Australian. A hangover from the British Raj.

My eyes fell on Andy in the corner, who was staring into his hand, a look of concentration on his face. I left Whitie, Phil and Blue without a word and joined him. 'So, Andy, what have you there?' I had approached unseen and made him jump.

Andy looked up in embarrassment.

I bent over his shoulder and stared at some palm cards.

'Oh . . . ah, I've written some palm cards out for the evening so I'll remember a few things, like who I should introduce to who first, men to ladies, juniors to senior rank. The kind of conversation I should avoid, like talking about religion, work and politics, and some other tips I've picked up.'

'That's a great idea, Andy. You won't mind if I use it some time?'

'No, not at all. Always pleased if I can help you out,' Andy cheerily replied, pleased that I appreciated his innovation.

I excused myself. 'Listen in, guys,' I said to Bluey and Phil. 'I can scarcely believe it, but guess what that sorry son of a bitch has with him? Palm cards. All lessons in social etiquette have been condensed, for ease of learning, onto three or four helpful palm cards.'

'Bullshit,' puffed Blue.

'Does it look like I'm joking?' I said quietly but forcefully, broaching no dissent. 'Bluey, you and I are sitting opposite him and the commandant tonight. Andy's cards don't allow him to talk about religion, politics and shop. Why don't we keep the conversation centred around those topics? That should throw a spanner in the works.'

We all took our seats and I smiled across at the commandant. Before Andy had even settled in his seat I asked the commandant for his opinion on a terrorist attack in Ireland, which immediately introduced both religion and shop into the conversation. This exhausted, Bluey introduced the problems of the Lebanese civil war. I steered this conversation into chatter on religious sects and terrorism, finally debating what could be done to stop legitimate governments who allowed terrorist organisations to base themselves in their countries.

Andy had a worried look on his face and every now and then glanced surreptitiously at his palm cards. 'What do *you* think of religious terrorism?' I asked him mischievously, but he steadfastly refused to be drawn into the conversation. Every now and then he attempted to change the topic by throwing in, 'Gee, there's been lots of rain about lately' or, 'Sir, how do you find living in Canberra?'

The commandant kept on giving Andy the strangest looks and Andy sat with a sulky expression on his face.

After the meal we moved outside for post-dinner drinks, but I was not about to let Andy off lightly and followed him and the commandant downstairs.

'Can I get you a drink, sir?' Andy fawned.

'No, I'm fine,' the commandant stated firmly. 'Thanks for hosting me tonight. You can go now and have some fun.'

'Thanks, sir.' Andy was now desperate. 'But I'd really like to buy you a drink. What can I get you?'

'I'm right. Really I am,' replied the commandant in a strained voice.

Andy was getting really frustrated. The night had not really gone as planned. 'What can I get you?' he almost pleaded.

I'd watched with a broad grin. 'Look, Andy,' I butted in. 'Why don't you go and buy yourself a drink, and while you're there I'll have a Scotch and Coke, Phil a Scotch and dry, Bluey will have a beer and that should just about do us.'

Andy looked at me in confusion before disappearing. I smiled at the commandant, shrugged and left.

A MEETING WITH THE GRIM REAPER

The Board of Studies sat a month into First Class. The charade in front of Panic Palace was repeated once more. And once more my name was read out. 'Sneyk—Commandant.' A low murmur followed the announcement of each of the seven cadets who was to see the commandant. No cadet who went before the commandant on a warning was at the college a week later. This was the end of the road and I only felt relief.

The next morning we assembled in the courtyard of Duntroon House, ready to see the commandant. Duntroon House was a beautifully kept Victorian mansion and had been the first building built in the Canberra area, by the Campbell family a century before. I looked around at my grim-faced companions. Most of them I regarded as hopeless. It was sobering to think that the staff thought I belonged in this company. Well, what did they know? They thought Andy was the best cadet in my class. Believe in yourself. I smiled.

I looked across at Hawkie, a genteel troublemaker who had fallen on the wrong side of his company commander. Hawkie smiled, but it was a sickly kind of smile which didn't fool anyone, least of all himself. His demeanour was grim. The others had the morbid intensity of the condemned.

'Well here we are,' I said to Hawkie.

'That we are, Tommy,' he replied. 'Just remember, no matter what happens here today we don't belong with these fuckwits.'

When I looked over his shoulder at Frog and the others, I couldn't help but agree. 'I know, mate, but we are and that hurts. You know.'

We spontaneously clasped hands. 'Yeah, I know,' Hawkie nodded in agreement.

An officer appeared and indicated for us to stand to attention.

'Staff Cadet Sneyk, you will go first. The rest will be in alphabetical order.'

I looked at Hawkie, held his gaze for a moment and took a deep breath before heading down the corridors in the direction indicated. Obviously they had something else planned for me. Instead of throwing me out of the college, maybe they intended throwing me out of an upstairs window. I just wanted to be left alone, but obviously they had one last game for me to play. 'Well, you vindictive arseholes,' I said to myself, 'let's play.'

I marched into a room, halted, did a left turn and faced the commandant. My hand whipped up in what I hoped was a smart salute, I puffed my chest out and drew myself up to my full height. I tried to look huge although I knew I was losing. The commandant's large desk seemed tiny in an enormous room with tall ceilings. The room was alive with accusing eyes. To my rear were the director of military art, the commanding officer and all the company commanders. The whole scene was intimidating and designedly so. However, that knowledge was of cold comfort. I wondered when they would stop playing their transparent psychological games.

'Listen in and hear what I have to say,' rasped the commandant. 'You are here because of your attitude. You were put on a director of military art's warning for your behaviour and bearing around the college and you have chosen to ignore it. In fact your flippant attitude might suggest that you are laughing in our face. Well, I find that behaviour unacceptable and I will not have the authority of my staff undermined by you. You have a final chance. You will march out of this office a new man and I do not wish to hear your name mentioned once more before graduation. Do you understand?'

I understood well. I didn't like the commandant and I didn't respect him, but I understood if you crossed the man you would lose.

'Yes, sir.' I tried to sound convincing but the quaver in my voice instantly told me I had lost.

'Go, and do not return.'

All the other members on commandant's warnings were thrown out. Even Hawkie, who didn't belong with those fuckwits. Hawkie's departure was felt sadly by the whole class.

SIMON THE PATRIOT

When we first marched into RMC we had been Sovereign's Company. However, we had lost the honour by coming last in the company competition at the end of that year. On our return to Duntroon, Beersheba was again the last company in the Sovereign's competition. Simon was intent on making it Sovereign's Company again. Each morning we'd be out of bed before dawn training. This was all well and good but few of the company shared Simon's visions of glory. In fact morale was noticeably low and there were a lot of sullen faces. Simon came to see me about the grumblings.

'What's wrong with the company?' he asked. 'I'm hearing a lot of dissent.'

I thought for a moment. 'The boys are just jerked off. You will win Sovereign's Company and that's fine, and you will receive the credit. We get nothing for being Sovereign's Company except being mucked around at 0600 hours on a winter's morning when we have to slide over an icy obstacle course.'

Simon nodded. From the thoughtful look on his face, I could tell he was listening.

The next week we were run up to the top of Mount Pleasant at 0530 hours in preparation, we thought, to doing the obstacle course. Instead, Simon had organised chicken and orange juice for breakfast which he'd paid for out of his own pocket. I looked around, I was seething. I grabbed a piece of chicken and a container full of orange juice and walked up to Simon.

'Personally, I'd rather do the obstacle course than sit on top of Mount Pleasant when the temperature's minus 5 and freeze my nuts off.' I brandished my chicken leg to add emphasis. 'You can shove your soda-fountain morale up your backside. I'm going back to bed.'

I walked down the hill and half the company followed. People power's much underrated, I thought. But it's still power . . . it still corrupts. Poor old Simon. He really didn't deserve what I'd just dished out.

FRIENDS TILL THE END

Simon and Jude grabbed me one evening as I came back from the mess.

'Come on in for a moment,' Simon said. I followed him into his room.

'I knew you wouldn't get thrown out like the rest the other day,' Simon continued. 'You're the great survivor, Tommy. I've spoken to Jude because we want to convince you to keep a real low profile to graduation.' I looked from Jude to Simon and didn't say a word. Simon continued. 'The company commander told me this morning that he will do anything to stop you becoming an officer. He suggested that if you were bished out of the corps he wouldn't be sorry. The gloves are off. I think he wanted me to organise it. You know that's not going to happen, but be warned. He has a few months to get you, and he intends doing just that.'

Jude cut in. 'Look, Tommy, just keep your mouth shut and a low profile till graduation. You can say what you want when you're an officer. You'll have a chance of achieving something as a lieutenant. Just play the game for a few more months.'

'Thanks, Simon, Jude, I'll watch it.'

I was full of mixed emotion, and grateful to Simon for the warning. It was big of him considering my recent behaviour. But I was disappointed with Jude. What game? I wanted to yell. It's my life; it's no game. Let's put off our responsibilities until tomorrow. When does tomorrow come, Jude? What is suddenly going to make me do what is right when I graduate? When are we supposed to stand by what we believe? When do we have courage and stand by our convictions?

I turned and left. The worst thing was that I knew I would do just what Jude said. I'd completed three years and nine months. With two months to go, I wanted the prize.

THE STAFF REMEMBER SOME OLD CADET HABITS

I returned to my room after work one day to find all my drawers emptied on the floor and my cupboards in disarray. I stared at the mess for a moment, locked the door behind me and started tidying up. As I cleaned, I fumed.

Who was it? Who have I pissed-off lately? No-one sprang to mind. Fourthies? Wouldn't have the guts. Besides, I haven't said boo to any of them. They had no reason. Second Class? Away on exercise. First Class? At lectures all day with me. Could have only done it during lunchtime. Who, though?

My room fixed up, I locked the door, went to the Rec Room and sat down, listening and watching. The first mistake people made when bished was to get angry and mouth off, swearing vengeance randomly to everyone they see. This immediately started rumours, which I had always capitalised on. Far better to say nothing. The average cadet was a mouth. He'd tell someone and I'd then be able to track him down. I sat for hours and observed. This was virtually the only time all year I had been in the Rec Room and I was amazed as people came in and glued their eyes to the television for hours on end. Nothing. Not a rumour, not a funny look.

The next day I returned to my room after lectures and again it was bished. I was now decidedly peeved. After two hours of cleaning I again went to the Rec Room. Nothing!

The only time available for my tormentor to do his work was lunchtime, so at lunch I dashed to my room ready to confront anyone who turned up. The room was already turned upside down and I found a note on my desk: 'Your shoelaces are missing, your socks are incorrectly placed, your clothes are still not folded neatly enough. Your Platoon Sergeant is obviously not doing his job! He should punch you in the nose because you keep drawing attention to his platoon's performance. Obviously you do not care about peer group acceptance.'

You have the last bit right, pea brain, I thought.

I knew then it must be one of the staff. There was no signature, of course. So, you bastards. You can't get me legally, now the staff are out to bish me. Well, you lack imagination and I now have the initiative. The staff had always pulled our strings like puppets, orchestrating by group punishment who would stay and who would go. Now it was more than that. The staff were bishing me because they couldn't work their system the way they wanted.

The next day I had Phil cover me for the morning lectures. I sat in the room next door and waited till I heard the rhythmic click of the sergeant's boots down the corridor. I heard my door open with the master key and waited 30 seconds.

When I walked casually into my room, Sergeant Lemon looked up with a start. He had the look of a little boy caught with a naughty picture by his dad. What he was doing was classified as break and enter and was, needless to say, totally illegal.

'Having fun, Sergeant?' I asked. 'I suppose you've been getting your jollies turning my room upside down, which really pisses me off.' I glared at the sergeant. 'Why don't we step out the back right now and fix this all up once and for all?'

Sergeant Lemon looked down at me. He was at least two inches taller and solidly built. He could have torn me apart in the physical confrontation I was obviously inviting him to.

'Look, Sneyk, I didn't want ta do this, I was directed ta,' he pleaded.

I looked back at him with disdain. 'You didn't have to do this. You did it because you could . . . because some little man suggested you have the power to . . . and because you're even less of a man.'

I stood toe to toe with Sergeant Lemon for a long time before I walked out.

THE LAST BATTLE

The class's last exercise at RMC was conducted at Puckapunyal, a dusty scrubby flat land 100 kilometres north of Melbourne. The object of this exercise was to practise fighting with armoured units. A bad performance while on a commandant's warning would have been the end for me.

The platoon and section lists were published for the exercise and I found my name quietly hidden as a number four rifleman. Whitie, Phil, Bluey, Jude and a few other close friends were in my section. This was more than a coincidence. Jude came and saw me.

'Someone on the staff has done you a favour,' he said. 'Now do yourself one. Shut your mouth. No funnies and we'll make sure you get good reports.'

They did. Every trick that four years of being a cadet had taught us was used to make me look good. I did not do a thing. Everything was done quietly for me behind the scenes. I received a glowing report and I thanked the lads, for we all knew these good reports would carry me safely through to graduation.

After reports were handed out the senior instructor informed the class that a live-fire attack had been organised for the next day. 'The best three performers in the class for this exercise will be chosen and briefed to lead a platoon assault on an objective. This is a dangerous activity as you will be joined in the assault line by Leopard tanks which will also be firing live ammunition.'

I was called aside with two others. 'You will lead the assaults tomorrow,' began the senior instructor. 'You have all conducted live-fire assaults before and you know what is required. The Leopards make this a particularly hard activity to command. They are noisy and make it difficult to be heard by your troops. In addition they can run over a soldier and kill him. If a soldier moves forward of the main armament when it fires, the chances are his eardrums will be blown by the noise of the blast.' He looked at us each in turn. 'Because of this you must ensure that the assault line goes no further forward than the tank's second road wheel. I rely on you to make sure this activity is conducted safely.'

In the morning I did my final checks with the platoon as we waited in our form-up point, ready to cross the line of departure. The Leopards' engines were growling and I looked to my platoon signaller Jude and my batman Phil, who were kneeling to my left rear. 'Noisy pricks,' I yelled. They nodded.

Captain Webster, the directing staff, signalled that all was ready and I waited as the seconds ticked by till H hour. I could see my section commanders watching me closely ready for the word. I stood, and the platoon stood. 'Go!'

The weight of responsibility rested firmly on my shoulders and I felt exhilarated by the power at my command. I may still be a cadet for a month, but today I was Lieutenant Sneyk.

Up the hill we moved. The noise was frightening and I fought to retain order. The tanks were moving painfully slowly and I sent Phil to hurry them up.

Captain Webster appeared close to my left ear. 'Get up the hill, you're too slow. The assault is too slow, you'll get your men killed out here in the open.'

'I can't. The tanks,' I yelled, pointing at them to remind him of the safety limitations.

Captain Webster persisted. 'Hurry it up!' He was inches from my face to make himself heard.

I felt myself losing control of the platoon as I concentrated on Captain Webster. This was dangerous and I had to act. 'Fuck off. Fuck off out of my platoon.'

Captain Webster grabbed me by the throat. I pushed him aside and continued with the assault.

On arrival back at Duntroon, Captain Webster called me aside and informed me I was being charged for insubordination.

I was called before a gleeful company commander who informed me that Captain Webster had supporting statements from two other captains who said that I had, for no apparent reason, rounded on him.

'Bullshit,' snorted Phil when I told him, Jude and Bluey at a crisis meeting. 'They weren't even there. They are out and out liers.'

'I know, but that makes it a lot harder to beat. It's now my word against theirs.'

'Our word,' corrected Phil.

I looked at Phil. '*Our word* is you, me and Jude versus three captains. Who do you think is going to win?'

A STRANGE ALLY

I was walking to the mess when Sergeant Lemon stopped me. 'You and I needs ta talk. Meet me behinds the gym at 1900 hours.'

At the appointed time behind the gym, Sergeant Lemon pointed to a group of bushes halfway up Mount Pleasant. 'Go up there and wait for me. Keep out of sight.'

I walked up the hill and crouched on my haunches. What was up? What did Lemon want?

Fifteen minutes later the sergeant joined me. 'Listen in Sneyk, and listen real good,' he said seriously. 'Don't let that charge of insubordination hit the courtroom. Youse goin' to be found guilty. Work is already in progress to disappears ya straight afterwards.'

Nothing that Sergeant Lemon said was surprising. I suspected as much already. What surprised me was to hear it from him. In fact I was speechless.

'I'm not telling ya this 'cause I like ya. I hate ya, but I hates Webster more. Fix him up.'

With that, Lemon was gone.

MAKING A PLAY

Panic Palace time for a last throw of the dice. I had written down my lines the previous evening and rehearsed them several times to make sure I had the tone and message right.

I strode to the adjutant's door. The preliminaries of saluting and greeting dispensed with, I fought to control my racing heart.

'Sir, as you are probably aware, I have been charged for insubordination by Captain Webster. While I can understand that this incident may have caused Captain Webster some chagrin, I feel at

229

this stage that a full account of what happened on that day is not likely to come out in the courtroom. Consequently, I feel my only way to bring all the circumstances into the open would be to counter-charge Captain Webster with assault. I don't particularly want to do this as it could cause ill-feeling but I don't know what else to do. You see, Captain Webster has two supporting statements from staff who were not even present. Now I don't want to suggest they're lying, but perhaps they have become confused. I thought you may be able to help me, sir. Give me some advice.'

The adjutant looked at me long and hard. 'You are right, Staff Cadet Sneyk. To charge Captain Webster would most definitely cause bad blood. How do you feel you were assaulted?'

Bad blood, I almost smiled at the well-chosen words.

'During the incident when I was allegedly insubordinate, Captain Webster pulled me aside by grabbing my collar and throat. It's fairly cut and dry. However, as most staff around here have become fairly personally involved, I thought I might exercise my legal right and ask for the charge to be heard outside of RMC.'

'Hmm. I will investigate your claims,' said the adjutant. 'My advice for the time being would be to organise your defence for the charge of insubordination as best you can. There is no need that I can see for you to have the charge heard somewhere else, as I assure you you will receive a fair trial at RMC. There will be no false statements in that charge room. Is that satisfactory?'

'I will accept your word, sir. Thank you for your time.'

THE CLASS RALLIES

The class took a petition to the commanding officer signed by over 80 members. It stated that they had no confidence in Captain Webster and asked for his removal from involvement in class instruction.

The organiser of the petition approached me to sign. 'I'm sorry, Andy, but I can't do that.'

'Sign it. It's for your benefit,' Andy looked exasperated.

'I can't. This is the army, not a trade union. There are correct channels for grievances and this just isn't military.'

'You're a queer bastard, Tommy. I'll never understand you.' Andy shook his head in frustration. I shrugged.

OFF THE HOOK

I looked around the room. Bluey, Whitie, Jude and Phil were all present. There was just one person missing, my defending officer. I looked at my watch for the hundredth time. I didn't say a word.

Phil was agitated. 'Fuck him. Where the hell is he . . . he knows we're due in the charge room in two minutes. I told you not to let him defend you. What the hell were you thinking?'

I stood in silence and straightened my dress uniform. It was spotless and I knew a pretty uniform wasn't going to get me off the charge, but there wasn't anything else to do.

'I'd better get going,' I finally managed. 'He'll probably be waiting for me inside.'

'Good luck.' Jude extended his hand. We looked at each other long and hard. I half-turned to go when the door burst open behind me.

Andy was red-faced. 'I've just been down at the adjutant's office. You're off. The statements and the charge have been pulled. No explanation, but Webster and his cronies were waiting around. They didn't look too happy. Am I the best defending officer in the world or what?'

I slapped Andy on the back. I was so relieved, I couldn't say a word.

'Port?' Phil offered a steel canteen full of the blood-red liquid and I gulped it down before handing it around to my brothers. A little port dribbled out of the edge of my mouth.

ON PARADE

The company stood on parade in the car park prior to marching on to the graduation parade. We were resplendent in our blue peaked caps with red bands, our white patrol jackets, and our blue trousers with a single red stripe down each leg. A white belt tied us in the middle. The company commander did his customary inspection and stopped in front of me. I was wearng a white plastic belt borrowed from the Defence Academy. They were banned at RMC, where cadets had to waste hours painting white house paint over a belt that was issued green.

I took the lazy option. Anywhere else in the world it would have been sensible, but at RMC it was lazy. The white plastic was far more practical, required no effort, and couldn't be spotted as being different from the painted variety at any more than a yard.

'Staff Cadet Sneyk, you even turn up to your own graduation parade defying orders. You will never be a good officer. It is an absolute indictment on this college that you are graduating. God knows, I have done my best to stop this occurring. I am speechless . . . you are a hopeless case. I want you to see the sergeant right after I'm finished,' raved the major.

Sergeant Lemon glowered at me for two minutes, stuck for words as the major moved further down the ranks. When the major was suitably far away, Lemon leaned forward with a smile and wink.

'You see me after, Staff Cadet Sneyk . . . right after graduation.'

From my position in the front rank of the parade I peered out. Unlike the remainder of my class, I still wore no stripes of rank.

I knew the remnants of my class were somewhere beside me. I

knew I would greet them in years to come as lost brothers. No. Blood brothers. Comrades who had taken part in the same crime, members of a tribe whose unusual values needed defence against people who could never understand. People who would impose judgments against us, after rationally thinking about the issues in the comfort of their lounge rooms.

I thought back to my first graduation parade, when I was a Fourthie, and wondered where the feeling of pride had gone. It wouldn't come back, and I didn't want it back. I would never believe in an institution again.

We marched off parade. The command was given, 'Graduates . . . Fall out.'

We threw our caps in the air in a spontaneous burst of theatrics. I turned and walked away. My fellow graduates were scrabbling around behind, trying to find their hats. Most undignified.

I was a few steps away when I heard Simon's voice calling from behind. He pushed his way through the throng. 'Tommy, your hat.' he held it out to me.

'Thanks, mate.' I tossed it back on the ground. 'Don't really need it any more.'

Simon looked at me for a long movement. 'You're mad,' he laughed, dropping his on the ground before grabbing me by the elbow.

I searched Dad out amongst the crowd. We hugged each other warmly and I could see the pride in his eyes. 'Well, Tom, despite everything, a shiver must have gone up your spine today?'

I froze, almost replied 'no', stopped myself and hugged him again. How could I explain this to him? Could I explain it to myself?

I excused myself from my guests and walked up to the barracks to change uniforms. On the way up I ran into Blue.

'That money you owe me, mate, can I grab it off you now?'

It was only a small sum but I'd been onto him for weeks and he'd never paid it back. Money was scarce for all cadets, and after graduation we had uniforms to buy. It was especially tight for me as I was travelling to Tasmania to spend Christmas with Dad, then flying to Brisbane to see Mum before returning to Albury-Wodonga where I was posted. Bluey had to drive to Sydney, where his parents lived and where he was posted.

'Tommy, don't bug me about that now. You know I'm tight for money.' It was a display that was characteristically arrogant.

I turned my back. I didn't feel angry . . . just relief. I'd finally been released from my pledge of four years before. The Musketeers no longer existed. The chains had finally snapped and now nothing bound us together.

BACK ON TRACK

At 0300 hours I left the graduation ball, weary but not sleepy.

I changed into my running gear automatically. My brain knew it wanted to think . . . alone . . . away from others. I jogged out into the cool air and headed around the lake one last time.

I felt the power and freedom of my legs.

A group of rabbits watched me as I ran in front of the American War Memorial, the concrete eagle's wings of the monolith stretched out for flight.

Hello friends. I smiled at the rabbits. They were old mates and had more right than most to be with me on graduation night.

My legs carried me on faster.

Who am I?

Do I have principles?

What are they?

My breathing was deep and regular, and I analysed the rhythm of my hands in synchronisation with my legs. I tried to feel every muscle movement.

Had I obeyed the rules of my society?

What were they? Integrity? Don't make me laugh. Mateship?

Well, it had taken four years but I knew that was a lie. The Musketeers had been an ideal. They were part of my belief in the Anzac legend. A tradition of mateship. The Musketeers had been a lie. I hoped that the tradition wasn't a lie.

Survival? Probably that more than most. Darwin was right. It wasn't the biggest and best that survived, it was the most adaptable. Birds and snakes survived. Humans . . . they thought and loved.

I halted on the bridge. Peering into the black water far below, I smiled. I couldn't see a smile reflected back at me. I accepted that, much as I had wanted to belong to Duntroon all my life, and much as I wanted that corner of the world to be my spiritual home, it never would be. I felt empty but deliciously so. No bitterness. No animosity. Just relief. I felt as if a hand had been holding my head under water, and finally I was released.

On I ran. Slower now. What's the hurry? You'll get there, you always do.

There is a duality in all of us. Not just in our actions but, intrinsically, in everything we are. There was the me I thought I was. Then there was the reality. The ugly me I became . . . and now perhaps there was a me I could live with. One where I didn't have to hide in an alcoholic stupor. I hoped Matthew, Mark, Luke and John, my Musketeer allies, found something they could live with. Maybe though, it was time for the disciples to stop following and start leading.

My strength was having the ability to believe in self. My weakness was having the vanity to believe in self. Long and slow. Relax. You're almost finished.

I leant into the hill. Power, not speed. Climbing hills requires energy.

The strength of your legs.

The steel in your arms.

The flexibility of your abdomen.

The concentration of your mind.

I felt the potholes in the road come and go. Further up the hill

I ran. It was black up here on Mount Pleasant and although I had enough light to see, it was black. The road was black as well.

I pumped the arms and flicked with my legs, feeling the burning pain grow as I reached for the summit. It was achieved as the pain became unbearable but I held that burning sensation for a moment longer, just so I knew I could, and then I walked. Hands on hips and gasping for air.

Over the last four years something had been taken away, and given away, that I never knew I had. Now that it was gone, I finally recognised it, and knew the next struggle was to get it back, and then no-one would ever take it away again.

It had been a long journey. First the landscape had been black, but the path distinct. Then the road I journeyed became as black as the landscape, until they merged. I knew my mistake. It was to close my eyes in the heat of the flames and to fall off the path.

The grey of the pre-dawn lit the horizon with just a glimmer of gold to suggest it would be a sunny day. I still wasn't sure. It could be imagination. The sky still had that washed look where I couldn't tell if it was covered in clouds or about to burst into a delicate blue. God I'm glad I've seen this dawn.

I thought back a lifetime to when I decided I liked good parties. Could that have been me? I was the one who had imagined the word 'good'. Last night was just a party and only perceptions separated participants. The sun was appearing and I moved to go.

I broke into a half trot down the hill. I didn't go down the road. I threaded my way deftly between rocks. I leant forward and let my body's weight do the work. It was more a glide than a run.

Back in my room I wondered how the others felt. I hoped it was proud. I'd want them to feel pride in their vocation, and perhaps, if necessary, die with pride. They could at least leave them that. They . . . who were they?

I sat at my desk. My officer's sword lay near a pen. I picked it up and slid it from its scabbard. I stared at its attractive sparkling hilt before placing it down with a click.

I wondered what my resolve was to defend Australia . . . a country that had placed such little value on the lives of its youth. My youth. Jude had asked me to leave my rebellious comments till after graduation. This changed our friendship in a way I couldn't explain at the time, but I now think I understood. He would have known what he asked was impossible if, like that soldier at Gettysburg, he'd seen what I'd seen that summer.

I picked up the pen and started writing.

January One, 156 cadets marched into the Royal Military College Duntroon.

Four years later, 41 of that class stood on graduation parade.

The rest were just statistics, unless you have laughed with them, or cried with them.